PENGUIN

Ink Ribbon Red

Alex Pavesi lives in Surrey, where he writes full time. He previously worked as a software engineer and before that, obtained a PhD in Mathematics. He enjoys puzzles, long walks and recreational lock-picking. His debut novel *Eight Detectives* has been published in more than twenty languages, and was picked by the *Sunday Times* and the *New York Times* as one of their books of the year.

Ink Ribbon Red

ALEX PAVESI

PENGUIN BOOKS

PENGUIN BOOKS

UK | USA | Canada | Ireland | Australia
India | New Zealand | South Africa

Penguin Books is part of the Penguin Random House group of companies
whose addresses can be found at global.penguinrandomhouse.com

Penguin Random House UK,
One Embassy Gardens, 8 Viaduct Gardens, London SW11 7BW

penguin.co.uk

First published by Penguin Michael Joseph 2024
Published by Penguin Books 2025

001

Copyright © Alex Pavesi, 2024

The moral right of the author has been asserted

Penguin Random House values and supports copyright. Copyright fuels creativity, encourages diverse voices, promotes freedom of expression and supports a vibrant culture. Thank you for purchasing an authorized edition of this book and for respecting intellectual property laws by not reproducing, scanning or distributing any part of it by any means without permission. You are supporting authors and enabling Penguin Random House to continue to publish books for everyone. No part of this book may be used or reproduced in any manner for the purpose of training artificial intelligence technologies or systems. In accordance with Article 4(3) of the DSM Directive 2019/790, Penguin Random House expressly reserves this work from the text and data mining exception

Typeset by Jouve (UK), Milton Keynes
Printed and bound in Great Britain by Clays Ltd, Elcograf S.p.A.

The authorized representative in the EEA is Penguin Random House Ireland,
Morrison Chambers, 32 Nassau Street, Dublin D02 YH68

A CIP catalogue record for this book is available from the British Library

ISBN: 978–1–405–94499–1

Penguin Random House is committed to a sustainable future
for our business, our readers and our planet. This book is made from
Forest Stewardship Council® certified paper.

Dedicated to Bailey, one of the greatest cats, who died of lymphoma while this book was being written, and his brother Lewis, who turned sixteen a few months before it was finished. Can I have my chair back, Lewis?

Author's Note

The major events of this novel take place during the late May bank holiday weekend, the year 1999; for the sake of completeness, the stories written by the characters over the course of that weekend have been included in the text at appropriate points.

PART ONE
Death

MONDAY
31 May 1999

The Scenic Route

'I don't want you to think I'm a bad person . . .'

The weekend had begun with hope but would end in horror, like every weekend. Anatol was looking sideways at Janika, waiting for her to respond. The steering wheel started to drift in her direction. They heard the crunch and tearing of nettles under the tyres, felt the front left wheel scrape the edge of the verge. Then Anatol brought his eyes back to the road. He had never been a very competent driver. He shrugged off the mistake, gave the steering wheel a reflexive wiggle, and carried on speaking. 'It's just that I haven't been feeling like myself lately. You see what I mean? I'm all over the place.'

Janika nodded diplomatically, but didn't answer. She was watching the passing countryside through the window beside her. A view of yellow fields and faded hills, under an unmarked white sky. Her hands clenched around the sleeves of her cardigan. She hadn't said a single word since they'd got into the car. She thought it was more in character to keep quiet.

'Everything feels like a dream,' said Anatol. He parted the fingers of his right hand and stared at the road through the gaps between the knuckles. A thick line of dirt capped each fingernail. 'When somebody close to you dies, nothing seems real. It's too much change to take in all at once. It makes everything feel like a dream. Do you understand?'

It was unusually cold for the last day of May. The day after Anatol's thirtieth birthday. A heavy, late-morning mist lay on the landscape. Every blade of grass looked haunted.

'But if nothing's real, then nothing matters. You lose your judgement about right and wrong. You do things you wouldn't normally do. Say things you wouldn't normally say. If I've been acting strange this weekend, then that's why.'

It was Monday morning. The bank holiday. Janika had spent the long weekend at Anatol's house with the rest of their friends. Now he was taking her to the station, so she could catch the train home. The car was a vintage forest-green convertible. Its bruised vinyl top had a tear down one side. The hole had been patched with layers of duct tape, but the cold air still managed to find its way inside.

'I'm probably not explaining myself very well . . .'

Anatol continued talking as he slowed down and signalled to turn off the main road on to a narrow byway where there were no white lines on the tarmac. He took his hands from the wheel and waited for a gap in the oncoming traffic.

'But grief is a shapeshifter. It manifests differently from one day to the next. Some days it's guilt, some days it's regret. Some days it's just sadness. And some days it's more like shock.' Anatol's father had died unexpectedly, five weeks earlier. 'I'm not trying to make excuses. I'm sorry if I seemed rude or short-tempered yesterday. But you can't help but lose your perspective on things when your mood keeps shifting like that. You'll understand this one day, when you've lost someone close to you, Janika.'

Cars streamed past them in stark primary colours. Janika looked beyond Anatol to their right. The road they were turning into seemed to lead nowhere. No signpost announced its destination. And there was nothing to be seen at the end of it. Just the feathery hedges that bordered the pitted road surface, pinched together by perspective.

'Anatol,' said Janika, speaking at last. 'Where are we going?'

'Grief,' said Anatol with a surge of enthusiasm. 'Grief is an awkward portmanteau of guilt, regret and disbelief. Because those are its three main ingredients.'

'Where are we going?' asked Janika again.

There was a sudden short gap in the traffic. Anatol accelerated into it, turning the wheel too late. The rattling convertible crossed over the opposite lane but missed the turning and ploughed into a patch of cow parsley. Anatol swore and put the vehicle in reverse. They jolted backwards, into the path of an oncoming car. Then forwards again, slowing to a crawl as they straightened out. The car passed by with a shriek of its horn.

'Exhibit A,' said Anatol. 'You lose your judgement.'

'This isn't the way to the station,' said Janika.

Anatol switched on the radio, changing the subject. But all he could find was local news, laced with static. He switched it off. 'The radio has a frog in its throat.'

Janika spoke again, with mounting urgency. 'Anatol. Where are we going?'

'Don't worry, this is the scenic route.' Anatol pointed into the empty distance. The road ahead of them was a blank page. 'We turn left up ahead here. We've been this way before, I'm sure.'

Janika checked the window beside her. The view was

obscured by a tall hedge but where there were gaps she could see only green fields, shaded grey by the mist.

'It's not scenic.'

'But it would be, on a brighter day.'

Janika twisted in her seat and looked through the back window, hoping that someone would have followed them into the turning. But the road behind looked the same as the road in front. 'The station's back that way, Anatol.'

'This might not be the most direct route, but it gets us there. And it's a nicer drive this way.'

Janika checked her watch. 'My train leaves in ten minutes.'

'Twelve minutes,' said Anatol. 'We have plenty of time.'

'I don't want to risk it. I want to get a good seat. I can't sit in the smoking carriage for two hours. I'll start arguments.' Janika sounded distraught. 'Take me back. Please.'

Anatol flinched at such a direct command. He drummed his fingers on the steering wheel, shaking his head. 'I'll tell you the truth, Janika. It's not about the scenery. I'm desperate for a piss. I'm going to have to stop somewhere further along here. It's only a slight detour.'

He pointed into the distance again. His fingers were thick and muscular, his hands huge. They must have made up at least an eighth of his six foot six inches. He was almost too tall for the car. His head pressed into its soft top, pushing the vinyl up like a tent pole.

'Don't worry,' he added. 'It won't take me long.'

Janika looked through the back window again. But there was no sign now of the turning they'd taken. 'There's a toilet at the station,' she said. 'Why don't you use that?'

'It won't take me more than a minute, in fact. There's a small wood just ahead of us. It's got a dirt track running through it. It's private property, but no one ever uses it.'

Anatol turned and gave Janika a misplaced grin. 'You could say it's nature's cubicle . . .'

The car drifted towards Janika again. Stony blackberries bounced off the windscreen.

'Anatol.' Janika tried raising her voice. 'You can hold in a piss. But I can't hold in a train, can I?'

'You won't have to, Janika. Look at the weather. The train will be late.'

'You don't know that.' She was almost shouting now, clinging to the handle of the door beside her. 'I don't want to risk it. I don't want to go to the woods.'

'I'm sorry, Janika. But I could injure myself if I don't stop. I've always been this way, ever since I was a child. It's my curse. Six foot six and a bladder like a Jif lemon. But it won't take me very long. Ninety seconds at the most. I used to time myself when I was a boy. Little boys like to do things like that. Not that I was ever little.'

'Anatol. If you don't turn around now, I'll open the door and jump out.'

Even though she thought she might be in danger, Janika was too obstinate not to escalate things further. She was known as the shy one of the friendship group, but she was also the most stubborn. When she did speak it was usually either to start an argument or admonish someone.

Anatol smiled. 'And how will that help you get to the station? And what about your luggage? Should I throw that out after you?'

'I know what you've done.' Everything that Anatol had said to Janika since they'd got into the car had been a lie. The route they were taking wasn't one that they'd taken before. She would have remembered. And there was no way it could be taking them anywhere near the train station. It was sloping downhill, while the road they'd turned off had been climbing upwards. And she'd heard Anatol use the toilet just before they'd set out, less than ten minutes earlier, while she'd been waiting with her shoes on by the front door. The sound of water drilling into water had been unmistakable. 'I know everything.'

Even his grief was greatly exaggerated.

Anatol laughed, his voice breathy with disbelief. 'What is it that you think you know?'

While Anatol had been speaking, Janika had reached down and pressed the button on his seatbelt. Now she sat calculating in quiet outrage, hiding its buckle in the palm of her hand. She was waiting for the perfect moment to let go.

'You're a murderer, Anatol.'

When they came to a straight section of road, she released the belt. It sprang up and juddered across Anatol's belly. 'What the . . .'

He caught the odd flat contraption in his palm and looked down at it. He'd always thought it resembled a dog. A metal muzzle with plastic ears. Then he looked up and saw that Janika had taken hold of the steering wheel. She was leaning across his seat. Before he could guess at her intentions, she'd swerved the car sharply to their right, towards a large chestnut tree at the side of the road.

'. . . fuck?'

The convertible climbed the short verge, leapt into the air and collided with the tree a foot above the ground. Anatol's body was thrown forwards. The half-worn seatbelt locked around his right shoulder, spinning him on to his side, so that his temple and jaw hit the steering wheel at the same time and his neck took the bulk of the impact.

His knee smashed into the underside of the dash. His left arm shot out and punched the windscreen.

The car swung in a quarter-circle, with the base of the tree as its pivot. Janika was thrown sideways. Her arm and shoulder hit the door beside her and her head whipped against the window. It felt like the muscles in her neck were tearing.

The car came to rest perpendicular to the road. Janika forced herself to turn towards Anatol, adrenaline pushing her through the pain in her neck. His head was resting on the steering wheel, facing away from her, his left arm lying inert on the dashboard. His hand was bent too far to one side. Blood was dripping down from his chin to his knees. Janika couldn't tell whether he was alive or dead. She studied the broad slope of his back and placed her palm between his shoulders, but she couldn't feel him breathing. She pressed on his neck but couldn't find a pulse. 'Shit,' she whispered.

Now it was her turn to stare at the world through the gaps in her hand and ask herself: was any of this real?

Had she really killed him?

SUNDAY
30 May 1999

Friendship Can Weather Anything

The weekend would end with Anatol's death, early on Monday. But the chain of events that led to it began the night before: on his thirtieth birthday.

It was Sunday, 30 May, the year 1999; the day before the bank holiday; two days before the start of summer; and seven months before the end of the millennium, which so many were convinced would mean the end of the world. Anatol had invited his friends to spend the long weekend at his house in Wiltshire, as they'd done every year since the year he'd turned twenty: 'A weekend without cards, cake or presents, with no singing and no acknowledgement whatsoever of the passage of time.'

After a decade, this tradition was about to come to a sudden end.

'I know what you all think of me . . .'

Anatol was slurring his words. He stood swaying at the centre of the drawing room, with his friends seated around him in a rough circle. There were four of them. Janika, Phoebe, Dean and Maya. Anatol towered above them all, standing as tall as a column of smoke curling from a campfire. 'I'm the convenient friend with the big house in the country.'

The room had been laid out in a style common to cavernous old houses, with oversized furniture in front of the fireplace and spindly antiques pushed up against the walls.

Maya was lying on a classic red Chesterfield, while Dean sank into a mossy-green velveteen couch opposite; Phoebe was sitting upright beside him. The long coffee table ran between the two sofas. Janika was sitting on the carpet, at one end of the table. Anatol was standing directly in front of her.

'I'm the wealthy host,' he continued. 'The grit in the oyster that caused the friendship group to form. But I'm not wealthy any more. And this was never really my house.'

Anatol's father had been an antiques dealer. Anatol had followed him into the family business. The drawing room was filled with old and obscure pieces of furniture. There was a red lacquer wedding cabinet opposite the fireplace; a pair of tall cloisonné vases straddled the door; a row of horse brasses had been pinned to the mantelpiece; a large, tarnished mirror hung facing the windows; and a series of animal horns covered one of the walls, with a scrap of white skull attached to each one. It looked like the horns had been planted in chewing gum. An old television set had been consigned to one corner, where no one could possibly watch it. There was a bronze floor lamp standing in front.

Anatol finished. 'So that means I'm back to just being grit.'

Janika crossed her arms and resisted the urge to argue with him; she felt that she'd said enough already that evening.

'Anatol.' The word rang with disapproval. Phoebe was sitting to Janika's left, her eyes wide with judgement. Phoebe was a schoolteacher by trade, but also by temperament; she often thought of herself as the only adult in the room. 'No one thinks you're grit, Anatol. No one has said that. I'm not going to let you invent things and blame them on us. We've spent the whole weekend doing what you wanted. We played that game, didn't we? We wrote those stories. And if anyone's the grit, it should be me. Most of you know each other through me.'

The friends had met at university. Janika had lived next door to Phoebe in her first year; Maya and Phoebe had grown up in the same semi-rural town in Essex; and Anatol had met Phoebe when he'd auditioned for a student play she'd been helping to produce: *Six Characters in Search of an Author*. Dean had been a friend of Anatol's and had met Phoebe at the cast party; he'd later married Phoebe's sister, Yulie.

'So who's the pearl?' Maya was pooled, like a cat, on the red leather sofa; she was an artist, interested only in interpreting the world, not in taking part in it. 'Sorry,' she added. 'I wasn't listening.'

Dean groaned and sank into his seat. A mild-mannered civil engineer with the Highways Agency, Dean had an aversion to conflict that was so extreme it could have qualified as a phobia. He pushed his glasses to the top of his nose. 'Haven't we all just had a bit too much to drink?'

The sixth member of their group, Marcin – who had a high-paying job in finance and was, in fact, the wealthiest of them all, wealthier even than Anatol, though he'd been raised in far more humble circumstances – had been missing since they'd woken up that morning.

'I know what you all think of me,' Anatol repeated, unfazed by his friends' interruptions. 'I doubt I'll see you again after you leave here tomorrow. Once I've sold the house, why would you bother? Friendship can weather anything except change.'

'What do you think we think of you?' asked Phoebe, shaking her head.

'You think that I murdered my father,' said Anatol.

And then the telephone started to ring.

Anatol hurried out of the drawing room, relieved at finally being able to escape the conversation, and headed towards the nook at the bottom of the staircase, where his landline was located.

'Hello?' he said, breathlessly, into the handset.

'Anatol?' He heard a woman's voice, speaking quietly. Anatol couldn't quite place it, but it sounded familiar. 'I'm glad I got through, Anatol. Something awful has happened.'

'Who is this?' asked Anatol. 'Who am I speaking to?'

'It's Marcin,' said the voice. 'Marcin is dead.'

THREE WEEKS EARLIER
7 May 1999

Mourning Socks

But before that there was the funeral. Anatol's father – Augustine, or 'Gus' for short – had died five weeks before Anatol's thirtieth birthday; he was buried two weeks later, on a chilly morning in early May.

The air was saturated with the smell of stone. Dean, Anatol's closest friend, was sitting at the back of the small, shabby church, wearing an austere black suit and black shoes. Anatol was seated several rows in front. Sombre voices filled the distance between the two men, but both sat in silence, waiting for the service to begin; Anatol was staring wide-eyed at the stained-glass windows in front of him, while Dean was passing the time by trying to rock the pew he was sitting on back and forth, until his calves started to scream from the exertion. Dean had the entire row to himself: his wife, Yulie, had balked at the idea of taking a day off work and he guessed that his friends had felt the same. He hadn't seen anyone that he'd recognized when he'd entered the church, except for Anatol. Dean didn't want to be there either, but his aversion to confrontation was sufficiently strong that when Anatol had invited him to the funeral, a few days earlier, he hadn't felt comfortable inventing an excuse.

'Absolutely,' he'd said, speaking slowly, his mind racing. 'I'd love to come.'

But at least it had given him a break from Yulie. Dean stretched out his legs to soothe his muscles and noticed that his trousers had risen slightly. Underneath, he was wearing a pair of lurid magenta socks, patterned with pictures of sausage dogs. They were the colour of gums or bubble gum, gaudy and disrespectful. Dean had put them on that morning as a sort of silent protest against the enforced solemnity of the occasion, since he'd never particularly liked Anatol's father – and although Dean didn't like conflict, he wasn't above pettiness – but he'd done so in the belief that no one would be able to see them, which had been true until he'd sat down. Now two bright strips of pinkish purple were clearly visible, even in the darkness below the pew.

Dean swore under his breath. He started to shift in his seat, trying to work some slack from his thighs down to his ankles, but his trousers were too tight. He would have to stand up. Though that would attract more attention than he was comfortable with. Instead, he crossed his legs and covered one of the socks with a cupped hand, hoping that the other one would be less noticeable on its own. He'd been sitting like that for several minutes, enduring the discomfort, when someone placed a hand on his shoulder. Dean's heart started to beat fast; he held his breath. There is nothing quite as isolating as being at the funeral of someone you'd never liked. Then he turned his head and felt sudden relief.

Phoebe, his second-oldest friend, his sister-in-law – who was always tolerant of her friends' imperfections – was standing behind him, looking concerned. 'Have a seat,' said Dean, patting the pew beside him. 'This is the largest armchair I've ever sat in and probably the most uncomfortable. But it's nice to sit on something that's not pointed at the television. You know what Yulie's like.'

'Dean.' Phoebe was speaking quietly. 'There's something important I need to talk to you about.'

TWO WEEKS BEFORE THAT
23 April 1999

Conversation Considered as One of the Fine Arts

But the story begins two weeks earlier, on a Friday evening in late April: the day that Anatol's father died. Maya was sitting lengthways on the couch in her small barrel-vaulted studio flat in the Barbican complex in the City of London. Her bed was directly above her, on a wooden mezzanine at one end of the room; Maya had done nothing with the day, since waking up at noon, except drop down from the bed to the couch. It had been nearly a week since she'd last left the flat.

She was sitting with her legs bent and her knees raised, with a glint of silver between her finger and thumb, holding a pair of tweezers. Her mint-green pyjama bottoms were pulled down to her shins, while she picked at an ingrown hair on her thigh: a comma, curling into her skin. Painful, and ungrammatical. She positioned the tweezers, held her breath and plucked. The hair came out without any audible noise, but the sensation itself was onomatopoeic: a brief resistance that melted into a quick twitch of the hand and brought the tiniest tingle to her fingertips. A stubborn pain followed by sudden relief.

'Pluck,' said Maya.

She leaned forwards and inspected the rogue follicle. A puckered eyelet with a wink of blood. Maya pictured herself taking a scalpel and a magnifying glass and cutting a small square around it, one millimetre by one millimetre, creating something like a carpet tile that she could then peel off with the tweezers. But this daydream was interrupted by the harsh metallic ring of the telephone: a restored vintage model in blood-red Bakelite.

Maya wiped her thigh with the edge of her palm, put the tweezers down on the coffee table and stared out of the window at the end of the flat.

The sunset was apocalyptic; a sheet of clouds rose above the wall of flats opposite, their pitted undersides coloured purple, pink and crimson. It looked like a mixture of blood and bubble bath. Maya blinked as she stared at the palette of light. It had been five days since she'd last been outside, snubbing even her studio nearby. The floor of her flat was littered with sketches that she'd abandoned, unfinished. They were part of a series of drab urban landscapes, representing the locations of every murder that had happened in London the previous January – the collection as a whole called *Happy New Year* – which hadn't turned out as evocative as Maya had hoped. She'd thought about daubing each one with just enough of her own blood to colour the skies red, but the practical difficulties of doing so seemed insurmountable and instead she'd fallen into a creative slump. Her flat was now a living diorama of the artistic process – stalled.

She stood and yawned and pulled up her trousers.

The phone had been ringing for more than a minute. Maya finally thought about answering it. There was a vanishing chance it could be something important. She walked over to the low table by the front door and lifted the handset.

'Hello?' she said cautiously.

'Maya? It's me.' The voice was Phoebe's; Maya and Phoebe had grown up in the same town and attended the same school, but had only become close at university. 'Do you have a moment to talk? I have some bad news.'

'I can give you two minutes,' said Maya, chewing on her hair. 'Three, at the most. Then I'm heading out to a private view. If I don't get there early the white will be warm.'

'The what?'

Maya glanced at the glass of lukewarm red that she'd left on the counter the night before. Dishes were piled high in the sink behind it. 'The white wine, Phoebe. It'll be radioactive.'

Phoebe declined to engage with Maya's obvious embellishments; she'd heard them all too many times before. 'Anatol's father died this afternoon. You should give him a call. Or send him a card, at least.'

'Gus?' Maya looked across the room at a set of drawers standing underneath the stairs to the mezzanine. Somewhere inside was a photograph of her friends, lined up in front of Anatol's house; Gus had been looking out from one of the windows behind them, until Maya had removed him from the image with a pair of nail scissors. She tried to picture his face but all she could see was that diamond-shaped absence. 'I'm not sure I'd call that bad news, Phoebe. I barely knew him.'

'But you know Anatol, don't you?'

Maya turned to the row of hooks, by the door, that held her keys. Anatol's watch was hanging beside them. He'd left it at her flat the last time he'd visited. 'Why? He wasn't involved, was he?'

'Involved?'

'In Gus's death?'

Phoebe sighed, unamused by the idea. 'No, Maya. It was an accident.'

'What kind of accident?'

'The tragic kind.'

'Why? What happened?'

'Maya. Don't get too excited, all right? I know what you're like. Don't make a big deal out of this.'

Maya hadn't felt anything resembling excitement in weeks. But the hint of intrigue underlying Phoebe's words had grabbed hold of her and was starting to pull her, slowly, out of her malaise. 'What do you mean? Was it something gruesome?'

Phoebe sighed once again: a long, tinny whistle through the wire. 'Just don't enjoy it too much, Maya. Don't start daydreaming. He was Anatol's father, remember.'

Maya scanned the paintings that were hanging from the walls of her flat, all violent shapes and morbid colours. She felt inspiration taking hold. 'I don't think I'll bother with the private view, after all, Phoebe. That means that I've got the whole evening free. Why don't you tell me everything? I want to know all the gory details.'

The surfaces in Phoebe's lounge were like tide pools, left behind by a sea of memories: every shelf, sill and table, as well as the top of the television, was crowded with ornaments, photographs and souvenirs. Slotted between these sentimental trinkets were the birthday cards from when she'd turned thirty, six months earlier. Everyone, except Anatol, had sent her a card. Dean had made his own, using clip art. It showed a blue cartoon dog chewing on a plant. 'It's all hound dill from here . . .'

Phoebe kept her small flat crowded with memories so she could feel like she had something to show for the three decades that she'd been alive: something better than a one-bedroom flat in Crouch End, with two-thirds of the mortgage left to pay, and a job teaching French to uninvested teenagers. Somewhere, safely packed away in a shoebox, were the birthday cards from when she'd turned twenty.

'I know you think I'm boring, Maya.'

Phoebe was sitting in a gold-fringed armchair with the telephone balanced on her knees. She could hear clanking pans and the sound of piano practice coming through the walls from the neighbouring flat. There was something infantilizing about living in London. Phoebe had always thought that adult life would consist of weekly dinner parties and drinks outside on long summer evenings, but she was still living like a student and hardly had enough space to entertain her friends; her flat was one half of the middle floor of a Victorian terraced house and she shared the garden with five other families. A small tabby cat bounded into the lounge from the adjoining bedroom and claimed half the space for itself.

'Just because I don't share your morbid fascinations,' Phoebe continued. 'But I'm proud to be boring. In fact, I don't think I'm boring enough. I should be living somewhere sleepy with a husband and a dog . . .'

The cat gave her a look that was half outrage, half helplessness. He was called Roundel, named for the dark patterns on his sandy fur. Phoebe had adopted him a month after her thirtieth birthday, but he was already getting too big for the flat.

'Nowhere too boring,' she added. 'But more boring than this.'

'You're the Goldilocks of boredom,' said Maya. 'Goldilocks and the three bores.'

Phoebe nodded, glad to have finally got her off the topic of death. 'And what a boring story that would be . . .'

After ending the phone call, Phoebe reached down and scratched Roundel's head, careful to keep the telephone balanced on her lap. Beside it was a spiral-bound notebook, where she'd written out a list of names; she'd volunteered to call each of her friends in turn and tell them the news about Gus, knowing that no one else would do it. For her own amusement, she'd written the list as if she'd been enumerating the suspects in a murder mystery: she crossed out 'Maya, the Artist', and moved on to 'Marcin, the Millionaire'.

What would that make her?

'The Teacher'?

Phoebe groaned and dialled Marcin's number.

'But that doesn't sound like an accident at all.'

Marcin's lust for gossip fogged the glass. He was standing in silhouette against his floor-to-ceiling windows, flanked by the abstract shapes of his furniture – with the handset of his telephone in one hand and its base in the other – looking down at the river, six storeys below. On the opposite bank was the ivory facade of the naval college in Greenwich; its exoskeleton of needless columns glowed in the low light.

'That sounds more like murder,' he added.

'Marcin. I've just had this conversation with Maya.' Phoebe's voice sounded small and exhausted, shrunk to the size of a fifty-pence piece and pressed into Marcin's palm, but her teacherly tone was unmistakable. 'I don't particularly want to have it again.'

'Then why don't you hang up,' said Marcin, 'and I'll call Maya and talk to her?'

'Marcin . . .' After a moment of wounded silence, Phoebe relented. 'Who do you think murdered him, then?'

The lounge was lit only by twilight. Marcin could never bring himself to switch on the electric lights until he'd been back from work for at least an hour, though the river would have usually turned black by then; he didn't want to acknowledge the end of the evening so soon after it had begun.

'Anatol,' he said matter-of-factly. 'I would have thought that was obvious.'

The air in the flat was scorching and stuffy. The heating had been set to come on at six, so it had been running for several hours by the time Marcin had returned from work, nearer to nine. He was a quantitative analyst at an investment bank. The job paid well, but he worked more than ten hours most days and drank almost every evening. A neat glass of whisky was warming on a hardwood pedestal beside him.

'Anatol has an alibi,' said Phoebe. 'He's been in London for the last two days, staying with Dean and Yulie.' Yulie was Phoebe's younger sister. 'I had dinner with them yesterday.'

'Murderers always have alibis, Phoebe.' Marcin opened the window in front of him – a sliding door that led out to a balcony – and felt a rush of fresh cold air. 'I suppose it could have been suicide.' He was looking down at the ground below, wondering what it would feel like to fall from such a height. A hard landing, cushioned by nothingness. Then the simple pleasures of not existing. 'But it doesn't sound like an accident. This isn't the sixties. People don't have those kinds of accidents any more. Electric blankets used to burn down houses. Deep fat fryers used to take out tower blocks. But modern appliances are much safer. And people know how to use them. Even Gus would know not to—'

'Marcin,' said Phoebe curtly. 'Do you have any evidence for what you're suggesting?'

'Evidence? Like what?'

'Exactly. This is all just speculation. But what happened to being innocent until proven guilty? Or don't you believe in that?'

The list of things that Marcin didn't believe in was long and multifarious and included God; the afterlife; the teachings of religion in general; an objective morality; the goodness of mankind; progress, which was in his view a fanciful concept that could be extrapolated from at most the last two or three hundred years of history, and then only if you ignored the majority of it; the power of positive thinking; marriage; monogamy; children; ghosts and the supernatural; nonsense such as the Loch Ness monster; the celebration of Christmas; horoscopes; the relevance of anything celestial to everyday life; the fitness for purpose of politics and politicians; dictatorship, democracy; communism, capitalism and ideologies in general; celebrity in all its guises; the wisdom of crowds; the profound nature of romantic love; and the jury system.

Marcin didn't really believe in anything when it came to the state of the world, except for the mathematical inevitability of complexity leading to chaos leading to cruelty and death. He would often describe himself as a nihilist, though he didn't like the connotations of extremism that came with the word; it was simply a way of summarizing what was, in his judgement, a sensible way of looking at things. But he hammed it up anyway and dressed mostly in black.

'No, Phoebe. It's a slogan for idiots. You're guilty from the moment you commit the crime. I would have thought that was obvious too. And Anatol is set to inherit everything. *Cui bono?*'

'Latin isn't an argument, Marcin. I know people like you would like it to be . . .'

'People like me?'

'Yes. Pretentious people.'

Marcin smiled, proud of having provoked Phoebe to the point of insulting him. 'Touché,' he said shortly.

'And I can't tell whether you're being serious or not,' Phoebe continued. 'But you don't really believe that Anatol's a criminal, do you?'

'I think it's possible,' said Marcin, with some restraint. 'People do bad things all the time. And not everything that's illegal is immoral. Smoking cannabis, insider trading. In my line of work it's illegal just to know things. How does that make any sense?'

'We're talking about murder, Marcin.'

'Technically. But it's not like Gus had much of a life.'

'Marcin,' said Phoebe with renewed disapproval. 'Anatol is one of your best friends. You should at least give him the benefit of the doubt.'

But Marcin didn't believe in the sanctity of friendship; friendship was often just a sign of shared history, or an indication of a few common interests; it had nothing at all to do with morality.

'You can't deny that it's possible, Phoebe.'

Phoebe felt a pang of guilt when she hung up the phone. Throughout the call her eyes had kept returning to the most impractical item in her large collection of memories:

a huge piece of driftwood which lay on the floor in front of the disused fireplace, flanked by a pair of empty Galliano bottles. It was more than a metre long and sanded smooth by the sea. Anatol had carried it back for her from a day out in Worthing, holding it over his shoulder like a club. It was easy to imagine him using it as a weapon. And it was only a short leap from that to picturing him as a murderer.

Phoebe sighed and shook her head and reached down to Roundel for comfort; he rubbed his forehead against her dangling hand. The conversation with Marcin had made Phoebe paranoid and anxious. She'd torn the first two pages of her notebook to shreds.

She crossed off 'Marcin, the Millionaire,' and moved on to 'Janika, the Professor'. It was Dean who had told Phoebe what had happened to Gus – and obviously Anatol already knew – so Janika was the last name on her list.

She picked up the phone and dialled Janika's home number.

Janika kept the lights in her office low so that she would always have a view, even when it was dark outside. The large window behind her desk opened on to a leafy section of the university campus and showed beyond it the giant clock tower piercing the night sky: a rocket ship, waiting to take the last surviving members of humanity up to the stars. Janika felt ready to join them. She had already conquered the philosophy department at the University of Birmingham and was keen to leave for somewhere new and exciting; maybe space should be her next step.

The clock's white dial floated like a second moon. Janika checked the time. It was a quarter past ten. The last of her colleagues had left the department several hours earlier. The lights in the corridor outside were switched off. Janika pulled the phone across her desk and dialled a number she knew by heart. She had no qualms about making the university pay for the call; it would be modest compensation for the fact that she was working late, though she was doing so out of choice. Janika spent most of her evenings working late.

After a minute, Phoebe picked up. 'Hello?'

She sounded concerned.

'Phoebe? It's me. Janika.'

'What do you want? You know it's after ten?'

'It's ten fifteen,' said Janika. 'Why? Were you asleep?'

'At ten o'clock on a Friday night? I'm boring, Janika, but not that boring. I was in the bath.'

'Then why did you answer?'

'Because I thought you might be Anatol,' said Phoebe.

Janika dealt with being shy by asking lots of questions, but also by arguing endlessly with the answers people gave. 'Well, why can Anatol call after ten if I can't?'

'Because his father died today. Don't tell me that yours did too? I sincerely hope not.'

'No.' Janika pressed the point. 'But I did get an email from you, Phoebe, saying that I should call.'

'Yes. You did. I was trying to reach you earlier. Anatol asked me to let everyone know. About Gus. But it's not that urgent.'

'You didn't say whether it was or it wasn't.'

'Well. It wasn't.'

Janika rolled her eyes. 'It's no use saying it now, Phoebe. How's Anatol?'

'I don't know. He seemed all right the last time I spoke

to him. But I don't think he'd processed it properly. That was a few hours ago.'

'I'll send flowers.' Janika picked up a pen, pulled a pad of paper towards her and wrote the word 'flowers'. Then she started to doodle, drawing a cramped auditorium, peopled with stick figures, strangling one another. 'Does he like flowers? He doesn't like presents.'

'I don't know,' said Phoebe. 'Send them anyway.'

'What about his birthday? What's happening with that?'

'Next month, you mean?'

'Yes,' said Janika. 'Are we still going to his house for the bank holiday?'

'I hope so. I didn't ask.'

'Why not?'

'Because I don't think it's particularly important right now.'

'Maybe not for you. But I need to make plans, Phoebe. I get back on the Saturday of that weekend. I'll be in Australia, remember.'

'Then you can ask him, can't you?'

'Maybe I'll mention it in the card.' Janika stopped doodling and wrote the word 'card'. 'Or would that be insensitive?'

In a fortnight, Janika was due to leave for three weeks in Sydney. It was a work trip. She'd spent the evening choosing sixteen photocopied articles and five textbooks to take with her, plus a collection of crossword puzzles to relax with on the plane. Her desk was covered in papers and books. A guidebook to Sydney sat on top of the pile. The five fingernails of the opera house reached out from its cover.

'I expect the plan will stay the same,' said Phoebe. 'I

don't suppose he'd want to spend his birthday on his own. Not after this. Would you?'

Janika nodded and wrote the word 'birthday'.

'So what happened?' she asked. 'How did Gus die?'

'He had an accident. It's a long story.'

Janika paused. A circle of ink started to spread from the end of her pen. It looked like a balloon being inflated. 'What kind of accident?'

'He electrocuted himself in the bath, listening to the radio.'

'That's unfortunate,' said Janika. 'There'll have to be an inquest, in that case.'

Phoebe groaned. 'Don't you start, Janika. Gus wasn't murdered. It was just an accident. And Anatol has an alibi. He was in London, staying with Dean and my sister.'

'An inquest is routine, Phoebe. It's not a murder investigation. My point was that the funeral will have to be delayed. I might not make it. I'm leaving in two weeks.'

'Sorry,' said Phoebe. 'I misunderstood.'

'I know you did.' Janika blinked at the distant clock tower; she began most conversations feeling irritable, as if she'd just been woken up from a nap, but she usually softened once the grogginess had passed. 'I'd like to be there, for Anatol's sake. But it might not be possible. There's so much I have to do in the next two weeks. This trip is very important for me, Phoebe. There'll be people there I need to impress. That means small talk. And that means practice. Practice and preparation.'

'Anatol will understand,' said Phoebe.

Janika turned to a new page and wrote the word 'inquest'. 'So who is it that thinks it was murder?' she asked.

SATURDAY
29 May 1999

Nicotine Yellow

Every single pore in Marcin's body is smoking its own miniature cigarette. A hundred thousand tiny white gloves are floating over those dewy openings, holding cigarettes to them and letting them inhale, then taking the cigarettes away again. And then his whole body is breathing out smoke, like a burnt roast chicken . . .

Marcin woke from this dream to the sight of the moon, fading into the sunrise. The overcast sky was stained nicotine yellow, the river below it silver and pink.

It was 5.00 a.m. on the Saturday of Anatol's birthday weekend, the day before his actual birthday, five weeks after his father's death and three weeks after the funeral.

The phone was ringing.

Marcin pulled his black bedsheets around his shoulders, making a cape, and stumbled through to the lounge. 'Hello?' he said, sceptically, into the handset.

'Marcin,' said a voice. 'It's me, Janika.' She sounded disgruntled. More so than usual. 'I know it's early, before you point that out. You don't have to tell me. I don't have much time. I'm going to be getting on a plane in a minute . . .'

'It's five o'clock in the morning, Janika.'

'Marcin. Concentrate. This call is costing me a lot.'

Marcin opened the sliding door and stepped outside, on to the balcony, taking the telephone with him. 'Me too, Janika.'

'But you didn't have to answer it, did you? The only reason I called you is because you have an answerphone. You could have let me leave a message.' Everything that Marcin owned was needlessly expensive, from the widescreen television to the squid-like lemon squeezer; the digital answerphone was no exception. 'Otherwise I would have called Phoebe.'

The sunrise looked the same as always. Marcin turned his back on it and found a pack of cigarettes hidden in a plant pot. He hadn't smoked at all since the previous morning, almost twenty-four hours earlier. He took one out and searched the balcony for a lighter. 'Where are you?' he asked. 'Still in Australia?'

'I'm at the airport in Singapore, halfway home. I thought you'd quit?'

Marcin plucked the unlit cigarette from his lips and looked at it like it was possessed. 'How did you know?'

'I can hear the wind,' said Janika. 'You're outside, on the balcony. What happened?'

Marcin had been trying to quit smoking since the start of the month. He'd been doing well for the first three weeks, but had lapsed over the last few days. 'I had some bad news earlier this week.' Marcin looked through the window at the marble-topped console table in the corner of his lounge; there was an envelope on top of it, addressed to his flat in anonymous, upper-case handwriting. 'And quitting takes practice, like everything else. You didn't send me a letter, did you?'

'I've sent you a postcard. But it probably won't arrive for another week. Why?'

Marcin sighed. 'Somebody sent me something. It's not important. Why are you calling, Janika? What do you want? Presumably it wasn't just to wake me up?'

'I need to know if this weekend is actually happening. Anatol was supposed to have told me by now. But I've been emailing him and he hasn't replied. And I've tried calling but he's not answering the phone. Maybe he's not at home, but it's hard not to feel like I'm being ignored.'

'He's probably not answering because it's the middle of the night.'

'I tried all day yesterday, as well. And the day before that. I'm supposed to be landing at Heathrow in about fourteen hours and I need to know what to do when I get there. Do I head back to Birmingham or stay in London? I'd like to see you all. I've got some news.'

'What news?'

'I'll tell you in person.'

Marcin dropped his rejected cigarette over the railing. Then he took the pack, which was still half full, and threw it carefully on to the balcony below his; it landed next to four other packs that he'd thrown down there over the previous week. Their bright red and white branding stood out clearly against the tawny decking, like a hand of cards laid down in a poker game.

'I hope he's at home,' said Marcin. 'I'm planning to set out in an hour or two.' He remembered the time. 'Or maybe three.'

'So the birthday party is going ahead then? I need to know.'

Janika's stress was infectious; Marcin already regretted getting rid of his cigarettes. 'I think so,' he said. 'Why wouldn't it be?'

'I don't know. I've been away for three weeks. Anything could have happened in that time, Marcin. Anatol could have died, for all I know. He could have moved house. He could have been arrested.'

Marcin stepped back inside his handsomely furnished flat and closed the door behind him. He had spent the last five weeks waiting patiently for news of Anatol's arrest, but it hadn't come. 'He's alive,' he said. 'He hasn't moved house. And he seems to have got away with murder.'

Scene at a Rural Train Station

A handful of people got off the train in front of Phoebe, later on Saturday morning. She followed them along the platform, then out through the station building. She was wearing a smart white and rainbow-striped pastel pullover with muted blue jeans, both covered in cat hair, and was carrying a brown leather travelling bag and a white bouquet of lilies and roses. It was raining heavily. The flowers were slowly filling with water. Phoebe stopped in front of the station building and tilted the bunch towards the ground, watching as the petals regurgitated liquid.

She was just outside the village of Tisbury in Wiltshire, a large settlement relative to the region, though still small enough to be hidden from view by a single line of trees. All Phoebe could see of it, on the slope of the hill opposite, were some pointed rooftops rising from the greenery, and the snaggle-tooth of a church spire jutting upwards at one end.

A small access lane joined the station to the road that led into the village. It was lined with parking spaces, painted on to the tarmac in white. A man in front of Phoebe got into a waiting taxi, but the rest of the people from her train hurried onwards towards the village. No one wanted to hang around and get wet. Phoebe followed them as far as the road, then turned and walked back towards the station. She hadn't seen Anatol's car in the car park. In fact, she'd hardly bothered to look for it, knowing that he would be late, as usual.

She found an unused doorway, set back slightly into the wall of the station building, and took shelter under the eaves. She took out her new mobile phone and checked to see if she'd missed a call from Anatol, but she hadn't; she didn't have any signal anyway. A curtain of raindrops dripped from the brickwork above.

'Come on,' she muttered, holding the phone up high.

There were few things in life that bothered Phoebe like lateness. Especially when it led to her having to wait in public, humiliated. She felt like a bride abandoned at an altar, the bouquet of flowers underlining her plight. But it was her own fault for telling Anatol the actual time that her train was due, when she knew she should have told him a time fifteen minutes earlier; it was her own fault for being thirty and not knowing how to drive. She plucked a leaf from the side of the bouquet and dug a thumbnail into its flesh, allowing her agitation to blossom into anger.

'Where the fuck are you?' she whispered.

With an answering sigh, the train that had brought her to Tisbury started to move. When its last carriage had passed out of the diminutive station, it felt like a great wall had been torn down. Behind it, Phoebe saw a steel fence, struggling to hold back a hedge of buddleia, and a high ridge of empty green fields. Train tracks stapled the horizon to the sky.

It was a scene as desolate as Phoebe felt.

But Phoebe had been feeling unsettled all morning. She'd left her flat much later than she had intended – worried that she would miss her train, though in fact she'd arrived at Waterloo with enough time to buy flowers on the concourse – after sitting in her cramped kitchen for as long as she'd felt able, clinging anxiously to a cup of tea, while her cat, Roundel, had pleaded for a second breakfast, just in case the post had come early, though she'd known on a Saturday morning that would be unlikely. But she'd received a strange letter the day before and had wanted to see if she'd get another one like it. It had consisted of a single sheet of A5 paper, folded twice, with two large words printed neatly in the middle, written entirely in upper case. The characters had been made up of short straight lines and most likely drawn with a ruler. The envelope had been written the same way, addressed to Phoebe at her flat in Crouch End. It had been posted from somewhere in London the previous morning, judging by the postmark, though she hadn't opened it until Friday evening, after she'd got back home from the school where she worked.

'I KNOW.'

That's all it had said, in large black lettering.

'I KNOW.'

And nothing else.

At that moment, Anatol's convertible came speeding down the access road, drawing a curtain across all of Phoebe's concerns. With a sudden screech, it swerved haphazardly into one of the empty parking spaces and came to a stop. The painted white lines sliced off its back left wheel. Then the door opened and Anatol clambered out. He was wearing corduroy trousers and a tweed blazer. As he climbed from the car, his knees and elbows bent into angles that made each limb look like the hands of a clock. When he was fully unfolded, he stood towering above his vehicle – six foot six inches tall – with an arm resting on its roof. He was holding a newspaper over his head to keep off the rain.

Phoebe picked up her bag and made a sudden, undignified dash along the access lane towards him. 'You're early,' she said, slowing down as she approached.

Anatol gave her a puzzled smile, tilting the newspaper back so it formed a peak above his forehead, out of his peripheral vision. He squinted bashfully. 'I'm late, aren't I?'

'Yes,' she said. 'You're very late.'

Anatol seemed unsure what to say to that. After a second of self-doubt, his arm came down and he offered Phoebe the newspaper. She shook her head, placed her bag on the ground, and gave him an aggressive, grunting hug, holding the flowers out to one side.

'Don't joke like that,' said Anatol as he patted Phoebe's back clumsily. 'I thought I was going mad for a moment. I thought I was turning into my father.'

Phoebe could feel soggy, cold newsprint slapping against her neck. She broke off their embrace, took the paper out of Anatol's hand and folded it under her arm. Then she picked up her bag and held it out towards him. The brown leather was turning to leopard print in the rain. 'At least if you were you'd have an excuse for being late.'

Anatol sighed and took hold of the bag. 'It's not my fault I was late,' he said, gesturing at the flowers. 'Do you want me to take those too?'

'No.' Phoebe stepped back defiantly. 'You'll crush them.'

Anatol walked around to the back of the car. 'There were ducks crossing the road. You wouldn't want me to drive over ducks, would you?' He took a careful, conciliatory look at his wristwatch. 'Was your train on time?'

'It was two minutes early. You're fifteen minutes late. There must have been a lot of ducks.'

'That train's never on time. One of us always ends up waiting.'

'Yes,' said Phoebe loudly, suddenly amused by her own hopeless indignation. She patted the convertible's vinyl roof, sending raindrops flying in every direction. 'And it should be you, Anatol. You have a car. You have shelter. You can sit in comfort and read the newspaper.'

'No. That's worse.' Anatol lifted her bag into the boot. 'The inside of a parked car is like purgatory. It's like being in a cage. I'd rather stand out here in the rain.'

'Is that right?'

Phoebe opened the passenger door and slid inside, placing the soaked newspaper on the floor by her feet and standing the flowers between her thighs. She thought about locking Anatol out, to teach him a lesson, but couldn't bring herself to be that cruel. He slammed the boot shut and came to join her in the car.

'I'm sorry,' he said as he climbed inside, straining to be heard above the sound of the rain. 'But I had to go to the shops this morning. I was out of almost everything. I tried to be quick.' He gestured to the space behind their seats. It was loaded with shopping bags, groceries showing through the stretched white plastic. 'Anyway, I'm still grieving.'

'What's grief got to do with being late?'

'Well. That's a good question.' Anatol struggled to think of an answer. 'It's not the grief, exactly. It's the work, Phoebe. It's relentless. Grief is a needle in a haystack of work. There's so much to sort out, so many things to throw away. That's what I've been doing this morning. That's why I'm a tiny bit late.' Anatol nodded at the nearest lily.

'Do you want me to put those in the back with the shopping?'

He placed a throttling hand on the bunch.

Phoebe moved the flowers away from him. 'No, don't. You might damage them. I've been holding them upright the whole way here. It's been like that game at school where you're given a bag of flour and have to pretend it's a baby.' Phoebe reached up to one of the petals and smudged a raindrop under her thumb. 'I can't get them to stop crying.'

'They look just like you.' Anatol took the car keys from his pocket and started the engine. 'I've got the perfect vase for them at home. It's just the right size for drowning a child.'

Phoebe gave the flowers a shake. 'I got them for Gus. They're going on his grave.'

'Gus?' Anatol sounded disappointed. 'Why? Weren't there enough flowers at his funeral?'

'Yes,' said Phoebe. 'But those must be dead by now?'

Anatol shrugged. 'I haven't been up there.'

'It's on the way, isn't it?'

'Now, you mean?'

'Yes. Why not?'

'Well. It's raining.'

'It'll only take me a minute,' said Phoebe.

But Anatol was shaking his head. 'There isn't even a headstone yet. The grave is just a pile of mud. You could sort of stab the flowers into the soil and they might stay upright. But they won't last long. Not in this weather.'

'That doesn't matter. It's the gesture that counts.'

The engine was still running, but Anatol had taken his hands from the wheel. 'Can't you go on your own? You could walk up from the house this afternoon.'

'In the rain?' said Phoebe. 'Don't you want to come with me? I thought it would be a nice thing to do together.'

'No.'

'Why not?'

'It's my birthday, Phoebe. What kind of party begins with a visit to a cemetery?'

'Your birthday's tomorrow, Anatol. Don't you ever go up there?'

'No. I don't. I find it depressing.'

'I'm sorry. I didn't realize.' Phoebe stared at the nearest rose. It looked like it could have been made of marble. 'Maybe if we go there together it won't be so bad?'

'I don't see why that would make any difference. I want to move on, Phoebe. He died five weeks ago.'

There was a small hole in one of Phoebe's sleeves. She worked a fingertip into it and worried at the wool. 'All right. But I'd feel bad if I didn't put them on his grave, now that I've brought them all the way here. It would feel like I was turning my back on him.'

Anatol put the car in reverse. 'He's not there, Phoebe. He won't even know about it.'

'Anyway. You owe me, for turning up late.'

'You're not going to let that go, are you?' Anatol looked over his shoulder and stepped on the pedal. The low convertible powered backwards. 'All right, I'll take you there. But I'm staying in the car.'

Artist in Residence

Maya was the first to arrive at Anatol's house, shortly after ten o'clock on Saturday morning. Her sleek silver hatchback, a Nissan Micra, trickled across the gravel driveway, lurching back and forth as she decided where to park, before coming to a stop under an overhanging section of hedge. It was raining heavily.

The house looked huge against the grey sky: a former Georgian rectory, built of red brick, it was three storeys tall and wide enough for five white-framed windows to fit in a line across its front, with four further windows in a row underneath and two dormers in the loft. Its rusted slate roof cut into the sky, while coils of rainwater hung from the gutters, banging like loose wires against the windows. Puddles of silt pitted the driveway.

Maya climbed out of her car and pulled on a knitted orange hat. She was wearing a beige duffle coat over a loose-fitting grey midi dress and a pair of Ugg boots. She frowned up at the imposing clouds, held out her hand and tested the rain with her palm. Her movements were unhurried, even while she was getting soaked; her only concession to the weather was the wounded furrow that formed on her brow. She walked around to the boot of her car and took out a white vintage suitcase with riveted leather straps. She carried it towards the house and put it down in front of the door, noticing, as she did so, a bright yellow note caught in the brass letterbox. That touch of fluorescence had the feel of something contemporary left by mistake in a historical film, exposing the whole thing as a fraud. Maya slid the note from its trap and sat down on her suitcase.

'Gone to pick up Phoebe,' she read. 'Back soon. Anatol. P.S. The door is unlocked.'

Maya had been hoping for a more salacious message but now she knew why there were no other cars on the driveway and why the house looked dead, or at least hungover.

'Hello?' she called out.

But there was no response.

Maya opened the front door and moved her suitcase into the hallway. She turned to her right and went through to the kitchen. The room was long, with windows at both ends and an arched recess for an oven in the middle. A section of the worktop jutted out near the door, making a sort of standing table or breakfast bar. Maya walked over to it and leaned her elbows on top, looking towards the back of the room.

'Is anybody home?' She spoke quietly, knowing the answer.

Maya had grown up as the youngest of five siblings, so in her opinion an empty house was something to be celebrated. The yellow note was still in her hand. Maya screwed it into a ball and turned to the tall fridge-freezer a few steps to her right. There were several nice things inside but nothing much took her fancy. She dug a fingernail into the butter and licked it clean. Then she balanced the ball of lurid yellow paper among the potatoes in the bottom drawer, making an instant work of art. But the note looked lost in the busy fridge; she picked it up again and left the kitchen.

There were five guest bedrooms on the first floor of Anatol's house. Maya emptied her suitcase on to the bed in the room that she usually slept in – and consequently thought of as her own – which was, coincidentally, the largest bedroom and the only one with an en-suite bathroom, and found a compact camera among her clothes. It was silver and black, with an inch-long lens. She left it sitting on one of the pillows.

Above the bed was a painting of John the Baptist being beheaded; Maya had hung her duffel coat from the edge of the frame; she fished a pack of cigarettes from one of its pockets. There was a small circular table by the window with two cushioned chairs pushed underneath. Maya extracted a black Mary Jane shoe from the pile of her belongings and placed it on the table. The yellow scrap of paper was still in her hand. She unfolded it, flattening it with her thumbs as best she could, and pressed it slightly into the neck of the shoe, making a shallow, makeshift ashtray. Then she pulled the top sash of the window down and lit a cigarette.

Smoking in the house was strictly forbidden – at least it had been before, when Gus had been alive – but Maya's room overlooked the driveway. She would get some warning if anyone arrived, though there were no signs of movement outside. Only the rain, tapping its weighty fingernails against the glass. When she went to knock the ash from her cigarette, Maya glanced at the note again. Anatol had gone to collect Phoebe from the station, it said. But Maya hadn't passed him on her way to the house. His vintage convertible was hard to miss: it usually trailed a cloud of black smoke. So either he'd set out before she was anywhere near and Phoebe's train was running late, or he'd gone to run other errands after picking her up and hadn't thought to mention them when writing the note. Either way, he could be gone a long time.

Maya tapped the table with indecision. She chewed loosely on the end of her cigarette. Then she took her camera from the bed and left the room.

Gus's bedroom and bathroom were up in the attic. Anatol had an identical pair of rooms at the other side of the loft, though both sides were served by separate staircases and kept apart by a pair of water tanks.

Maya stood in the doorway and surveyed Gus's room. At some point in the last five weeks, all his belongings had been removed. Most of the furniture had been taken as well. The only thing left inside was a large double bed with a wrought-iron frame and a white mattress, waiting to be skinned. A fifteen-inch promotional statue of Bibendum, the Michelin mascot, made of immovable cast iron, held open the door. It dated from the early twentieth century but was in good condition. Maya knelt, pinched the cigarette from her mouth and took a photograph of the corrugated figure. The flash gave its skin the texture of meringue. She moved it out of the way and found a host of dead insects behind the door. Maya knelt and took a picture of the swarm. It was obvious that the room hadn't been cleaned after being emptied; there were thick gatherings of dust along the base of the wall. They must have been lying dormant for years behind cupboards and under tables. Now they were free to drift across the lacquered floor.

Maya took photographs of everything she found. She followed the wall around to the side of the bed, where the stains from a spilled cup of tea traced the obvious outline of a missing bedside table. But the dirt was thickest under the bed itself. The clumps of dust that clung to the bedposts looked like handfuls of fur torn from an animal, and the gaps between the floorboards were littered with fingernails. The bedsheets above were webbed with hairs. Maya walked through to the adjoining bathroom and spat her cigarette into the toilet. She flushed and came back and lay down on the floor by the bed. She felt a wicked urge to slide underneath it, if only for the joy of climbing into the bath afterwards and watching the filth be washed from her body – picturing pellets of mouse shit being propelled from her hair like tiny torpedoes – but contented herself with taking photos.

Maya rolled on to her side and pointed the camera. The shutter clicked; the flash whined; there was a gentle knock on the open door.

'Maya?' said Dean. 'What are you doing?'

Safety First

Dean had found the three-hour drive unbearable. It was the fifth time he'd done it in as many weeks: on the night Gus had died, he'd driven Anatol back to Wiltshire from London and had stayed there for the evening, so that Anatol wouldn't have to be in the house by himself. Then he'd returned to London the following day. And he'd driven to Anatol's house again for the funeral. But none of those journeys had been as bad as this one, the day before Anatol's birthday, when the roads were busy and the rain torrential; Dean had been forced to drive with his hands clamped to the steering wheel, with wide eyes and rigid elbows, barely able to see even the vehicle in front of him.

Dean was a nervous driver in good weather, despite working for the Highways Agency; he sweated in the rain. The downpour had started as soon as he'd set out that morning. At first it had just been a few large droplets, falling infrequently – sloppy semibreves bouncing off the windscreen – but by the time he'd reached the M25 the noise had become constant. On the M3 it had been even worse; the chaotic weekend traffic had been nothing but a blur of white froth and blaring horns. A conga line that could have killed him instantly.

He'd stopped at a service station, near Fleet, for a hot drink and a few minutes of calm. He bought a takeaway coffee and took it into the toilet, where a long line of urinals faced a bank of cubicles. Dean ignored both and went straight to the sinks. He stood at one of the basins for almost a minute, taking tiny, cautious sips of his coffee, until he grew self-conscious – he was the only one there with refreshments, after all – and, for something to do, prised the top from his coffee and poured an inch or two of it down the drain. The brown liquid coiled into the porcelain depression. Dean took his time replacing the lid.

At last, he had the area by the sinks to himself.

Moving quickly, he felt in his trouser pocket for the corrugated rims of three pound coins and turned to the condom machine on the wall beside him. It was a white metal cabinet with a strip of instructions across the top. Dean pressed his three coins into the machine, then jabbed at one of the buttons below. A sapphire pack of three condoms fell into the tray at the bottom with a weightless clunk.

Dean picked them up and hid them in his palm. Normally, the transaction wouldn't have caused him any embarrassment – if anything, he'd have enjoyed a slight sense of triumph – but it felt different doing it for the sake of adultery.

It felt like everyone was watching him.

Dean turned to the mirror above the sink. He was wearing his driving clothes: grey tracksuit bottoms, a loose-fitting denim shirt and his most practical pair of glasses. But the pockets of his tracksuit were unreliable, so all his valuables, except for his loose change, were packed into the two breast pockets of his top. One had his car keys and a pair of sunglasses, the other his wallet and the keys to his house. Dean unbuttoned one of the pockets and pushed the condoms in with his wallet. The corner of the pack stabbed at his heart. He picked up his coffee and left the toilet.

There was a row of payphones at the back of the sprawling service station. Dean pulled a fourth pound coin from his pocket and used it to call his wife, Yulie. Phoebe's sister. He was the only one of the six friends that was married.

'Hello? Yulie? It's me, Dean.'

Yulie had originally been planning to accompany him for the long weekend, but had decided the week before that she didn't feel up to it. Secretly, Dean had been relieved.

'Nothing,' he said into the phone. 'I just wanted a break from driving. The weather's terrible.'

The large black handset bracketed his head; Dean was holding it like a disguise. Together with the styrofoam coffee cup, which he kept close to his mouth, it covered almost his entire face. 'You won't miss anything, Yulie, I promise. The moment something interesting happens, I'll leave the room and call you immediately. If anyone says anything funny, I'll write it down. If it's me that says it, I'll send a telegram.'

Dean wiped a sheen of sweat from his brow. 'No, I won't tell anyone,' he said. 'I won't tell Phoebe. I love you too.'

He hung up the phone and returned to his car.

Artist in Residence (continued)

Maya breathed in sharply as she looked towards the doorway, too lethargic to be startled, though she was certainly surprised. Dean was standing at the top of the stairs, hovering on the threshold with his hands in his pockets. Maya let her head loll back against the floor.

'Dean,' she said. 'How did you know I was here?'

'I could hear the toilet all the way downstairs.' The cistern hadn't finished refilling after Maya had flushed her cigarette. 'It sounds like a dying swan.'

'I didn't hear you arrive,' said Maya.

'No. Well. I didn't go out of my way to make noise.'

Dean walked through to the bathroom and fiddled with the toilet. The sound of the pipes halted abruptly, leaving only the clattering rain. 'It smells like someone's been smoking in here.'

Maya studied the ceiling. 'It wasn't me.'

Dean reappeared in the bathroom doorway. 'What are you taking pictures of?'

'Gus's shadow,' said Maya enigmatically. 'There are traces of him everywhere. Look. These are his fingernail clippings on the floor down here. And some of this dust must be his dead skin.'

'Why would you want to photograph that?'

'I want to turn his death into art. It's my way of dealing with it.' Maya prised a wispy grey hair from the side of the mattress and held it between her finger and thumb. 'These are the things that outlast us all.'

Dean sounded unconvinced. 'But only until someone vacuums.'

'It's a way of photographing loss,' said Maya. 'How else could you take a picture of absence?'

'Sorry,' said Dean, concerned that his previous comment had been too dismissive. 'You know that I don't know much about art.'

Maya raised her camera and took Dean's picture, his pained face framed by the doorway. 'It's just an idea I'm exploring. It's part of my job, Dean.'

'It sounds very interesting.'

Maya sat up and nodded indifferently. 'Do you know what happened? When Gus died? Do you know the details?'

The question coaxed Dean out of the bathroom; he tried to lean casually in the corner of the room, but ended up bouncing between the walls. 'Details like what?' he asked.

'Like where it happened?'

'In the bath,' said Dean blankly. 'In the bathroom, Maya.'

Maya got to her feet and brushed the dust from her dress. 'I know that. But there aren't any plug sockets in the bathroom.'

'It was plugged in there.' Dean indicated the socket beside the bed. 'The extension cord ran across the floor into the bathroom. The radio was balanced against the wall.'

Maya crossed the room. 'Which wall?'

Dean nodded at the distant end of the bath. 'That one.

Presumably, Gus didn't realize how dangerous it was. I don't know if that was due to dementia or just carelessness.' He pointed down at the patterned beige flooring and gave Maya a sheepish grin. 'He should have put it down there, shouldn't he? Music always sounds better on vinyl.'

'The bath is the only thing in here that's been cleaned.' Maya sounded disappointed, but she took a picture of the tub, regardless. 'Then what happened?'

'I only know what Anatol told me. It fell in, somehow. Maybe Gus was trying to tune the radio with his toes. Once it was in the water, that was it. He couldn't have climbed out. He'd have been jelly.'

Maya bit her lip. 'Would it have been painful?'

'I hope not.' Dean frowned. 'He would have been panicking. The heart can't beat properly when there's electricity passing through it. And sometimes panic can override pain, can't it?'

'Don't modern appliances have anything to prevent accidents like that?'

'Electricity is always dangerous,' said Dean. 'And I doubt it was a modern appliance. You've seen the kind of stuff that Gus had.'

Maya gestured at the empty bedroom. 'Not recently,' she said.

Dean glanced behind him. 'Anatol's been busy. But don't you remember what it used to be like in here? Even his toothbrush was an antique. I'm sure it was made of horsehair.' Dean was still wearing his driving clothes. He caught sight of himself in the mirror. The shape of the condoms showed in his top left pocket. He shivered at the realization and turned to leave the room. 'I should get changed. The others will be here soon.'

Maya followed him. 'So who found the body?'

'There's a woman that comes to clean every Friday.' Dean lowered his voice when they reached the staircase. 'She was here the day it happened.'

'And no one thought she might be involved?'

'The cleaning lady? There's no motive.'

'And Anatol has an alibi?'

'He was with me. It wasn't murder, Maya. The inquest said it was most likely an accident. And the police agreed. If it wasn't Anatol or the cleaner, who else could it have been?'

They stopped on the landing outside Maya's bedroom. She threw her camera back on to the bed. 'I'm offended no one thought it was me.'

Car Trouble

Marcin's pricey BMW had an automatic transmission, which at the time of its purchase had seemed the height of indulgence, and so he had taken to driving with a gavel instead of a gearstick; as he judged it, every single car that he'd encountered that morning had been doing something wrong. But Marcin had been seeing enemies everywhere lately, ever since that letter had arrived. He felt for his mobile phone with his free hand, finding it amid the clutter on the passenger seat, and held it against the steering wheel: a little bolt of alien technology, with a short stubby aerial and an LCD screen.

Marcin's eyes jumped back and forth between the road and the phone as he jabbed at the buttons, searching for Anatol's number in its memory. Ten seconds later, he could hear it ringing. By some miracle it had signal: minimal, but sufficient.

'Hello?' said a voice. 'This is Dean speaking.'

'It's me,' said Marcin.

'Marcin. Where are you?'

'I'm in the middle of nowhere. I'm calling on my mobile. Is Maya at the house yet?'

'Yes,' said Dean. 'She's here. It's just the two of us at the moment. Anatol's gone to pick up Phoebe. Do you want to speak to Maya?'

'Not particularly,' said Marcin, 'but can you do me

a favour? Can you go and ask her if she's got any cigarettes?'

After hanging up the phone, Marcin stamped on the accelerator. But he couldn't escape everyone else's bad driving, no matter how fast he went.

Forbidden Glove

The police car didn't seem real at first glance. Its bright colours and swirling blue lights looked out of place in the quiet countryside on a miserable day; the scene behind it only added to this sense of unreality. A silver car, crumpled into a fist, had been thrust into the base of an oak tree. Its metal bonnet was bent into peaks and tents. Phoebe couldn't see its driver anywhere. They might have been on their way to hospital or off making a phone call. Or they might have been sitting in the back of the police car. She couldn't tell. Her view was blocked by the flowers she was holding.

It was eleven twenty on Saturday morning. Anatol switched lanes and rolled past the accident, tapping his thumb to the tick of the indicator.

'That was lucky,' he said. 'They'll probably close this road in a minute.'

'I hope no one was hurt,' said Phoebe.

'Less lucky for them, of course. But strangers don't count, do they?'

Phoebe sighed but said nothing; she felt like she was being provoked. They turned on to a single-lane byway that led into the village of North Hatch, where Anatol's father was buried. The road was overgrown with hawthorn bushes; their buoyant white flowers broke against the windscreen as the car rattled past. Phoebe imagined reaching out through the window, rescuing the fallen flowers and adding them to her bouquet; it seemed a shame to waste them. But it was still raining and the delicate petals were soon shredded by the windscreen wipers.

'I should come to Wiltshire more often,' she said. 'Even when it's grey here, at least it's still green. And you can see the stars at night.'

'It's nice around here,' Anatol agreed. 'But you'll have to be quick. I'm not going to be living here much longer.'

'What do you mean?'

'I have to move, Phoebe. That's what I was trying to tell you before. About why I was late. Grief is change, whether you want it or not. I owe half the value of my father's house in inheritance tax. I can't afford that, so I'll have to sell. The sharks are already circling. I've got about a year.'

'Can't you get a loan or something?'

'Not without a steady income.'

The car accelerated out of a curve. Phoebe clung to the door handle. 'I'm sorry,' she said. 'I did wonder if you'd want to stay in that big house by yourself.'

'I want to,' said Anatol, 'but death is expensive. And inheritance is a myth.'

'What will you do? Will you stay in Wiltshire?'

'If I can find somewhere nearby. I'd like to take over my father's business. It's not really work, looking at antiques all day. And I don't know how to do anything else.'

Phoebe studied her fingernails; they were almost mirrors. Five glints of light gleamed back at her. 'What if I moved out here? We could work together.'

'Selling antiques?'

'Why not? I've been looking to make a change, since I turned thirty.' Phoebe was afraid she would spend the next few years watching her social life turn to stone, as her friends got married and moved away from the capital, leaving her alone with her cat, who was currently in the care of one of her neighbours, and a job that she didn't particularly enjoy. 'It's not like I've always wanted to be a teacher. Mostly I want to move out of London. I'm fed up with spending two hours a day underground.'

'Then why don't you?'

'Because it's hard, doing it alone.'

Anatol shook his head. 'I can't tell if you're being serious, Phoebe. You wouldn't really want us to work together, would you? I'm not very methodical. I'd drive you mad.'

'I don't know. Probably not.' Searching for a change of subject, Phoebe opened the glove compartment and took out a bag of toffees. 'But I don't know what I want. Just to be settled somewhere.'

'You don't even drive.'

'No. I know. Forget I said anything. I've been having all sorts of wild ideas lately. Do you want a toffee?'

The bag was half filled with empty wrappers. Phoebe pulled them out one by one and crushed them into a ball in her fist.

Anatol held out his hand. 'Can you open one for me?'

Phoebe moved her bouquet, so that it rested against the window beside her. 'Anatol,' she said. 'There's a gun in here.'

She was looking down at a tiny silver revolver sitting in the glove compartment where the bag of toffees had been half a minute before. She picked it up and laid it across Anatol's palm. Its barrel was only an inch long, its handle nothing more than a stub. The gun looked at least a hundred years old.

'Is it loaded?' asked Phoebe.

'I hope not.' Anatol balanced the gun on Phoebe's thigh and brought his hand back to the wheel. 'I forgot that was in there. It belonged to Gus; it's nothing to do with me. I found it with his things.'

'But it's illegal to keep it, isn't it?'

'I don't know. I don't think so. But you probably know more about it than me, Phoebe. You read the news. I just skim the headlines.'

'It's a handgun?' Phoebe covered the revolver with her palm. 'I don't know much about guns, but I know that's about the size of a hand. So Gus was supposed to get rid of it last year?'

'Yes. Technically, it's a handgun. But there's an exemption for antiques that I need to look into. Otherwise all the museums would be empty. That one's a Webley. A British Bull Dog. Made in Birmingham. It's a classic. Someone shot an American president with a gun like that. Doesn't that make you proud to be British?' Anatol smiled and pointed at the glove compartment. 'It's the bullets that are illegal. I don't know what to do with those.'

Phoebe peered past the flowers she was holding. At the very back of the glove compartment was a worn yellow cardboard box with a picture of a bullet printed on top. The illustration was angled towards her, the bullets inside probably pointing at her chest. She wondered if the warmth from the engine could ignite them.

'Will they still work?' she asked, moving the bouquet in front of her body.

'I don't know,' said Anatol. 'I was planning to drive somewhere quiet at some point and shoot them into the sky, just to get rid of them. Only there's about thirty in the box. Shooting that many might attract some attention. But I don't suppose anyone would mind if I just shot them into the woods, two or three at a time.'

'That depends on what you hit,' said Phoebe. She put the gun back in the glove compartment and closed it carefully. 'Haven't you ever seen *Bambi*?'

'No, Phoebe. It's a children's film.'

'And you were never a child? You're like the reverse Peter Pan.'

'I haven't seen that one either,' said Anatol.

It wasn't long before they reached the tiny village of North Hatch, less than a mile from Anatol's house, where steep driveways sloped up to houses hidden behind trees and hedges. Only the shabby church made any impression. It could be seen from several miles away, the sepia skeletons of last year's leaves still stuck to its pointed roof. Anatol parked across the road from it, in front of the village's only other point of interest: a small shop that would be closing shortly. There were some dim jars of damson jam in the window. Phoebe looked beyond them and saw magazines and milk, a bright display of cigarettes and a rack of local postcards.

Anatol switched off the engine and Phoebe turned to him expectantly.

'Do you remember where it is?' he said.

The beating rain filled the ensuing silence. Phoebe pointed mutely at the ramshackle churchyard. The ground inside sloped upwards, so most of the cemetery was visible from the road. There were no extravagant tombs or statues, just simple, modest stones; each one marked a story that had come to its end, then been bound in pinewood and buried. The graveyard was a kind of library, seen in the right light.

'Just go through that gate,' said Anatol.

'You're not seriously staying in the car?'

'It's raining, Phoebe. I don't want to get wet.'

'Anatol. I'm going to put flowers on your father's grave.' The small hole in Phoebe's sleeve had widened to the point where she could fit a finger through it. 'I know you had a difficult relationship with him, I know his illness was hard on you, but he was your father. And you only get to grieve once. Don't you even want to watch from a distance?'

'I've always been susceptible to the cold and the wet. You know that. I'm like a child that way.'

'So you're going to make me go on my own?'

'It was your idea, wasn't it?'

'Fine. Is there anything that you want me to say to him?'

Anatol shook his head. 'I told you, he's not there. You'll be talking to yourself. I had to endure enough of that with Gus, when his mind started going. It wasn't pleasant. Sometimes I think he's better off dead.'

'If he's not there then I don't see why you can't come with me. I thought a parked car was like purgatory?'

'That's true,' said Anatol. 'I'll open a window.'

When Phoebe got back to Anatol's car, a few minutes later, she opened the passenger door and found that the bag of toffees had taken her place. She picked them up and tossed them on to Anatol's lap.

'I'm done,' she said as she fell into her seat.

Anatol was sitting with the door wide open, his long legs spilling out on to the pavement. His ankles were getting wet. 'Did you manage to find it? Even without the headstone?'

'Yes.' Phoebe wiped her palms on her soaked thighs. 'It's still the newest grave there. The last one along the row at the back.'

'This must be a slow time of year for death. I suppose that bodes well for the weekend.' Anatol grinned and held out his hand. There were four small bullets lying on his palm. 'I've been thinking,' he said. 'Why don't we go somewhere and shoot these into the air, like we discussed? Just a few of them.'

'Won't the others be at the house by now?'

'They can wait. I left it unlocked.'

Phoebe shook her head. 'We just passed a police car.'

'I know somewhere private. A small patch of private woodland. We won't be there long enough for the police to find us.'

'But what if they did? I'm a teacher, Anatol. I can't risk doing anything illegal.'

'Two bullets each, Phoebe.'

Phoebe had never seen bullets up close before; to her, they looked like foetal mushrooms, or primitive chess pieces. She picked one up and inspected it. 'I don't want to, Anatol,' she said firmly. 'You should put that gun away, before someone gets hurt. If this was a story that's how it would have to end, now that you've shown it to me. The gun in act one always goes off in act three.'

Anatol grinned again. 'Then it's lucky that this is reality, isn't it?'

MONDAY
31 May 1999

The Scenic Route (continued)

But the answer to Janika's question was: No.

She hadn't killed Anatol.

He breathed in suddenly and raised his head from the steering wheel. The half-worn seatbelt had slowed his body just enough to save his life.

'Anatol?' Janika pulled her hand from his back, as if she'd been burned. She knew that this was her chance to escape. But she lingered for a moment, anchored by guilt. 'How badly are you hurt?'

Anatol turned towards her, his eyes struggling to stay open. His nose was shattered. His lips were in pieces. A beard of blood ran down his chin. The chestnut tree loomed over the wrecked car, casting their conversation in shadow. 'Why did you do that?' His words were quiet, barely audible above the sound of the struggling engine. 'It's my birthday.'

'Your birthday was yesterday. And you're a murderer, Anatol. I had no choice. You were taking me somewhere secluded. Against my will.'

'But I wasn't going to hurt you.'

'Then why the woods?'

Anatol spoke through bubbles of blood. 'Not to kill you, Janika, to confess.'

Janika turned her back on him. She watched the sky slowly shift: clouds within clouds within clouds within clouds. Somewhere in the distance a hot-air balloon hovered. She made a conscious effort to calm her breathing. 'Then it's true? You are a murderer?'

Anatol pulled an antique silver revolver from the narrow compartment in the door beside him. He held it with his good right hand, pointing it at the back of Janika's head. She couldn't see him. 'Yes. It's true.'

Anatol squeezed the trigger. There was a brief, bloody explosion. Then Janika's body fell forwards with a thump.

A NOTE FOUND TORN INTO SEVERAL PIECES

Dear friends,
I am not a murderer. I want to make that clear.
   You shouldn't believe everything that you're told.

PART TWO
Murder

SUNDAY NIGHT
30 May 1999

Moon Shot

Dean had arrived at the house with hope; he would leave it in horror, late on Sunday.

'I know it's your birthday,' he was saying. 'But that doesn't change anything, Anatol.' He looked down at his hand. It was curled into a clam on his knee. He watched it form a fist. An unconvincing fist, more question mark than full stop. Then it started to pick at a thread on his chinos. He caught himself and crossed his arms. 'I'm not going to lie any more.'

'I'm not asking you to lie,' said Anatol gloomily. 'I just don't want to discuss this now. Not on my birthday. It's my thirtieth, Dean.'

It had started raining ten minutes earlier. The two men were sitting in Anatol's low-slung convertible, parked in the woods, with the engine switched off and the doors wide open. The smell of wet earth rose from the soil underneath them; fledgling raindrops landed on the back of Dean's hand, as it clenched and unclenched.

'I know,' said Dean. 'I'm not asking you to discuss it. There's nothing to discuss.'

'Then why are we talking about it?'

'Because I want you to agree with me. There's nothing to discuss. I'm not going to help you cover up a murder.'

Anatol checked his watch: it was eleven fifty-four. 'It's only six minutes, Dean. Three hundred and sixty seconds until midnight. Then it won't be my birthday any more. Then we can talk.'

'What will you say in six minutes that you can't say now?'

'You'll find out in six minutes.'

A full moon punched through the clouds. The rain drew dotted lines across its pitted surface. Dean pulled the door beside him shut. 'You're going to have to deal with the consequences of your actions sooner or later.'

Anatol grinned; for a moment his face looked as large as the moon. 'My life is nothing but consequences these days, Dean. They've got me cornered. It's like I'm losing a game of chess. This one moves sideways. This one can jump. Consequences are like raindrops. And I'm standing outside in a storm.'

Anatol thrust a hand out into the rain, to illustrate his point. Water trickled down his wrist and dripped to the floor.

'I want to swap seats,' he said.

Dean was nonplussed. 'Why?'

'Because I'm bigger than you. And there's more leg room on the passenger side. It doesn't have the steering wheel in the way.'

'Why aren't you taking this seriously?' Dean was staring straight ahead, watching the rain make constellations on the windscreen. 'You probably think I wouldn't do it, don't you? But it's only a phone call.'

'It's four minutes now. Then we can talk.'

Adrenaline had always disagreed with Dean. He was clinging to the handle of the car door, trembling imperceptibly, already light-headed. 'I know I'd be incriminating myself if I told the truth now. But there's got to be a grace period, hasn't there? A month or two when I can say I was just confused. Overwhelmed. In shock.'

'Why don't you sit here?' said Anatol. 'I'll sit in the

passenger seat. Then I can close the door.' The rain was getting heavier, coming down at a slant. Anatol's knee, thigh and forearm were already wet. 'Aren't you cold with the door open?'

Dean was almost always cold. He watched the rain paint the window across from him. 'We'd get soaked switching seats.'

'No. Look. I'll go round and you can climb over.'

Without waiting for Dean to respond, Anatol leapt out into the leafy night. Dean heard his shoes hit the soil, then watched his silhouette dash past the windscreen.

The door to Dean's left opened suddenly. He looked up. Anatol's towering midriff was level with his head. 'Have you even been listening to what I've been saying?'

'Come on, Dean. Move over. I'm getting wet.'

Dean sighed as he moved into the driver's seat. 'It feels weird sitting here when I'm not insured.' He put on his seatbelt and pushed his hands into his pockets to keep himself from driving out of habit. 'And I'm over the limit. I've had three glasses of champagne.'

The chassis sagged as Anatol fell into the passenger seat. He shut the door and opened the glove compartment. 'Two minutes now,' he said. 'Would you like a toffee?'

'Why don't we go back to the house?' The countdown to midnight was making Dean nervous; sitting in the driver's seat felt all wrong. 'I've already said what I wanted to say.'

Anatol unfastened his watch and laid it along the length of the dashboard. It made a slack-jawed cyclops with the glove compartment hanging open underneath it. He leaned forwards and watched it twitch. 'Which hand hits the twelve first? When it gets to midnight?'

'What do you mean?'

'Which hand on the watch gets there first?'

'It depends on the watch.' Dean was secretly glad of this change of subject; he sat up straight. 'In theory, they should all hit twelve at the same time, shouldn't they? But you'd probably need a camera to know for certain, like Muybridge with his horses.'

'The same time?'

'Midnight, to be precise.'

The next thirty seconds passed in silence.

'It's no longer my birthday,' said Anatol. 'Now we can talk.'

'Is it midnight?' asked Dean. 'So which hand hit first?'

Anatol pulled from the glove compartment a small, mottled revolver, about the size of a five-pound note. 'I don't know,' he said. 'I wasn't paying attention.'

Dean caught the glint of silver in Anatol's hand; it was roughly the same shade as the moon. He smiled, puzzled. 'Do you get a lot of werewolves out here?'

Anatol showed him the gun. 'It's an antique,' he said.

'Don't do anything you might regret,' said Dean.

An owl cried out in the darkness. Anatol held the gun to Dean's head. 'I'm not going to let you send me to prison.'

He pulled the trigger. There was a sharp flash of light. An antique crack echoed throughout the car. Dean's broken head was thrown back against the door. A red asterisk appeared at the centre of the window. His body curled slowly into a question mark.

'Don't ask,' said Anatol. 'You know why.'

And Dean died with his hands in his pockets, curled up like commas.

SATURDAY
29 May 1999

The Gift of Murder

'This must be a dream,' said Anatol as he came into the drawing room, carrying four shallow cocktails on a silver tray. Each one was an upturned triangle of black liquid, with a thin lid of pale foam. There was a fire burning in the grate; its flickering orange threads showed in the four glasses. 'Why else would there be a giant gold present on the coffee table?'

A large box stood upright in the middle of the room, wrapped in glittering paper. It was a metre tall and forty centimetres square at its base. Anatol placed the tray beside it.

'We got you something,' said Phoebe. 'It's only something small.'

'About the size of a post box,' said Dean.

'It's huge,' said Anatol. 'What's inside?'

'Open it,' said Phoebe.

It was shortly before noon on Saturday. Marcin and Janika were yet to arrive at the house. Maya, Dean and Phoebe were sitting in Anatol's drawing room, watching the fire writhe and flame. Anatol handed out the cocktails, taking the last one for himself. Dean made a joke they'd heard him make many times before. 'Are we sharing a pint of stout, Anatol?'

'These are hard times, Dean. But not that hard.' Anatol sat down on a granite-grey armchair near the fireplace and hooked a leg over its arm. He looked like a spider, spilling out of a thimble. 'It's an espresso martini. I hope I didn't make them too strong.'

'Aren't you going to open your present?' asked Phoebe.

Anatol swirled the glass in his hand. The drink inside looked like ink and cream. 'I don't like getting presents,' he said. 'You know that, Phoebe. Every year I tell you not to bother.'

'Yes. But we thought we'd make an exception this time, since it's a special occasion. It's your thirtieth.'

'You're thirty,' said Anatol. 'I didn't get you anything.'

'I'm aware of that,' said Phoebe, frowning. 'A card would have been nice. But it's not just your thirtieth, Anatol. It's your golden birthday.'

'Gold? Wouldn't that be when I'm fifty?'

'No. You're thinking of wedding anniversaries. It's when your age is the same as the date you were born. So your birthday is the thirtieth of May and you're thirty this year. It only happens once in your life.'

'And it happens to most of us as children,' said Dean.

'This sounds like something you've made up,' said Anatol.

'Not me,' said Dean, shrugging innocently as he sipped his drink; he had changed out of his driving clothes twenty minutes earlier, hiding the condoms he'd bought in the drawer with his socks. 'I hadn't heard of it until Phoebe mentioned it.'

'It's real,' said Phoebe. 'Not that it matters. I like buying presents. It was just an excuse to get you something. Aren't you going to open it?'

Anatol put down his drink and reached for the box. 'Presents make me uncomfortable, Phoebe. Gus never got me presents. Presents were one of those strange things that other families did, like eating in front of the television or going to church. Gus just gave me money.' Anatol tilted the box towards the blustery light coming from the fire, searching for any messages that might be hidden on the paper. 'Is it from the three of you?'

'Yes,' said Phoebe, undeterred by Anatol's lack of enthusiasm. 'Marcin was working late when we went to get it. And Janika was out of the country, obviously.'

'You should open it before they get here,' said Dean. 'It'll be less awkward that way. It's from Yulie too.'

Marcin was due at any minute; Janika would be joining them the following afternoon.

'I didn't contribute much,' said Maya. 'I just met Dean and Phoebe at the wine bar and followed along. They got you a good gift though.'

'Well, it was really Phoebe's idea,' said Dean, 'if we're getting forensic.'

'Then let's not get forensic,' said Phoebe. 'He hasn't even opened it yet. He might not like it. I've still got the receipt.'

'But it's the thought that counts,' said Dean.

Maya had been lying on the sofa since she'd come down from Gus's room in the attic. She reached out with her naked foot and placed it reassuringly on Phoebe's forearm; Phoebe flinched away from the gesture.

'Honestly,' said Maya. 'It's one of your best.'

Anatol lifted the present on to his lap and frowned down at it. 'It's the web of obligations that concerns me. Every gift comes with a debt, doesn't it? So what happens now? I have to get each of you something of equal value? Or do I take the price of this and divide it by three? How much did you spend?'

'There's no obligation, Anatol.' Phoebe finished her drink and placed her glass pointedly on the table, in an attempt to force the conversation to a close. 'You don't have to get us anything in return. Just open it. Before Marcin gets here. I want to watch you.'

Anatol shook his head at her naivety. 'Denying the web exists only makes it more of a trap, Phoebe. You've got me something, so now I'm expected to get you something back. I know enough to know that's how it works. Then we'll all end up slightly worse off than if we'd just spent the money on ourselves. I don't understand it, but it's not from lack of knowledge.'

'You spend a lot on food and drink when we come here, Anatol. That's why we wanted to get you something. It's just to say thank you. You don't owe us anything. Either way, you're going to have to open it. I'm not going to graciously accept your ingratitude.'

Anatol's hand made the long journey to his chin; he tapped a knuckle against his front tooth. 'I don't actually spend that much, Phoebe. But there is one thing you could do for me, now that I think about it. Instead of getting me a present.'

'We've got you a present,' said Phoebe. 'You're holding it.'

'In addition to this, I mean.'

'Schrödinger's present,' said Dean. 'If you don't open it, does it even exist?'

'What do you want us to do?' asked Maya.

Anatol stood the box on the floor. 'Just the tiniest, easiest favour, Maya. I'd like us to play Motive Method Death again . . .'

*

Motive Method Death was a simple parlour game that Anatol had invented two years earlier: a game for three or more players, suitable for anyone with a dark sense of humour, that required its participants to imagine one another's deaths, then write them down as short stories or sketches.

Anatol had written up the rules as follows:

Before the game begins, a number of small, identically sized slips of paper should be prepared and handed out. There must be exactly two slips of paper for each participating player. The players should write their names on both slips, fold them over and place one into each of two separate containers. One container will represent murderers, the other victims. Every name must appear in both containers, but only once.

At the commencement of the game, each participating player will take one name at random from each container, thereby choosing a *murderer* and a *victim*. They must not reveal their chosen names to any other players. In the event that any player draws the same name from both containers, that player must announce this fact to the group and the draw will be declared invalid. When a draw is invalidated, all of the names should be placed back into the containers and all players should draw again. This process is to be repeated until a valid draw has been obtained, in which case the game can begin.

The object of the game is simple. Each player must write a short scene or story in which their chosen murderer kills their chosen victim. The circumstances of the murder are at the player's discretion, but players are encouraged to make their stories plausible, brutal and exciting, in equal measures. Once complete, the stories should be shuffled into a random order and read aloud by a designated *reader*. When a story is being read aloud, the author of the story must take care not to reveal themselves. Each story is then scored out of ten by all participating players in three categories: *motive*, *method* and *death*. The scores must be written on an otherwise blank piece of paper. One player should be designated as the *counter*. When all the stories have been read out, the *counter* will collect the pieces of paper containing the scores and total each story's score in each category, as well as calculating a combined overall score for each story, which will be the sum of the three. When a player is scoring their own story, it is accepted that they may give it the maximum score of three tens. But otherwise the scoring must be honest, unbiased and anonymous.

When all the scores have been totalled, the highest-scoring story in each category should be announced by the *counter*, as well as the story with the highest overall score. This latter story is the winning story. At this point the players may choose to reveal which stories they wrote, though no one should be forced to do so.

And this is where the game ends.

'We got you a telescope, Anatol.' Phoebe pointed at the unopened gift. 'It seems a shame to live somewhere as nice as this and not have one, since the sky in London turns orange at night. But clearly it was a failed experiment. Do you want it or not?'

Anatol had the kind of bashful, self-deprecating smile that, when it appeared, could erase whole paragraphs of preceding conversation. He grinned at Phoebe, then at

Dean and Maya. 'That's very kind of you, Phoebe. All of you. Now I can do my own failed experiments. But what about the game? Are you going to play?'

'Yes,' said Phoebe, crossing her arms; her clothes were still wet from the cemetery. 'I'd rather write about something nice. But it's your birthday. We can spend it however you want.'

'But, Anatol,' said Dean, 'don't you remember what happened the last time we played that game? We stayed up until two in the morning finishing those stories. It took us forever. Then you had to read them out in the early hours. Then everyone started arguing. We didn't get to bed until half past four.'

'Yes,' said Anatol. 'I remember that. But we began late. It was already evening. And we'd been drinking. This time we can play it properly, the way it was intended to be played. We can start as soon as Marcin arrives.'

'And spend all weekend writing stories?'

'It will take us most of today, maybe. But it's my birthday, Dean, and the weather is lousy. What else are we going to do with the time?'

'Anatol.' Phoebe leaned forward. 'Are you sure that this particular game isn't a bit too morbid? Especially now, a month after your father died?'

'That's why I want to play, Phoebe. I think it will be therapeutic.'

'Therapeutic?'

'Yes.'

'I don't see how.'

'Isn't that why people like watching violent films? And reading violent books? They make horrible things feel familiar and comfortable. They make them feel routine and dull. Bad things don't seem so bad after that. Isn't that why people watch the news?'

'Not exactly,' said Phoebe.

Anatol stood and walked over to the window with his drink in his hand. Daylight poured through the shallow martini glass, turning the tarry liquid a lucid brown. 'People like to say that life is short, when somebody dies. I must have heard that a thousand times at my father's funeral. But the real lesson of his death is that life is glass. It's fragile. Gus was killed by a radio cassette player. Doesn't that sound ridiculous? But the truth is that almost anything can kill you at any moment. You have to learn to see death for what it is, something normal and natural. Something familiar and dull. It's the only way to make a tragedy like that bearable. Animals eat each other alive, after all.'

'Mine will definitely be dull,' said Dean. 'You know I'm not very good at this kind of thing, don't you? I'm an engineer, Anatol. What do I know about writing stories?'

'It doesn't matter, Dean. Murder always makes an interesting story. It has a beginning, a middle and an end built into it. A motive, a method and then death. That's why this game works so well. It's why it will make me rich one day.' Anatol turned to Maya. 'What about you? Are you going to play?'

When Anatol had stood up, Maya had moved her feet to his vacant chair; they sat there like a pair of pushy cats, claiming their place.

'I've already started,' said Maya, nodding.

The Complications of the Passage of Time

Marcin's black BMW swung through the gap in the hawthorn bushes and pulled on to Anatol's drive, shortly after midday on Saturday. Through the shapes made by the windscreen wipers, he saw the house ahead of him as two overlapping arches of sodden red brick, while the rest of his view was obscured by raindrops. Maya's face appeared at the bottom of one of the arches. She was looking out of a window. The front door opened and she stepped outside, holding a half-filled martini glass and a packet of cigarettes. She sat down, hitched her graphite-grey dress up past her knees, out of the rain, leaned back against the door and started to smoke. A slight chevron of wood formed a porch over her head.

Marcin parked and took his backpack from the back seat. He was wearing a burgundy cashmere jumper over a black shirt, black trousers and a pair of black canvas shoes. He climbed out of the car and hurried to the house, weaving past the puddles on the driveway.

'Move,' he said to Maya, but without conviction.

Maya picked up the pack of cigarettes and held it out towards him, sliding it open with the edge of her thumb. A lime-green lighter had been squashed inside. Marcin crossed his arms, tucked his hands into his armpits and shook his head. 'No,' he muttered.

'But Dean told me you wanted one.'

'Later,' said Marcin. 'I'm trying to make it to forty-eight hours. That's nine o'clock tomorrow morning.'

Marcin pushed under the porch with Maya and attempted not to inhale her smoke. Quitting seemed much easier when it was just a case of saying no to things. It would be effortless, he thought, if only he could perceive the passage of time as the constant turning down of cigarettes: one every second, every microsecond. But that kind of positive thinking was never more than scaffolding and although you might be able to climb high on it, you couldn't make a home inside.

'So why am I smoking this?' asked Maya. She looked at the butt of her cigarette as if it had just appeared in her hand that moment. A channel of ash ran down her torso. 'I thought you were going to join me.'

'Then why didn't you wait?'

'I got impatient. Why do you want to quit, anyway?'

'My hair's started falling out.'

Four weeks earlier, standing in the bathroom, holding one mirror in front of another in search of an inflamed spot on the back of his head, Marcin had noticed for the first time that the hair around his crown was thinning. It was undeniable in the cold bathroom light. He could even see the spot that he'd been seeking – a docile bump, about to burst – poking through his wispy hairs. It was a sight that Marcin had never even considered: acne and hair loss shaking hands. His youth and his old age, conspiring against him.

'I always thought getting old would be a gradual process,' he continued. 'But it's more like a series of downward leaps, straight into the grave. As soon as you stop growing, you start to die.'

'I can't see anything wrong with your hair.'

'It's at the back,' said Marcin. 'You'd have to get up.'

'Oh,' said Maya. 'You mean your bald spot? That's not new.'

'It's new to me. I don't have eyes at the back of my head.'

'Just an eyelid,' said Maya. 'But you're getting older, Marcin. We're all getting older. Giving up smoking won't help with that.'

'It might,' said Marcin. 'Stress and smoking both cause premature ageing. It's work that makes me stressed, but I can't quit my job. Not yet. I need to make enough money to retire first. If I'm lucky I'll manage that before I'm thirty-five. Quitting smoking should keep me alive until then.' Marcin looked back at his expensive car; it was pointing at him like an accusing finger. 'As long as no one ruins it for me.'

'What does that mean?'

'Never mind.'

Maya finished her cigarette and flicked the butt across the gravel. 'Don't you want to enjoy your life while you're young?'

'I don't enjoy anything,' said Marcin dismissively, 'except for physical comfort and complaining. You know that, Maya. And I get enough of both.'

Maya picked up the half-drunk cocktail that was on the step beside her – black liquid with a layer of fine white foam – and held the glass up towards him. 'Do you still enjoy alcohol?'

Marcin took the glass, had a sip and handed it back. 'That's nice,' he said. 'Where can I get one of those?'

'You're too late,' said Maya. 'Anatol made them fifteen minutes ago.'

'That's a shame,' said Marcin. 'But cocktails are a good sign. I was worried this weekend would be more subdued than usual, with it only being a few weeks since Gus had his accident. If that's what it was.'

Maya finished her drink. She ran a finger around the glass and licked off the froth. 'I don't think that will change anything,' she said. 'Wait until you hear what he wants us to play.'

The Grump

'Look, I like murder as much as the next Maya,' Marcin was saying as he followed Anatol into the drawing room, after getting a drink from the kitchen. 'But the last time we played that game it took us all night . . .'

Noon on a wet day is when things have the fewest shadows. Everything blends into everything else. Marcin found Phoebe, Dean and Maya melting into the furniture, with only the skittish light from the fire throwing shapes across their bodies. He stood between them, holding an open bottle of beer, his hair still dishevelled from the drive. He looked like someone found at a party at three in the morning: bedraggled but unguarded, with energy only for gossip and argument. 'Everyone's exhausted, Anatol.'

'I'm not exhausted,' said Phoebe.

'I've just driven for three hours in the rain,' Marcin continued. 'I want to relax. And this is meant to be a holiday. It's a bank holiday weekend. It's got holiday in the name. Doesn't that mean anything?'

Anatol sat down. 'They're just short stories, Marcin.'

'Yes. But in my experience, short stories are quite long.'

There was a stack of six red notebooks on the coffee table, next to a row of blue ballpoint pens. Anatol picked up one of the books. 'It's just a few pages in here. Between three and ten, maybe? A scene. A few short scenes.'

'That will take me all weekend,' said Marcin. 'I'll be writing all day tomorrow. I'll still be writing on Monday morning. I'll have to move in with you. Why don't we make it a paragraph instead? Maya killed Dean. She stabbed a pair of nail scissors into one of his eyes and pulled out his brain. Throw in a bit of blood. The end.'

'Leave me out of this,' said Dean with his hands held high.

'I like that,' said Maya. 'What happened next?'

'Or a limerick,' said Marcin. 'We could each write a limerick. I could do that in forty-five minutes, with a drink. There once was a man called Anatol . . .'

'Who didn't like Marcin's plan at all.' Anatol nodded towards the garden, visible through their faint reflections. 'What will we do today, if we don't do this? Look at the weather.'

It was still raining furiously; it sounded like a swarm of tiny birds breaking their necks against the glass.

'Drink,' said Marcin, raising his bottle. 'I was hoping to drink away my troubles.'

'But this is my golden birthday,' said Anatol. 'It's a special occasion. I'd like to remember it. It only happens once in a lifetime.'

'Your birthday isn't until tomorrow.'

'But it is the reason we're here this weekend,' said Phoebe. 'If Anatol wants to play this game, then that's what we should do.'

Marcin turned on her. 'But it's work, Phoebe. Don't you understand? It's a lot of work. I do enough work during the week. Twelve hours, most days. This is meant to be a party.'

'Birthday parties always take work,' said Phoebe. 'Maybe it's usually someone else doing it, but they still take work.'

Marcin collapsed on to a mustard wingback armchair

that stood at one end of the coffee table. He massaged his forehead. 'So it's like Paper Scissors Stone, then? Birthday beats holiday. Holiday beats what? Sick day? Then sick day beats birthday, presumably?'

Phoebe nodded. 'And I suppose you're sick, are you?'

'Essentially, yes. I've been feeling terrible since I gave up smoking.'

'So have we,' said Maya.

'I thought you'd started again,' said Phoebe.

Anatol raised his hands in surrender. 'You don't have to play, Marcin. Not if you don't want to. But you didn't get me a present. I thought you might do this instead.'

'You always say you don't want presents.'

'Normally,' said Anatol. 'But this time is different. It's my thirtieth birthday. Everyone else got me a present.'

'Did they?'

Phoebe had moved the telescope, in its gold wrapping, out of sight behind the sofa. Any disappointment she felt at the fact that it was still unopened had been similarly set to one side.

'Anyway,' Anatol continued. 'You might get bored, if you're the only one not playing.'

Marcin looked around the room for support. Phoebe was smiling tolerantly, as usual, with the look of a teacher waiting out a tantrum; Maya was half-asleep; it was only Dean that seemed to be following the conversation, open to whatever conclusion it might reach. Marcin made eye contact with him. Dean thought for a moment and then shook his head.

'I'm going to give it a go,' he said. 'I'm not very good at this kind of thing. But I don't think it'll be as bad as last time. Not if we get started earlier.'

Marcin sighed, resting his head on his hand, with his sleeve pulled up around his fingers and precious goat's wool pooled on his palm. 'Remind me how it works,' he said. 'We each have to write a murder mystery? With the five of us as suspects?'

'Not a mystery,' said Anatol. 'Not with a detective. That would take far too long. Just a simple depiction of murder. A scene or two. Here's the murderer, here's the victim—'

'Splat,' said Maya.

'Exactly,' said Anatol.

'Some light reading,' said Phoebe.

'More misery than mystery,' said Dean.

'And it's the six of us,' said Anatol. 'Not the five of us. Janika is taking part too. She'll write hers when she gets here tomorrow. She should be on a plane by now.'

Janika was due to get back from Australia late that evening.

'All right.' Marcin frowned. 'Fine. Just don't expect too much from me. I'm on holiday, birthday or no birthday.'

'So you just wanted to complain?' said Phoebe.

Marcin batted away the criticism with a swig of his beer. 'You should never do anything, Phoebe, without lowering people's expectations first.'

Motive Method Death

Is it possible to have too many murders? The last time the six friends had played Motive Method Death – two years earlier, in May 1997 – the game had gone on until three in the morning and had ended, as expected, with six stories of murder being read out back-to-back, slowly, in the slurred words of the early hours. But, though the game had in many ways been a disaster, the stories themselves had been dark and enjoyable. Anatol had reread them, for inspiration, in the week leading up to his birthday.

Anatol had picked Dean's name, as well as his own; his story that year had involved Dean treating him to a trip in a hot-air balloon for his twenty-eighth birthday, then pushing him out of the gondola, somewhere over Wiltshire, while its operator was distracted. The motive had been simple: Anatol had promised to leave Dean some money in his will and greed had taken care of the rest. At the climax of the story, Dean had watched, unmoved, as his friend had plummeted five hundred metres to his death. The final line had expressed a sentiment that often came to Anatol when he saw hot-air balloons pass his property: 'Man has always dreamed of flight, but aren't there better ways to do it than in a picnic basket?'

Marcin's story had been more prosaic. It had started with a scene in which Phoebe had visited Janika at her house in

Birmingham and been offered a cup of tea laced with antimony. The bitter taste had been explained away as a result of bad milk; Janika was too busy to visit the supermarket. But the poison had sent Phoebe upstairs with a stomach ache, turning a passing visit into an extended stay. This had been followed by a series of short scenes showing Phoebe's decline over the subsequent weeks, as Janika had continued to poison her. Their interest had derived mainly from their depiction of Janika as the domestically dominant one and Phoebe as the dependant, forced to endure stained bedsheets and too weak to do anything about it. After a month of bickering, Phoebe had died in the final scene, with her last words being: 'I know it was you.'

But Marcin hadn't bothered to include a motive.

Janika's story had started like an essay, with a lengthy preamble musing on humanity's relationship with the outdoors and the violence it took to keep nature at bay, before eventually segueing into a short scene of Anatol mowing an overgrown lawn (his own, presumably, though Anatol had never once mown a lawn in his life) while Maya lay sunbathing in the long grass nearby, hidden from view. The resulting collision had been brief but bloody. 'A fountain of organs and intestines rose into the sky, scattering blood over the surrounding geraniums.'

Phoebe's story had been short and economical. Marcin and Dean had both driven into Anatol's driveway at the exact same time, from different directions, causing a minor collision. An argument had ensued over who was to blame. The scene had primarily consisted of dialogue.

'You drive like a wrecking ball, Marcin.'

'Better that than driving like an accountant.'

And had been relatively plausible; at least, more plausible than the rest of the stories. It had even led to Marcin stopping the game and asking whether the story was meant as some kind of confession, since he'd noticed a scratch on his car that afternoon.

The argument had continued to escalate (in the story) until Marcin had pulled a penknife from his coat pocket and stabbed Dean straight through the heart. Dean had died quickly, in less than a paragraph.

In Maya's story, Phoebe had trapped Marcin in the swimming pool (a fictional swimming pool, in the grounds of Anatol's house) by pulling the cover across it while he was still swimming, preventing him from climbing out. The rest of the word count had been reserved for a detailed, if unscientific, description of Marcin's death by drowning, largely via simile.

So the dark was 'disorientating, full of echoing noises, like being trapped in a cave with a colony of bats'; the ache in Marcin's arms as he struggled to swim felt like 'a pair of elephants pulling him apart'; and breathing in water was 'like being forced to swallow someone else's fist, only to then struggle helplessly as they scrunched his lungs into a ball . . .'

Dean had felt more comfortable dealing with fantasy than reality, so in his story Maya had been possessed by some kind of creature or curse that had engendered an extreme, if not unexpected, bloodlust; she'd then chased Janika through the woods with an axe. The story had involved more exercise than violence, except in its uncharacteristic final line. Maya had caught up to Janika, thrown her to the floor then brought the axe down on to her head. 'The blade went in better than butter; the goo that came out was thicker than lard.'

After Anatol had finished reading out the stories, the friends had stayed awake for another hour, arguing; no one had been happy with the way they'd been depicted. Maya hadn't been pleased that her motive for murder was mostly supernatural, while Phoebe had resented the implication that she could be outsmarted by Janika; Marcin hadn't liked the slight on his physique during the description of his swimming, while Dean had felt that the comments on his driving were a little too barbed; and Janika hadn't enjoyed the dreary descriptions of her house in Birmingham.

Only Anatol had sat back and savoured the chaos.

Twelve Names

'The murders should take place this weekend,' said Anatol as he came into the drawing room, carrying five fresh cocktails on a silver tray. Vodka martinis. Each one was an upturned triangle of silty liquid, with a skewered olive listing against the glass. 'And be set here, in this house, if possible.'

Anatol handed out the drinks and took one for himself. There were two glasses left on the tray, both filled with small pieces of paper, folded into squares, and covered with tinfoil. One had a green elastic band around its stem, the other one red.

'Here?' said Dean. 'That's different from last time.'

Anatol picked up the green-banded glass and peeled off its foil lid. 'I know. It's to make the stories feel more authentic. They shouldn't have anything supernatural in them, either.'

'But we don't want them to be too authentic, do we? It's meant to be a bit of fun. They could get personal.'

'Besides,' Marcin mused sarcastically, 'if they're too authentic then how will anyone tell the difference between fiction and reality?'

'It doesn't matter, Dean. No one here is easily offended.' Anatol laid his wide hand over the glass's rim and shook its contents up and down. His palm was roughly the size of a coaster. 'Everyone gets a turn to be murdered and everybody gets to commit one murder. So nobody should end up feeling left out.'

'I just hope I don't have to murder one of the girls again,' said Dean. 'I don't feel comfortable writing about things like that. Maya, maybe, but not Phoebe or Janika.'

'I'm sure we'd survive,' said Phoebe.

'Who wants to go first?' asked Anatol. 'These are the victims.'

'It's your birthday,' said Phoebe. 'You should go first.'

Anatol nodded. He closed his eyes and felt inside the glass, stirring the folded slips with his fingers. He pulled one out, then gave the glass to Phoebe.

'Pass it along.'

Phoebe took out a name, then handed the glass to Dean, who gave it to Maya. Marcin took it from Maya and studied the two remaining pieces of paper for almost a minute before choosing one at random. Then he placed the glass back on the tray, with a single stub still inside.

'Should we open them, then?'

Anatol nodded. 'Just don't let anyone see who you've got. The victim's name should be written in green pen. If it's written in red, something's gone wrong.'

They opened their scraps of paper surreptitiously, the five of them leaning back in their chairs.

Marcin groaned. 'Can I take another?'

'Why?' asked Anatol.

'Because I got the one person I didn't want.' Marcin pointed at the last slip of paper, sitting alone in the glass. 'I could swap it for that one.'

'That one's for Janika. If you gave her yours, you'd know who she had.'

'So?'

'It would ruin the game.'

'I don't see why,' said Marcin. 'In fact, I think Janika

would prefer this person. She'd certainly like them more than I do.'

'No one is supposed to know anybody else's names. The rules are not negotiable, Marcin. I put a lot of thought into them.' Anatol removed the foil from the second glass. 'If I'd had time, I'd have carved them in stone. Now choose a murderer.'

Anatol angled the glass towards Marcin. The six unopened squares of paper formed a shallow heap at the bottom of the cone. 'Fine,' said Marcin, taking one from the top.

'Open it,' said Anatol. 'If it's the same name you picked for your victim, you can put it back and draw again. Otherwise we'd get six stories about suicide. But you can't put the victim back.'

Marcin hid the scrap of paper in his hand and unfolded it between his thighs. The others watched his expression for clues; he raised an eyebrow, but shook his head.

'It's not the same name,' he said.

Anatol moved the glass towards Dean. Dean took one of the names and read it discreetly. 'What happens if we pick ourselves?'

'Well, don't tell us about it,' said Phoebe.

Dean shrugged. 'I didn't say I did. I was just wondering what would happen if I had.'

'You're allowed to pick yourself,' said Anatol. 'Just don't give us any hints about who you've got.'

'I didn't,' said Dean.

Phoebe and Maya chose their names next. They both opened them and shook their heads. Neither had picked the same name twice.

'Good,' said Anatol, taking one of the final two slips for

himself. 'Now we all have a victim and a murderer. And no one has the same person twice.'

There was a scrap of paper left in each glass. Marcin gestured towards the tray. 'How do you know those two aren't the same?'

'I don't,' said Anatol. 'But it's not very likely, is it?'

'It's possible,' said Marcin.

'I'll take my chances.'

'If you like I'll look and see what they are. Then if they are the same, I can swap one of them for one of mine.'

'There's no swapping,' said Anatol shortly. 'Those names belong to Janika. She can open them when she gets here tomorrow.' He tipped the final two names on to the tray and turned the two glasses upside down on top of them. Both bands fell slack, in sulking loops. 'If there's a problem with them, we'll deal with it then.' Anatol carried the tray to a glass-fronted display case near the fire and locked it inside.

'It's all right,' said Marcin. 'Maya will swap with me.'

'I won't,' said Maya. 'I've already worked out what my murder is going to be.'

'How? You've had the names for less than a minute.'

Maya shrugged. 'I just took the person that I picked as my murderer and thought about the worst thing they'd ever done. Or the worst thing I can remember them doing. The rest flowed from that.'

Anatol grinned. 'So you've been sitting here quietly judging us?'

'Only one of you,' said Maya.

'I doubt it's me,' said Dean. 'I don't think you'd know the worst thing I've ever done. I'm not sure I know it myself.'

'I could probably think of something,' said Maya.

'What about me?' asked Anatol. 'What's the worst thing I've ever done?'

'I might not have picked any of you.' Maya held up her pieces of paper. 'I might have picked myself. I could be writing a confession.'

'That's true,' said Anatol. 'But I'm curious anyway. I won't be offended.'

'The worst thing you've ever done?' Maya gave it some thought. 'We were driving near here once. And you hit a deer with your car. It wasn't dead. So you finished it off with a kitchen knife. You cut its throat. Remember?'

'That was the kind thing to do,' said Anatol. 'It was in pain, Maya. It got hit by a car.'

'I know. But it stuck in my mind, the way you just cut into it while it was still alive. You didn't even seem upset.'

'Not being sentimental doesn't make me a monster.'

Phoebe winced. 'Can't we talk about something a bit more pleasant? I don't want to think about animals getting hit by cars. I have a cat at home.'

'That gives me an idea,' said Dean.

Marcin was the first to finish his drink. He put his glass down on the table. 'Maya. What about the worst thing that you've ever done?'

Maya considered the question carefully. 'I used to enjoy killing insects,' she said, 'when I was a child. I remember emptying a kettle on to a line of ants. They were just crossing the patio. They weren't doing anyone any harm. I probably shouldn't have done that.'

'No,' said Marcin. 'That's not it. Do you remember we were having lunch once at a pub in Hampstead? On the terrace outside? And you stubbed out a cigarette in the sharing platter? While the rest of us were still eating?'

Maya rolled her eyes. 'That was years ago, Marcin. I thought you'd finished.'

'Even if we had finished, it was still disgusting. And I say that as a smoker. I remember the look the waitress gave us.'

'You're always bringing this up,' said Maya. 'It's time to let it go, Marcin.'

Two Typewriters

'One last thing,' said Anatol. 'When you've finished your stories, I'd like you to type them up. That way I won't be able to recognize your handwriting when I'm reading them out. I'll type mine too. I've put two typewriters in the dining room. They're antiques, of course, but they're still functional. And there's another in my bedroom if anyone gets desperate.'

'My laptop's in the car,' said Marcin. 'Can't I use that?'

'Did you bring a printer?'

'No.'

'Then what would we do with it? We'll stick with the typewriters. I've planned this all out, Marcin. Stop causing problems. Now, once you've memorized your names, you should throw them on the fire. Then we can begin.'

Anatol picked up his drink and took the two pieces of paper that he'd chosen from the end of the coffee table, where they were folded shut. He bundled them together and pitched them into the tangerine coals, where they were consumed by flames in less than a second. Dean stood and did the same. Maya didn't move; Marcin held out his hand towards her and she gave him her names, crushed into two tiny balls. Then he walked over to Phoebe and stood in front of her expectantly.

Phoebe tilted her hand away from him. Her two slips of paper were lying open on her palm. 'So the one in red kills the one in green?' she asked.

'Yes,' said Anatol. 'Red is for danger.'

Phoebe looked up at Marcin and shook her head. 'I'll do it myself. I don't trust you.'

Marcin shrugged; he threw the contents of his fist at the fireplace.

Four Short Scenes

Marcin followed Anatol to the kitchen to get another drink. On the way, he collected one of the typewriters from the dining room and carried it along the corridor, under his arm. When he got to the kitchen, he placed it down on the work surface, next to the kettle, and pressed a few keys at random.

'This is going to be a long, long weekend,' he said. 'I type very slowly, Anatol.'

'Why don't you just cheat, Marcin?'

'What do you mean?'

'If you don't like the names you got,' said Anatol, 'then choose some different ones. Write a different story altogether. I didn't want to say this in there because I don't want everyone doing it. But it doesn't matter so much if it's just you. No one will know about it until the game ends, anyway. I can read your story out last, if necessary.'

'That means someone would be murdered twice,' said Marcin. 'Or they'd end up committing murder twice. Or maybe both. I thought the rules were set in stone?'

'Yes. But it's better than hearing you complain all weekend. Just don't tell the others about it. If everyone cheats it will be anarchy.'

Marcin shook his head. 'I'm not sure,' he said. 'I do want different names, but on the other hand I've been enjoying being difficult.'

*

With great reluctance, Maya got up from the couch and left to use the toilet. Phoebe watched her go, then followed a moment later. She caught up with Maya in the nook by the staircase.

'Maya,' she said. 'What's the worst thing that I've ever done?'

'I don't want to tell you,' said Maya.

'Why not? I won't be offended.'

Maya looked at Phoebe sceptically. 'Do you remember Marcin's thirtieth birthday? You threw his cigarettes off the side of his balcony?'

'I remember,' said Phoebe, leaning back against the wall. 'But surely that's not it? The worst thing that I've ever done?'

'It was mean,' said Maya. 'And unnecessary.'

'I was drunk,' said Phoebe. 'It was maybe a little bit rude. But it's hardly a bad thing to stop someone smoking.'

'It was mean,' said Maya, shaking her head.

Sitting by himself in the drawing room, Dean noticed that two of the pieces of paper that had been thrown at the fire a few minutes earlier had bounced out of the grate, only slightly singed.

He checked that the corridor was clear, then stole over to the fireplace and retrieved the two scraps of paper with a brass poker. He unfolded them with guilty hands but was immediately disappointed: the two slips were the two that he'd thrown at the fire himself. He'd never had a particularly good aim. The name 'Janika' was written on one of the slips in green pen, while the other had 'Anatol', written in red.

Dean was supposed to write a story about Anatol killing Janika.

He picked up both names and dropped them carefully on to the coals.

The group gathered in the drawing room again. 'I think that's everything,' said Anatol. 'Does anyone have any questions?'

Nobody did. Anatol raised his glass. 'In that case, let the fiction begin.'

SATURDAY NIGHT
29 May 1999

The Incest Paradox

Atlas held the heavens on his shoulders. Anyone still awake, alone, at two in the morning has to carry the moon on their back. Anatol was sitting at the end of his bed, watching the stars. Marcin knocked on the door behind him. The door was half open.

'It's late,' said Anatol, looking around.

'Better late than never . . .' Marcin was balancing the room on his eyeballs. He was too well practised at talking to slur his words, but he was leaning heavily against the frame of the door, holding a bottle and two shot glasses. 'I'm sorry I didn't get you a birthday present. I didn't know we were doing that. But I found you something. This was in the boot of my car. It's whisky. Single malt. Expensive.'

Anatol walked to the door, took the bottle from Marcin and examined the label. 'It's already been opened.'

'I know that. But the present's not the bottle. Or the contents. The present is a drink in my company. I don't like drinking alone.'

'Now?' Anatol handed the bottle back.

'Why not? We're both awake.'

Anatol checked the room behind him. 'All right. Have a seat.' He pulled a circular table to the side of the bed and sat on the mattress, with the duvet pulled across his legs. The table had a chessboard inlaid at its centre. Rows of squares of light and dark wood. Marcin took a chair from under the desk and sat down opposite. They looked as if they were about to play a game of chess, wearing pyjamas.

Marcin placed the shot glasses on adjacent squares and poured them both a drink. 'Are we going to play? Or would you rather talk?'

'Which is more likely to help me sleep?'

'We don't need to choose one. Conversation can be a game of chess, can't it?' Marcin tapped his forehead. 'Chess of the mind. Or would it be chess of the tongue?'

'You're here to gossip, Marcin. Gossip isn't a game of chess. I suppose the whisky will knock me out, whatever we do.'

They both raised their glasses and drank. The whisky tasted like earth and fire. Marcin rubbed his jaw. 'That reminds me of an interesting story I heard once. Do you know the one about the chessboard and the grains of rice?'

'The grapes of wrath?'

'The grains of rice.'

'I don't think so,' said Anatol. 'It doesn't sound very interesting.'

'It depends how you tell it.'

'Was it worth waking me up for?'

Marcin produced a cigarette from somewhere. 'You weren't asleep.'

'But I would have been by now.'

'Counterfactuals are a bad habit. Do you mind if I smoke?'

'Not in here, Marcin. I sleep in here.'

'All right. Then I'll smoke when you're asleep.'

'You might not have to wait long. Are you going to tell me this story?'

'That's what you wanted, isn't it? Stories, for your birthday.'

'About murder,' said Anatol, 'not about chess.'

Marcin sucked the unlit cigarette. 'But chess is about murder.'

'Regicide,' said Anatol. 'It's not very relatable.'

'But you have to kill a lot of other pieces before you get to the king. Knights, bishops, parents.'

'What did you say?'

Marcin forgot where he was and lit his cigarette out of habit. Anatol plucked it from his mouth and placed it upside down in one of the shot glasses. A smear of whisky extinguished the tip. The butt stuck up like a miniature drinking straw.

Marcin fished it out and filled both glasses, taking the ashy one for himself. 'I'd like to tell you that story now, Anatol.'

'The rice board and the grains of chess?' Anatol pulled the duvet up around his shoulders. 'Let me get comfortable.'

They both downed their second shots. Marcin filled their glasses again. 'Once upon a time, a wise old man invented the game of chess. He was asked to teach the king how to play. The king was so impressed by the game that he told the wise man he could have anything he wanted as his reward. So the wise man asked the king to take the chessboard and place a single grain of rice on the first square, then two grains on the second square, four on the third square, then eight on the fourth, then sixteen, and so on to the end of the board, each time doubling the number of grains from the square before. When the last square had been filled, the wise man would take the rice that covered the board. That was all he wanted. The king was amazed at this humble request and granted it without hesitation.'

Marcin moved his glass around the board as he spoke, playing an imaginary game against an imagined opponent. Anatol watched, trying to follow his movements. 'I suspect he'll regret that.'

'But the king didn't realize that if the grains of rice double with each square and there are sixty-four squares on a chessboard, starting with a single grain, then the final square will need two to the power of sixty-three grains of rice.'

'And how many grains of rice is that?'

Marcin drank, slowly this time. 'Let's work it out. Two to the power of ten is slightly more than a thousand. That's one with three zeros. Let's pretend it's one thousand exactly, to get a rough estimate. Then two to the power of sixty will be one with six times three zeros. Eighteen zeros. A billion has nine zeros. Nine plus nine is eighteen, so that's a billion billion. And two to the power of three is eight. So two to the power of sixty-three will be just over eight billion billion. Call it nine billion billion.'

Anatol sat up and tapped the squares. 'In that case, how about we play a drinking game, Marcin? We go along the board. The shots double with each square. I can start.'

'There's no need, Anatol. Conversation can be a drinking game, can't it?' Marcin tapped his forehead with the empty glass. 'A drinking game of the mind. Every sentence leaves you slightly intoxicated. Now listen carefully or this will get you sloshed. Imagine that instead of a chessboard, this table had a picture of your family tree. Starting with you, down here. You have two parents; your parents have two parents.'

'Had,' said Anatol.

'Had,' echoed Marcin. 'That's four grandparents. And they had two parents each, as well. So you had eight great-grandparents. But they had sixteen parents between them. That's sixteen great-great-grandparents. Thirty-two great-great-great-grandparents. And so on. Every generation you go back, you have to double the number from the generation before.'

'I see. So it's the same as the grains of rice?'

Marcin tapped his glass on the table, drunk with excitement as much as with alcohol. 'Exactly the same. That means when you've gone back sixty-three generations, you'll have got to eight billion billion great-great-great-and-so-on-grandparents. Isn't that dizzying?'

Anatol cringed. 'No one likes to picture their ancestors having sex.'

'But that's not the end of the story. Because how far back does sixty-three generations actually take you? Not that far, it turns out. A thousand years, if everyone had children at sixteen. They don't, so let's say it's sometime between the last millennium and the birth of Christ. How many people were even alive then?'

'About nine billion billion?'

'No, Anatol. Nowhere near. The world population is six billion now. It was one billion at the start of this century. It would have been much lower a thousand years ago, much less than a billion. So how can you have nine billion billion great-great-whatever-grandparents, when there weren't even a billion people alive at the time?'

'I don't know. What's the trick?'

Marcin shook his head. 'There is no trick. Everyone has two parents. Even Jesus. The rest is just arithmetic. Let me ask you a different question. How would we write out the names of your nine billion billion ancestors, if we only had a billion names to use?'

'We'd have to use some of the names more than once?'

'Exactly. But not just more than once, Anatol. We'd have to use each name nine billion times. Nine billion times in the same family tree.'

'I see. My mother's great-grandfather is also my father's great-grandfather, that kind of thing? You're talking about incest?'

'Precisely, Anatol. Your family tree is riddled with incest. Distant incest, but incest, nonetheless. It's the same few names repeating over and over and over and over. And so is mine and everyone else's. They have to be. It's basic mathematics. And yet people get so sentimental about their families, don't they? When really everyone ought to be slightly ashamed.'

'So what happened to the wise old man?'

Marcin poured out two more shots. 'He was killed or made king. There are different versions. Take your pick.'

'That wasn't much of a story, Marcin. Why did you tell me all that?'

'Because I'm not sentimental about my family. And I don't think you are, either. We have that in common. And that's why I'd like you to tell me the truth, Anatol. You killed your father, didn't you? I'm not going to hold it against you. Like I always say, I can forgive you anything except not telling me.'

Anatol swallowed his drink in one. 'Are you trying to get me drunk, Marcin? Get me to confess to all sorts of wild things? It'll take you a while. It's these long limbs. One. Two.' Anatol measured off segments of his forearm.

'You could get three bottles of wine in there. And that's just one arm.'

Marcin shrugged. 'What do you think I'll do? Call the police? We're friends, aren't we? I know that you did it, I just don't know the details.'

Anatol tapped his foot on the floor, thinking things through. 'Has this all been building up to some kind of blackmail attempt, Marcin?'

'I can't blackmail you. Yet. I don't have enough proof.'

'Good. Because I don't have enough money.'

'Like the whisky,' said Marcin, 'I have about fifty per cent proof. But it's still enough to get you wrecked. Here. Have a look at this.'

Marcin pulled a thick brown envelope from his trouser pocket and handed it to Anatol. Anatol looked inside, frowned at the contents, and passed it back.

'Fifty per cent.' Anatol nodded. 'Where did you get that?'

'Fifty per cent,' Marcin said again. 'That's check but not mate.' He finished his whisky and put the shot glass down. Queen's bishop three. Then toppled it on to its side. A glob of amber liquid rolled on to the board and stained the square brown. 'But it's not far off. We should play again tomorrow night,' he said, getting to his feet. 'There might be more to discuss. Have a think about what I've said, before then. You can keep the whisky. I'm feeling generous. Happy birthday.'

'Yes. I'll think about it.'

Marcin's cigarette was still on the chessboard, joining two adjacent squares. A game of cigarettes and ladders. He picked it up and made his way to the door. A dark staircase led down to the landing. Marcin stopped on the second step to light his cigarette. He breathed in smoke, thick and warming. Then something cast a shadow across him. The flame in his hand was thrown into darkness. Marcin looked back and saw Anatol standing above him. The size of the door frame. A walking murder weapon, grinning maniacally. His knuckles were swinging beside his shins. 'I've thought about it,' he said.

Marcin felt two huge hands on his shoulders. And then came the push. He fell forwards, face first. The staircase liked to chew its food slowly, one tooth at a time.

Marcin landed at the bottom with a broken neck.

A NOTE FOUND TORN INTO SEVERAL PIECES (CONTINUED)

I repeat: I am not a murderer.

I didn't murder my father, any more than I shot Janika on our way to the station, after she crashed my car into a chestnut tree. Neither of those things actually happened. They're both just stories. One of them written down as part of the game we've been playing, the other spread through smears and gossip.

But they're both fiction.

PART THREE
Blackmail

SUNDAY
30 May 1999

Stranger on a Strange Train

Janika turned her head at the sound of an engine. The oily plastic of the payphone's receiver slid from her ear across her cheek and brushed against her lip. But it was just the noise of the road, thirty metres away. Now a tinny, distant voice was speaking into her mouth.

'Hello? Anatol's house.'

But Janika could tell from the tone it wasn't Anatol. She took two steps back and once again checked the side of the access lane that formed the station's small car park, then the length of road that ran parallel to it. But both were empty: no cars had sidled past while she'd been dialling Anatol's number or waiting for his phone to ring. She brought the handset back to her head.

'Who is that? Dean?'

'Yes. It's me. Where are you?'

'I'm at the station,' said Janika. 'Where's Anatol?'

It was early afternoon on Sunday, Anatol's birthday. Janika was in the small village of Tisbury in Wiltshire, where Anatol had met Phoebe the day before.

'Anatol,' said Dean, speaking slowly, a note of doubt entering his voice. 'Isn't he with you?'

'No,' said Janika. 'He's supposed to be here, but he's not.'

'He's not here either. He's gone out somewhere. We thought he was going to meet you.'

'He's on his way, then?'

'I assume so. He said you'd be arriving today.'

Janika felt her muscles relax, her shoulders melting with relief. She turned her back to the wall and crouched down, resting her head on the waist-high suitcase beside her. The cord of the payphone cut across her neck. Her morning up to that point had been a struggle. She'd spent the whole train journey drifting in and out of sleep. Each time that she'd woken up she'd had no way of knowing whether or not she'd missed her stop, until the next station announcement had come. Those extended periods of panic had exhausted her more than the moments of rest had helped. The whole journey, all the way from Australia, had been a constant back and forth between extreme stress and forced inactivity. And the stressful moments had left her too frazzled to do anything productive with the downtime.

'How long will he be?' she said into the phone.

'You know as much as I do,' said Dean.

'I doubt that,' said Janika. 'I don't know anything. What time did he set off?'

'About an hour ago.'

'An hour ago? It's a ten-minute drive, Dean.'

'Yes. No. I know that. But he hasn't taken his car.'

'What?' Janika felt the same disorientating panic that she'd experienced waking up on the train. She got to her feet and searched the station again.

'His car,' said Dean, retreating into the wires, humming to cover the silence. He sounded maddeningly uninvested; she could have been asking him about a clue in a crossword puzzle. 'It's here, on the driveway. I'm looking at it right now.'

'Then he hasn't left yet?'

'Yes. No. He's definitely left. Maya saw him go. I heard the door slam. He's not here.'

'On foot?' asked Janika.

'Yes.'

'Then he can't be coming here, can he?'

'I thought he might be walking over to meet you.'

Janika wondered if she was still asleep, dreaming. 'Why would he do that? I need a lift, Dean. I have luggage.'

'All right. I don't know. Don't shoot the messenger.'

'Then make sure the message makes sense.' Janika glanced at the payphone's olive-green display. Her pound coin was about to run out. She had another, but it was the one she kept back for shopping trolleys and emergencies. She'd donated the rest of her change at the airport. 'I don't have long, Dean. Can you run up and check that Anatol's not in his room?'

'There's no point, Janika. I was in there earlier.' Dean lifted his glasses and massaged his eyebrows with his index finger and thumb. Janika couldn't see him, but she knew him well enough to know that's what he was doing. 'I was looking for him. But I don't think he's in the house. I'm certain he's gone out.'

'Then where did he go? If he's not coming here?'

'I don't know. He did say he was planning to pick you up. Today. Last night.'

Janika sighed and pushed her final pound coin into the payphone. 'But he'd be here by now, Dean. Even if he was coming on foot. It wouldn't take him an hour to walk here. Did he definitely leave an hour ago?'

'I don't know. Give or take.'

'Dean. I need to know.'

Dean groaned; he sounded like a ghost being forced through a sieve. 'Have some sympathy, Janika. I'm hungover. It hurt just to answer the phone. I only answered because the ringing hurt more. I don't know when it was. It was roughly sixty minutes ago.'

'Can you come and pick me up, then?'

'Me?'

'Yes. You have a car, don't you?'

Dean sounded panicked. 'I don't think it's safe for me to drive in this condition, Janika. I have a thumping headache. I can't look directly at the light. I can barely concentrate.'

'It's only ten minutes.'

'I think I'm still drunk from last night,' said Dean. 'I must be over the limit. I'd be breaking the law.'

Something moved in the bushes. Most likely a bird. 'You won't be over the limit. It's the afternoon.'

'I might be.'

'Can you go and ask Marcin, then? Marcin won't mind.'

'I don't know where Marcin is. He's gone out too. You could try Maya, but I think she's just got in the bath.'

'So I'm stranded here?'

Janika scanned her surroundings once again, wishing she had stayed in Australia. The train station was profoundly empty. She saw a child's shoe, lying abandoned next to one of the rails in the pit between the platform and the opposite bank. Mustard cigarette butts filled the gaps in the ballast. But there were no other markers of human existence. A lone magpie flew from the bushes. The few people who'd disembarked with Janika had left long ago.

'Not exactly,' said Dean. 'You can call a taxi, can't you?'

'Where would it come from? Salisbury? I'd be standing here another thirty minutes at least. I've been here twenty minutes already. That's an hour wasted. I'm too tired to do any work. I don't even have the money to make another phone call.'

'I'm sorry,' said Dean. 'I don't know what else I can suggest.'

'Why didn't you answer the phone fifteen minutes ago? I called then. I called last night.'

'It was unplugged,' said Dean.

'The phone?'

'Yes.'

'Why?'

'I don't know. I just found it like that. I plugged it back in. I was about to call Yulie.' Dean lowered his voice. 'Everything's been a bit of a mess this morning, Janika. We all drank too much yesterday. I'm definitely still drunk. Do you want me to call a taxi for you?'

Janika could hear the reluctance in Dean's voice. 'I'll walk,' she said, reaching down decisively and conjuring the handle from inside her case. She knew a path that led through the fields to Anatol's house. It was a route that she'd jogged occasionally when she'd been staying there before. But that was back when she was younger and fitter. Now she was in her thirties, tired and loaded with luggage.

Dean winced in sympathy. 'How long will that take?'

'It's a fifty-minute walk,' said Janika. 'An hour, maybe. An hour fifteen. I've done it before, just not with luggage.'

'Are you sure you can manage?'

'I don't have much choice, Dean. If Anatol's walking here then I'd have to walk either way, wouldn't I?'

'I'm sorry I couldn't be more helpful. But I'll see you soon?'

'An hour, give or take.' Janika was watching her money

tick down. They'd gone past the point where the phone would give change and she wanted to make sure she used every penny. She could hear Dean's patient breathing. She spoke up at the last second. 'Goodbye, then.'

'Good—' The call cut off. Dean's meandering voice was replaced by the constant, droning hum of the dial tone.

Anatol's house was set back twenty metres from the road: orange, austere and familiar. Its large garden was surrounded by a lofty, unkempt hedge, which kept the house hidden from its few neighbours. An hour or so after leaving the station, Janika stepped carefully through the gap in the hawthorns and pulled her suitcase on to the gravel. But the case's tiny wheels were insufficient against the gathered stones; it suddenly felt like she was dragging an anchor. She stopped, turned around, collapsed the case's telescopic handle and took hold of it by its leather strap. Then she heard the slam of a car boot behind her.

Maya's silver hatchback was parked at one side of the drive, halfway between Janika and the house. Maya was standing behind it, leaning back against the boot.

'Did you actually walk?'

Janika struggled over with her leaden suitcase. 'Yes,' she said. 'Why?'

'Dean told me you were walking. I thought he was joking.'

'I didn't have any choice,' said Janika.

'That's not true. You could have waited. I was in the bath. But I would have picked you up. I wasn't even washing. I was just bored. It would have been nice to have a reason to get out of the house.'

'There was nowhere to wait.'

'You could have gone into Tisbury. Had a coffee.'

'On a Sunday?'

Maya shrugged. 'Somewhere would have been open. You just like making things difficult, Janika. I know you too well. The pubs would have been open.'

'I was too tired to think of that, Maya. I'm too tired to be having this conversation. My best friend just left me stranded at the station. Is he back yet?'

'No. Not yet.'

'I told him three weeks ago what time train I'd be getting. Look at me.'

Janika's trainers were filthy. The bottoms of her jeans were fiery with dried mud: splashes and splatters that licked up the sides to her knees. She'd followed the footpath through the wet grass until she'd found herself sinking into a spreading doormat of mud at the entrance to a field, then she'd given up on the path and continued along the road. Now that she'd stopped moving, she could feel how damp and sweaty her T-shirt was underneath her cardigan. She'd been wrestling with her case for over an hour. Her whole body ached. There'd even been a flurry of leftover rain, thirty minutes into her journey. Janika had waited for it to pass, hunkered under the armpit of an oak tree.

'Do you know where he's gone?' she asked.

Maya shook her head. 'Phoebe's inside. She might know something. I was just looking for a pack of cigarettes. I thought I had one in the car. You don't have any, do you?' Maya tapped the roof of her hatchback, keeping her other hand flat against the boot.

'No,' said Janika. 'I don't smoke. You know I don't.'

'I should have asked you to fetch some from Tisbury. Marcin smoked all of mine.'

'You could have asked. I wouldn't have done it.' Janika looked to her left; Marcin's car was missing from the driveway. 'Where is Marcin?'

'No one knows. He was gone when we got up this morning.'

'He didn't go with Anatol?'

'No. Anatol left a couple of hours ago. I was awake by then. Marcin left a few hours before that. He's taken all his stuff with him. His room's empty. I tried his mobile but he's not answering. It's a mystery.' Maya said this brightly, as if she was being helpful. 'You like mysteries, don't you?'

'Do I?'

'You like puzzles, at least.'

'Not when they're at my expense. Is he coming back?'

Maya shrugged. 'I wouldn't be surprised if he'd gone back to London. He tends to disappear when he owes people money. Even if it's only a packet of cigarettes.'

'So it's just the four of us? You, me, Dean and Phoebe? I don't know why I bothered, Maya. It's nice to see you, obviously.' Janika softened slightly. 'But it wasn't exactly convenient for me to get here. I could have just come up to London.'

'No,' said Maya. 'I don't really know why you bothered, either. If I'd had to walk here, I would have got straight back on the train and gone home.'

'That's not very logical.' Janika lifted her weighty suitcase. 'If I'd got back on the train it would have been the opposite of going home. Are you coming inside?'

'No,' said Maya. 'I'm going to drive into the village and buy some cigarettes. Do you want a lift to the front door?'

Janika looked doubtfully across the driveway. 'Not really,' she said. 'It's ten metres, Maya.'

Janika opened the door and stepped through into the hallway, where a short corridor connected with the house's main staircase. To Janika's left this corridor turned to its right, giving access to the study, drawing room and dining room, while to her right it passed a small toilet and shower and led through an archway into the kitchen. There was a faint pale rectangle on the wall beside the staircase, where an imposing painting had previously hung. Janika traced its outline with her fingertips.

'Anatol's been making some changes,' said Phoebe as she emerged from the archway at the end of the corridor. 'I saw you from the kitchen. Dean told me you were on your way. I'm sorry that you had to walk. We thought Anatol was picking you up. We'll have to start chaperoning him when he goes out to run errands. He can't be trusted when he's by himself. But you're all right, aren't you?'

'It looks weird in here without that painting.'

'It's better,' said Phoebe, giving an exaggerated shudder as she pulled Janika into a hug. 'It was only Gus that liked that picture. I thought it was horrible.'

The painting had shown a hunting party pouring over a hedge, with fussy red coats and a froth of white and brown dogs.

'I keep forgetting that Gus is actually gone.' Janika stepped sideways, out of Phoebe's embrace. 'I've barely spoken to Anatol since it happened. Has he been all right?'

'I think so,' said Phoebe. 'He's back to normal, as far as I can tell. Not that there was anything normal about last night. How was your holiday?'

Janika sat down heavily on the stairs and started to pick at her wet shoelaces. The aches and pains of the walk were slowly giving way to a numbing tiredness; the stress and frustration that she'd been feeling all morning curled up into a ball inside her, leaving in their place a pervasive sadness. 'I'm not sure that Anatol wants me here. He didn't reply to any of my emails. I couldn't get through to him on the phone. And then he left me stranded at the station, after I spent almost forty-eight hours travelling here.'

Janika slipped off one of her shoes. It landed on the bottom step and the mud under the sole shattered like glass.

'I was hoping you'd tell me that he's getting forgetful,' she continued. 'That he can't concentrate on anything. That he can't even get out of bed. I was hoping he'd at least have an excuse.'

Phoebe took out a tissue, crouched down and began to pick up the pieces of mud that had scattered across the floor. 'I'm sure he wants you here. But you know what Anatol's like. If it's any consolation, he was late collecting me from the station yesterday.'

'How late?'

'About fifteen minutes.'

'You're obviously his favourite, Phoebe. And it was a conference, not a holiday. I was out there working.'

'A conference for philosophers?'

'Yes.'

Phoebe gave Janika a dubious smile. 'So it wasn't even ten per cent holiday, with the sun and the sea and the sand and everything?'

Janika slipped off her other shoe and let it fall to the

floor, making a fresh mess where Phoebe had cleaned. 'It's winter over there,' she said, looking forlornly at her exposed sock. 'Sorry,' she added. 'I didn't mean to do that.'

'Winter?' said Phoebe, nodding sagely, as if winter was something she'd heard of but didn't truly believe in. 'But isn't their winter warmer than our May?'

'It was jeans-and-a-cardigan weather.' Janika pulled her black cardigan close around her. 'And it was dark by five o'clock.'

Phoebe crushed the tissue into a ball and stood up. She threw it playfully at Janika and they both watched as it bounced off her knee, but neither of them made any effort to catch it. The ball came to a stop at the base of the stairs. Phoebe bent down, picked it up again and crushed it further. 'Where was the conference, then?'

'In one of the university buildings.'

'So you got to leave the hotel room at least?'

Janika shrugged. 'We went out in Sydney a couple of times. To some restaurants and bars and places like that. But that was after work. It wasn't a holiday.'

'And what was that like? Paradise?'

'It's just a normal city, Phoebe. It has a lot of beaches, if that's what you find interesting. But I spent most of my time working. I'm not really a beach person.'

'No. I never imagined you were.' Phoebe picked up Janika's shoes and put them on the rack in the nook beside the stairs. 'But I've always wanted to visit Australia.' She frowned. 'Maybe one day I'll make it.'

'All right. Well, I'm not your travel agent. But if I go there again I'll let you know.' Janika swept the rest of the dirt to one side with her sock. 'Phoebe. Did something happen here last night?'

'Like what?'

'I don't know. An argument? A fight? Anything that would explain where Anatol's gone? Or Marcin? You said it wasn't a normal night.'

'Oh. We just drank too much.'

'Aren't you worried about them?'

Phoebe seemed surprised by the question. 'Should I be?'

'You're always worried. About everything.'

'That's not true.' Phoebe dug a thumbnail into the tissue. 'Anyway. Anatol only left two hours ago. It's his birthday. He could be anywhere. He could have gone to pick up a cake. Maybe he just lost track of the time.'

Janika crossed her arms and leaned against the wall, closing her eyes. 'I could have made him a cake,' she muttered.

'Could you?' asked Phoebe sceptically.

'I don't see why not. How hard can it be?'

'As for Marcin, who knows? Maya said he ran out of cigarettes. Maybe he went to get some more.'

Janika shook her head, feeling the first shallow wave of sleep wash over her. 'It's like that painting on the wall. Everything here feels slightly different. It's unsettling.'

'If you mean me,' said Phoebe sharply, 'I'm just hungover. Everyone's getting older, Janika. We can't drink like we used to.'

'I didn't mean you. I meant everything. That's why I said everything.'

Janika felt the tissue hit her square on the forehead. She opened her eyes. Phoebe was standing in front of her with her hands in her pockets, smiling impishly.

'Maybe a cup of tea will help?'

*

Janika was watching the end of the driveway, willing Anatol to appear; she was sitting at the kitchen table, making patterns with the coasters. The kettle rumbled at the far end of the room. Phoebe was standing between the two, beside the open refrigerator.

'I don't know what Anatol expected us to do about lunch,' she was saying, straining to be heard above the noise of the kettle. 'Probably starve. But there's plenty left over from yesterday if you want it.'

'I had a sandwich on the train,' said Janika.

The kettle finished boiling. The sound of a suitcase came from the corridor: its small, hard wheels were unmistakable. Dean appeared in the archway, slouching apologetically. He was dragging Janika's case behind him. 'Janika, is this yours?'

'Yes. What are you doing with it?'

'I didn't realize it was so big. You're only here for one night, aren't you?'

'It's the case I took to Australia, Dean. I haven't been home.'

'Sorry.' Dean frowned. 'I thought you had.'

'No. I stayed in a hotel last night. Near Heathrow.'

'I didn't realize you'd brought so much stuff with you. I would have walked to the station and helped you carry it, if I'd known. Or met you halfway at least.'

'I told you I had luggage,' said Janika.

'But I'd pictured a backpack.' Dean sounded distraught. 'You usually have a backpack.'

Phoebe took a bottle of milk from the fridge and went over to the kettle. The ribbon of steam from its spout spiralled erratically. 'You didn't know, Dean. You did your best.'

Dean shook his head helplessly. 'I could have met you at the airport yesterday, if you'd asked me to. That would have been the best thing, I think. Then we could have driven straight down here. We'd have arrived just in time to hear Anatol read out the stories.'

'It's fine, Dean.' Janika closed her eyes. 'I needed to sleep. I still need to sleep. I didn't sleep at all on the plane. I didn't sleep much in the hotel, either.'

'But you could have slept in the car,' said Dean. 'I wouldn't have minded. I would have put the radio on or something.'

'There's no point discussing this,' said Janika.

'No, I don't suppose there is.'

Dean started rolling the suitcase away, along the corridor.

'Wait, Dean . . .' Janika rose from her chair. 'What stories?'

SATURDAY
29 May 1999

Pen to Paper

Maya, Dean, Phoebe and Marcin made a start on their stories shortly before one on Saturday afternoon, roughly an hour after Marcin had arrived; they were sitting in the drawing room, as far apart as the furniture made possible. Anatol left them there and went to make lunch.

Phoebe put down her pen, threw an elbow over the back of the sofa and turned to watch the raindrops exploding on the windows. Dean caught her movement out of the corner of his eye and looked where she was looking. They were both sitting sideways on the sagging green couch, with their feet sharing the middle cushion.

'The isobars of our cage,' said Dean, pointing outside with his pen. 'We're being held prisoner by the weather. And this is our forced labour.'

He held up his red notebook. But there wasn't enough light in the room for it to cast a reflection in the glass; he waved it back and forth but could barely see any movement. The only clear reflection was the shifting orange shape of the fire. Dean sighed and tossed his notebook on to the table. He'd spent the last half-hour picking at it like it was a plate of leftovers, whenever inspiration struck.

'You haven't finished?' asked Marcin, with pre-emptive outrage.

'I haven't started,' said Dean; he held his pen in one hand and stabbed it playfully through a gap in his fingers, then grasped it with the other hand and stabbed it back. 'All I've done is make a list of different ways you can kill someone. But there's no story there yet.'

Marcin looked at Phoebe, who was resting her notebook on her raised left knee. Its pages were covered in her neat, coiled handwriting. 'You've written a lot, Phoebe,' he said. 'You must be nearly finished?'

'I'm not keeping any of that.' Phoebe looked back at him glumly. 'I'm finding this much harder than I thought I would.'

'It's only been half an hour,' said Dean.

Marcin frowned and turned to a blank page. 'It should be easy for you, Phoebe. You studied literature.'

'I studied French,' said Phoebe. 'Only a small part of it was literature. The part I never get to use any more.'

'It's still more than me,' said Marcin. 'Why can't we play a game where we sit and do something I'd be good at for the afternoon instead? Maths or something.'

Maya was lying on an opulent red rug by the fire, with cushions under her chest and neck. Her face hovered a few inches from the floor. She was stroking her pen lid across her lips; she slid it into her mouth and breathed through it for several seconds, then took it out and put it down on the rug, where lint stuck instantly to her patchy saliva. 'It's not that hard, Marcin. Just imagine one of us dying painfully, then describe it in detail.'

'Why does it have to be painful?' asked Phoebe.

'It's easy for you.' Marcin was talking to Maya now. 'You have a creative job, Maya. You're an artist. I work in finance. Creativity atrophies after a while. It evaporates. It's eviscerated. It's . . .'

Phoebe concurred. 'It's easy for everyone except you,

Marcin. The rest of us write stories like this all the time. We often get together and play this game without you.'

'And me,' said Dean, failing to pick up on Phoebe's sarcasm. 'I studied engineering.' He took his notebook from the table and started to doodle, drawing first a random polygon, then determinedly subdividing it into smaller and smaller triangles. 'I might try working upstairs, where I can concentrate. I'll be in my bedroom, if anyone wants me.' But no one responded and Dean didn't move. He looked at Phoebe; then he glanced out of the window again. 'I think there might be a storm coming.'

'Maybe it's the end of the world,' said Maya. 'Nostradamus said it would end this July. He could have been out by a couple of months. Or maybe July will be the end of the end and this is just the beginning? Maybe it'll take two months to run its course?'

'That would be ideal,' said Marcin. 'I could give up smoking and get out of writing this story, without having to work at either.'

'Killing two birds,' said Dean, 'with one apocalypse.'

Phoebe was staring wistfully at the window, transfixed by her view of Anatol's garden, shattered by the rain. 'You three can die if you want. But I don't want to die this weekend.'

A Walk in the Rain

The group had their third round of cocktails straight after lunch. Anatol made each of them a cosmopolitan: a nub of sticky red liquid, nose-down in a martini glass. The drink tasted insipidly sweet, until the alcohol found its way to the tongue and overwhelmed everything else.

'I'll sip that one slowly,' said Dean.

The five friends were sitting in the drawing room. They raised their drinks, but nobody felt the need to touch glasses with their neighbours; they'd done it too many times in the past.

'What happened to the rain?' said Maya as she looked out of the window at the dripping garden. 'It's stopped, Dean. You said there was a storm coming.'

Dean looked embarrassed. 'I meant later.'

'Then I think I'll go for a walk,' said Maya. 'Before the rain comes back.'

Marcin looked up. 'You haven't finished your story, have you?'

The Arrivals Lounge

Dean had arrived at the house shortly after Maya; his midnight-blue Ford Mondeo had turned cautiously through the gap in the hawthorns and slumped on to the gravel at twenty-five past eleven that morning. After more than an hour of driving in the heavy rain, since his previous stop at the service station, Dean had felt as relieved as if it had been his own body collapsing on to a feather bed, though the small shifting stones had been hard and sharp. With halting progress, its wheels scratching at the soupy gravel, his car had continued across the driveway and pulled up alongside the only other vehicle there: Maya's silver hatchback. Dean had wondered briefly how she'd managed to get to the house before him, when she'd almost certainly set out later. But then he'd remembered: Maya had no regard for human life, least of all her own. She must have driven there at speed, without giving a single thought to what could go wrong.

Dean sighed heavily and switched off his lights, his wipers and then his engine. Within a matter of seconds the windscreen was flooded.

It wasn't even midday and he was exhausted.

'I survived,' said Dean, ten minutes later; he was talking on the phone to his wife, Yulie. 'Don't laugh. It was dangerous. You didn't see how bad it was.'

The front door of Anatol's house opened on to a

bright hallway, where a short corridor joined with the central staircase. The staircase proceeded towards the back of the house, turning left at its midpoint, leaving a small nook beside it, opposite the front door. This narrow recess was cast in shadow, bordered by the rising stairs, and like most of the house was filled with old furniture. There was a needless hatstand in one corner; an umbrella stand in another; a florid walnut sewing table, where Anatol stored his keys and post; a cast-iron shoe rack; and a large, doomy grandfather clock that was no longer functional and tricked everyone that entered the house into thinking it was either midnight or noon.

Dean was tethered to the middle of this jumble by the spiralling cable of Anatol's telephone, mounted on the wall above the shoe rack. He was leaning against the newel post, holding the slim red handset up to his head. 'I'm not checking up on you. I just didn't want you to worry. I could have died.' He had changed out of his driving clothes and was wearing a powder-blue jumper and grey trousers, though both looked navy in the dim light. 'All right. In future I'll only phone if I'm actually dead. Yes. All right. I love you too.'

Dean hung up and walked through to the drawing room; Maya was lying on the red leather couch, facing away from the door. She'd heard him coming and had tilted her head back in expectation. A gaudy magazine lay open on her stomach, like a shotgun wound. Dean flinched at the sight of her upside-down face. He rested his elbows on the back of the green sofa and looked down at her. Anatol's present was by his feet, wrapped in gold paper. Dean had brought it to the house in the boot of his car. 'I don't know how you can sit like that after being cramped in the car for three hours. Don't you want to stretch?'

'If it was up to me,' said Maya absently, 'I'd have driven here sitting like this. How's Yulie?'

'She'll survive. She's just got a cold. It's a nasty one, though. You wouldn't want to catch it. Her nose has been dripping like a tap all week. It's like she's wedged an ice cube up each nostril.'

'No. That doesn't sound pleasant.' Maya gathered together a number of magazine pages, curled their corners over, and used the point to clean underneath her nails. 'She's not pregnant, is she?'

'No,' said Dean, taken by surprise. 'Why? Does your nose run when you're having a baby?'

'It's just that she wasn't drinking the last time I saw her. Not even a drop. I think she thought I wouldn't notice. But Yulie's always drinking.'

Dean came casually around to the front of the sofa and collapsed on to it in mock exhaustion. 'She probably had a hangover,' he said. 'You know how bad her hangovers are.'

Maya had grown up in the same village as Phoebe and Yulie and had known them both since secondary school. 'It was last Monday, after work. No one has a hangover on a Monday evening.'

'Were you drinking?'

'Of course,' said Maya. 'Two double gin and tonics.'

'Then maybe she did have a drink and you don't remember?'

'I was drinking, Dean. I wasn't drunk.'

'All right. But I don't know what to tell you, Maya.' Dean pulled a magazine from the pile under the coffee table. It was something about the countryside. He didn't look at the title. 'She's not pregnant. You know she gave it up for Lent?'

Maya looked across at him. 'What, sex?'

'Alcohol,' said Dean.

'Lent finished weeks ago, didn't it?'

'I know, but she drinks less now. She hasn't got back in the habit. Not yet.'

Maya went back to tending her nails. 'She wouldn't be the first person to panic after turning thirty and immediately have a baby. My sister did the exact same thing.'

'She's twenty-eight, Maya. She's not having a baby.'

'You're thirty. Maybe she's panicking vicariously, on your behalf.'

'Maybe.' Dean opened his magazine loudly. The pages were filled with property listings, most of them priced at more than three hundred thousand. The photographs alongside were decadent and tasteless: they showed thatched cottages with clay tennis courts, exposed beams that loomed over swimming pools and sweeping balconies looking out on to farmland.

'In that case, I hope I haven't spoiled a surprise.' Maya chewed her collar. 'Sometimes the husband isn't the first to find out. Maybe I should ask Phoebe instead.'

Dean tossed his magazine on to the table. It landed with a slap. 'All right, Maya. I'll tell you the truth. Yulie is pregnant. But nobody knows about it yet. Not even family. It's too early. You know what can happen. We can't tell anyone. Even Phoebe.'

'I can keep a secret,' said Maya, smiling at this small victory.

'Can you?' Dean shook his head anxiously. 'I mean this

in the nicest possible way, Maya, but you have a mouth like a tabloid newspaper. Please don't tell anyone.'

Maya mimed putting a safety pin through her lips. 'Well. Congratulations, anyway. I assume it's a good thing?'

'Yes, it's a good thing. But can we please stop talking about it?'

'I promise,' said Maya. 'Now I have to imagine the two of you having sex.'

'Please don't,' said Dean.

'And Phoebe definitely doesn't know?'

'No. She doesn't. And she'd be offended if she found out from you instead of Yulie. You know what sisters are like.'

Maya shrugged. 'I won't say anything.'

Dean sat on his hands and tried to relax, but he couldn't get comfortable on the wilted sofa. He stood up again and walked to the door. Maya was surprised to see him leaving so soon.

'Where are you going?' she asked.

Dean groaned. 'To call Yulie back.'

'I won't tell anyone else. I didn't tell Maya, anyway. She already knew. You gave it away. Couldn't you have ordered a shandy or something?'

Dean was on the phone again. He was toying with the coiled cable that attached the handset to the wall, stretching out small sections of it, slotting his fingers between the loops and then releasing the slack, so that the rubbery circles pinched at his skin. It felt like he was putting his hand in a toast rack. He continued talking. 'All right. I'll relax. I've already relaxed.'

He tried to pull his hand free, but the cable clung to him.

A shape moved across the panels of clouded glass that surrounded the front door: a comet or a car or something else. Dean couldn't tell over the sound of the rain, though it would most likely be Anatol returning from the station. Or maybe Marcin arriving. Dean moved as close to the door as he could manage – the phone cord releasing his hand as it straightened and lengthened, more narwhal tusk now than corkscrew – and tried to look out through the garbled windows. But all he could see were some smears of colour. He tilted his head away from the receiver, letting Yulie's voice fade a little, and pressed his ear against the wood. Through the constant rain he heard the soft clunk of a car door being closed, then the glassy crunch of shoes on gravel.

Outside, somebody spoke. 'I count two cuckoos in the nest.'

Dean recognized Anatol's voice, followed by Phoebe's. 'Can you open the boot?'

He unlatched the front door and let it swing inwards, towards him, nudged on its way by the pounding rain, then he moved back to where the phone was fixed to the wall. Yulie was saying something, her distant speech flecked with static.

'You're probably right,' Dean interrupted her. 'I overreacted. I'd better go now. Anatol's just got here.' He raised a hand to cover the mouthpiece, just in case Anatol blurted out something indiscreet, or – worse – tried to embark on a tedious exchange of pleasantries with Yulie, with Dean as the grudging go-between. 'Yes. I'll tell him. I love you too.'

He hung up as he heard the approaching rustle of polythene bags. Anatol pushed the door open wide, bashing the bags against the wood. He was holding three in each hand, hoops of wiry white plastic criss-crossing his skin.

'You made it OK?' he said, when he noticed Dean in the recess opposite.

'I made it,' said Dean. 'But I'd have come by boat if I'd known the weather was going to be like this.'

'Just give me a minute.' Anatol held up a cluster of shopping bags: a white flag, by way of apology. 'Some of this food is already thawing. I forgot that I'd bought some things for the freezer.'

'Can I help with anything?'

But Anatol didn't respond. The question was lost in the chaos as he crashed his way along the corridor to the kitchen, the shopping spinning into his knees with each step. Then the noise shrank to a point and stopped, replaced by the sound of approaching footsteps. Phoebe appeared in the empty doorway, holding a hefty leather travelling bag in front of her chest.

Dean laughed. 'You look like you're about to saddle a horse.'

Phoebe squinted up at him through beaded eyelashes. She ran a hand back through her hair and shook off the water that gathered in her palm. 'What are you doing there? Were you waiting for me?'

'I was on the phone,' said Dean. He reached out and pressed on the handset, making sure that he'd replaced it properly, letting his fingertips linger on the smooth plastic. He never knew what to do with his hands.

'With Yulie?' asked Phoebe.

Dean gave her a nod. 'It's only a cold. She's resting. She'll be fine.'

'I know she will. My sister's a hypochondriac.' Phoebe placed her bag down next to the door. 'She's definitely not coming?'

'No.'

'What about if she feels better? Will she join us tomorrow?'

'It's unlikely. She'd have to drive.' Dean slid his hands into his pockets. 'It's nice to see you,' he added sadly. 'Are you pleased to see me?'

Phoebe avoided the question, stepping to one side. 'Could you help me carry my bag upstairs?'

Dean reached down dutifully and lifted the bag. He started up the staircase, waiting on the second step for Phoebe to join him. 'Is something wrong?' he whispered.

'I think we need to talk,' said Phoebe.

A Walk in the Rain (continued)

Maya's walk took her to the back of the cemetery in North Hatch, where she collected the thirteen white flowers – lilies and roses – that had been placed neatly on Gus's grave, and laid them to one side. Without them, the grave had an austere majesty, whereas with the flowers it had just looked neglected and sad. A scraggy barrow of scar tissue. It was a long mound of sodden earth, with no headstone and nothing near it but grass. At its furthest tip a skinny wooden cross bore the name 'Augustine Bloom'. Underneath were the dates of his birth and death.

Maya knelt and started taking photographs. It had stopped raining, but the ground was still soaked. She could feel the wet grass sticking to her legs. She lay down flat and took more pictures, trying to get the grave against the cedar trees behind. But the wooden cross looked lost with the huge mound of mud in front of it: like a tiny torso staring down dejectedly at a gigantic stomach. Maya stood up, grabbed it by the handles and yanked the cross out of the ground.

It came out easily, though its stem was longer than Maya had been expecting. And its bottom was flat. She'd been picturing something more like a stake. She moved it to the foot of the grave, where it would have more visual impact – with the mound as a background – and tried to push it into the soil. But its blunt end got stuck after just a few inches, leaving it standing absurdly tall, like the prow of a Viking ship. Maya leaned her weight on it, with her elbows on its arms, but the cross just sank to one side and toppled over, gouging out a chunk of earth as it fell. Maya ended up with her face in the grass.

'Balls,' she said as she got up and brushed the soil from her hands.

The cemetery was deserted. Even the birds had fled in the bad weather. Maya looked around for a shovel or a trowel, but she couldn't find anything useful. She knelt again and tried plunging her hand into the loose dirt, digging with her fingers, wondering how far she'd be able to reach and whether it would be enough to knock on the coffin lid. But she could soon feel her fingernails lifting away from her skin. She pulled her hand out sadly and wiped it on the grass.

Then she moved the cross back to its original position. But the wet mud had shifted slightly in the few minutes since she'd taken it out. She could only slide it partway into the hole. It stood there at a slant, like an old, weathered scarecrow. 'For fuck's sake . . .'

Maya removed the cross and laid it flat, adding desecration to her list of vices. 'Oh well.' There was bound to be a caretaker or something. Someone would fix it. She took a final photograph of the ruined grave, then tossed the flowers back on the heap. 'Goodbye, Gus. You horrible old man.'

The Arrivals Lounge (continued)

The rotting window in Phoebe's room had been left open; while she reached over to close it, Dean put her bag down on top of the bed; then, worried that the bottom of the bag might be wet or dirty, he moved it to the floor and finally to the top of a chest of drawers. 'Where do you want me to put this?' he asked.

'Anywhere,' said Phoebe indifferently. She was reaching up towards the top of the curtains, trying to open them as wide as they would go, but the stained white linen kept springing back, covering five inches of glass on each side. Phoebe's room was the darkest and smallest of the five guest bedrooms, tucked away at the end of the landing, with a window half the size of the rest. She'd volunteered to take it on their first visit to the house – in an act of showy humility – and had been stuck with it ever since. Its colour scheme was cream and grey. A gaunt carving of Christ on the cross was fixed to the wall above the bed.

Dean folded his arms and looked at the bag, then moved it down to the floor again. 'So what do you want to talk to me about?'

Phoebe abandoned the curtains and turned around, leaning back against the desk. 'Where's Maya?'

'Downstairs,' said Dean.

'What about Marcin?'

'He's not here yet. We can talk, Phoebe. We're safe. No one can hear us. We can do anything you want.'

'There's something I need to show you,' said Phoebe.

'Are you angry with me?'

'What?'

'You haven't given me a hug,' said Dean. Phoebe was in the habit of hugging everyone; Dean was sure she would hug Maya in a minute, though Maya, he knew, wouldn't even raise her arms – she'd just let herself be squeezed; and Phoebe had probably hugged Anatol already that morning.

'I'm not angry with you, Dean. I'm the opposite of angry. I'm just worried.'

'Worried isn't the opposite of angry.'

'I am happy to see you, believe me . . .'

Emboldened, Dean put his arms around Phoebe. She was tense, but he soon felt her shoulders resign themselves to his wrists, her cheek to his chest.

'But I'm worried about what happens next,' she whispered.

An embrace is just a hug where the participants have lost track of time; after half a minute, Dean lowered his head to kiss Phoebe, but she put a hand on his chest and pushed him away. 'I think Yulie knows about us.'

SUNDAY NIGHT
30 May 1999

Window Pain

Tragedy struck late on Sunday evening, when spring was at its most fickle. The rain had stopped suddenly and the night had filled with the sibilant ticking of insects; a gentle breeze brought floral whispers through the open window; the murmuring curtains glowed white in the moonlight. A glass of lemonade trembled on the desk.

Dean was pacing around his room. He'd gone to bed shortly after midnight, but had stayed awake for another hour since then, walking circles in the dark. He was fighting sleep, with his fists clenched. The floorboards in his room were brittle and loud. But he'd learned where the quiet parts were, prodding and probing at the floor with his feet, until he could walk the whole circuit in silence, from the door to the bed to the wardrobe and back again. He stopped by the desk and picked up his drink. The cold liquid walked slowly down his throat, waking him up.

Dean moved to the window and leaned against the glass. Through the layered panes he could just see the pond at the bottom of the garden: a black spot on the dark blue lawn. Dean had been down there earlier that day. He'd positioned one of the stones at the edge so that it reached out over the water, enough that if someone put their weight on the wrong part they would fall into the pond. Especially if they'd been drinking alcohol. And if they hit their head on the way down – either by accident or with a little assistance – they could end up drowning in the shallow water. It would be an easy death. Three minutes later, the garden would be quiet again: the moonlight renewed and the black water turned back to vinyl.

And there would be no way of knowing that it hadn't been an accident.

Dean went to the oak wardrobe, took off his Fair Isle jumper and held it with a hug of indecision, then hung it from one of the hangers. He took off his string vest and his corduroy trousers and slid off his socks. He dithered over his boxer shorts, but decided to keep them on. Then he put on his dressing gown and his driving gloves, and switched on the light and looked in the mirror. There was no denying that the gloves looked suspicious. They would certainly make things easier, but his body was royal-blue terrycloth and his hands were black leather. He took them off, then took off his underwear.

His genitals stared back at him.

It was the pond water that posed a problem. Anything that touched it would come away filthy. And there was no way that Dean could wash his clothes without attracting suspicion. He couldn't rely on hiding them either, not if the police might end up investigating. He could hide a pair of boxer shorts, perhaps, but nothing as big as a jumper. So his plan was simply to do the act naked. The cold would be uncomfortable, emasculating even, but at least it would be brief. Then he'd return to the house and take a hot shower, in the downstairs bathroom where no one would hear. After that, he'd go to bed, with a slug of whisky to help him sleep. When he woke up in the morning all his troubles would be gone.

Dean switched the light off and knelt by the door, looking out through the keyhole. The landing was dark. He couldn't hear anything except the ragged sound of breathing, coming from one of the rooms to his left. It sounded like someone had swallowed a rattle. He sat down on the bed and removed his wedding ring, then unfastened his watch. The time was one twenty-nine.

He held his breath.

And then came the knock: a single knuckle against the wood.

Dean opened the door. Phoebe was leaning against the frame, smiling faintly in the speckled darkness. Even drunk she was punctual. 'Are you ready?' she said.

'I'm ready,' said Dean.

Phoebe nodded. 'Whenever you're ready.' She was slurring her words. There was a shapelessness to her vowels. They were like overripe fruit. She reached in and kissed him.

'The others . . .' mumbled Dean through smothered lips.

'They're all asleep. I can hear them breathing.'

'I was worried you might have drunk too much.'

Phoebe put her hands on her hips and shook her head. 'I held back,' she said. 'When that second bottle of champagne came around. I poured mine into a plant pot.'

Dean nodded. 'I held back too.'

In actual fact, he'd gone to the toilet and vomited his champagne into the sink, filling the porcelain with thin white foam. It was the third time he'd been sick that evening, partly due to nervousness and partly as a form of forward planning. But he didn't share that detail with Phoebe. She kissed him again, forcing her way into the room.

Then she closed the door and turned on the light.

Dean and Phoebe had been fucking in secret for almost

a month, keeping the affair hidden from their friends as well as from Yulie.

'Dean,' said Phoebe. 'Why are you naked? I thought you were ready?'

'I'm only naked underneath,' said Dean, gathering his dressing gown around him. 'No one will see me. Except you.'

'You can't go out like that. You'll catch your death.'

Phoebe was dressed for the outdoors. She was wearing jeans, a raincoat, a pair of boots and a lambswool scarf.

'It's not that cold,' said Dean.

'Don't be ridiculous.' Phoebe had her hands on her hips again, looking like a schoolteacher. 'You'll get pneumonia. Put on some trousers.'

'What's the point of putting on clothes if we're just going to take them off again?' Dean tried a sheepish wink but Phoebe turned away from him, smacking the gesture back like a tennis ball. 'Besides,' he added, 'they'll get wet on the grass.'

'We're not going to have sex outside,' said Phoebe, opening the wardrobe and running her hands through the clothes that were hanging there.

Dean sat down heavily on the bed. The mattress sagged. The springs inside him sagged even more. 'What are we going outside for then?'

'I thought we were going for a walk in the moonlight. Somewhere romantic. Then we'd come back here, where we have a warm bed.' Phoebe took out the jumper that Dean had been wearing before. She took out the same sandy trousers and fresh pairs of pants and socks. 'Here, why don't you put these on?'

Dean sighed as she passed him the clothes. The jumper

was soft and absorbent, a woollen sponge. He pulled it over his head unhappily. If he got it wet, he'd never get it dry again. 'It's May, Phoebe. We're not in the Arctic.'

He would have to take it off when they were outside. Along with everything else. There was a Gothic Revival pillar near the pond. He could hide behind that and get undressed. No doubt Phoebe would kick up a fuss, but it wouldn't matter what she thought by then.

'What about a coat?' she asked. 'And an umbrella?'

'I don't need a coat,' said Dean. 'It's stopped raining.'

Phoebe went to the desk and leaned her head and shoulders out through the open window. Her hips were level with the bottom of the frame. She kept one hand on the sill and held the other to the sky. 'It is raining,' she said, bringing her head back inside. 'Why don't we just stay here?'

Dean looked startled. 'I thought it had stopped?'

'Then it must have started again.'

'Are you sure?'

'My hand's wet,' said Phoebe. 'There's no mistaking that.'

Dean stood up, naked from the waist down. He hurried to put on the rest of his clothes. 'I don't mind the rain if it's only light. I'll wear a jacket.'

Phoebe shook her head. 'I don't want to go outside. You had the right idea before, being naked.' She started unbuttoning her bulbous coat.

'But what if someone hears us?'

'I don't think they will. They've all been drinking.'

'But isn't it more romantic outside?'

'It's raining,' said Phoebe. 'I'm not Lady Chatterley.'

Dean looked at the window and shook his head. He was

trying to remember where he'd put his gloves. 'Are you sure it's raining? It wasn't just water dripping from the roof? That happens sometimes.'

'I don't think so,' said Phoebe.

'Can you check and make sure?'

'I can hear it in the trees.' Phoebe leaned out of the window again, resting both hands on the windowsill. 'It's a shame. It's a nice night otherwise.'

Dean found his gloves in the pockets of his dressing gown and pulled them over his shaking hands. Then he did the only truly impulsive thing that he'd ever done in his life. He marched over to the window and lifted Phoebe's legs and tilted her forwards and let her fall. It was four and a half metres from there to the ground.

The whole thing was over in less than a second. Phoebe spun as she plummeted and landed on her back, thumping her head against the flagstones.

'Ninety-eight. Ninety-nine . . .'

Dean finished counting to a hundred. He was still in his room, looking out of the window. Phoebe hadn't moved. She was either dead or unconscious. Dean took a deep breath. Either way, he would have to see it through now. He would have to put her body in the pond, hold it under the water, then topple the loose stone to make it look as though she'd fallen in. The rain would wash the blood from the flagstones. There would be no way for anyone to work out what had actually happened or to link it back to him.

He went to the wardrobe and peeled the gloves from his hands. He took off his jumper and put it back on the hanger. Then he took off his trousers, folded them and placed them inside one of the drawers, along with his socks. He dithered over his boxer shorts again, before sliding them off. Then he took his dressing gown from the bed, found the arms and put it back on.

There was a knock at the door.

Dean froze. He thought about pretending to be asleep, but the lights were on in his bedroom. There would be light leaking out through the keyhole and under the door.

Whoever it was knocked again.

Dean wiped the sheen of sweat from his forehead and opened the door.

Phoebe was leaning against the frame. She looked unsteady. 'Dean?' she said, slurring her words. 'You're naked?' She put a hand to her head. 'I think I'm having déjà vu.'

'Phoebe, I had to do it.' Dean stepped back. He felt in the pockets of his dressing gown but found them empty. 'You gave me no choice. I didn't want to hurt you.'

Phoebe looked at him without comprehension. Her eyes could barely focus. 'Slow down, Dean. My head is ringing. I think I just woke up in the garden. I don't remember how I got there.'

'You had an accident.' Dean spoke in a hurried whisper, hoping that with this change of tone Phoebe would forget what he'd just said. 'You were leaning out of the window and lost your balance. Come over here, into the light.'

Dean ushered Phoebe into the room and closed the door behind her. He held her shoulders and turned her around, under the overhead light. The whole back half of her head was glossy with blood, seeping from a wound that looked like a bald spot. It was a patch as big as an apple. Luckily the blood was sticking to her hair, not dripping down on to the floor.

'Does it look all right?' she asked.

Dean bit his lip. 'You really don't remember anything?'

'We were going to go for a walk outside. Weren't we?'

'Move forwards a few steps, Phoebe. I need to see the back of your head in the light. There. That's better. You look just fine.'

Dean pushed Phoebe forcefully towards the window. She fell and caught herself on the sill. Dean lifted her legs, placed a hand under her stomach, and threw her forwards, out of the window. It was four and a half metres from there to the ground. Phoebe landed in the same spot as before.

This time Dean didn't hesitate.

He shed the dressing gown and ran outside naked.

SUNDAY
30 May 1999

The Display Cabinet

'Is this some kind of joke?' Janika was shaking her head in disbelief. 'Anatol reads out your stories about murder and then goes missing the next morning? Marcin too? You're not making fun of me, Dean?'

'Does it look like I'm having fun?' A handful of birds were circling outside. Dean was watching them as if they were television. He had no choice. He was trapped at the desk in Janika's room, facing the window. Janika's suitcase was open on the floor behind him, pushed up against the legs of his chair, its lid leaning against the back of his seat. 'I hope not,' he continued. 'I don't want to be stuck here all day.'

Janika was sitting beside the suitcase, unpacking the things she would need for the evening and the following day. She found her pyjamas and laid them on the floor behind her, next to a pile of books. Her clothes were folded as flat as envelopes. It looked like she was sorting through post. 'You can leave when you've answered my questions,' she said.

There was an antique typewriter at one end of the desk. Dean pulled it towards him and peered into its mechanism, pressing the keys intermittently. He found a single sheet of paper, barely used, in the bin underneath the desk and fed it into the top of the carriage, twisting the platen until it turned white. Then he started to type, speaking the words out loud as he did so.

'"Send help,"' he said. '"I'm being held captive."'

'What are you doing?' asked Janika.

'Clack clack clack,' said Dean. 'Don't you love the sound of a typewriter?'

'Not particularly. It's making me sleepy.'

'Exactly. It's soothing.'

'I don't like feeling sleepy,' said Janika. 'I find it stressful. I like my brain to be functioning, not taking time off.'

Dean pushed the typewriter back towards the window. 'I've finished, anyway.' He turned the platen again and pulled out the page that he'd been typing on, then folded it five times, into the shape of an aeroplane. 'Hopefully someone will read this and rescue me.'

Janika's room was the second smallest of the five guest bedrooms. It overlooked the garden and had a bright colour scheme, with lilac walls, an oak wardrobe, a white-painted chest of drawers and a wrought-iron bed. The desk by the window was also white; the sheets on the bed were daffodil yellow. Hanging above the headboard was a large navy painting of the *Titanic* sinking in the middle of the night, its ominous stern jutting out of the dark, fibrous calm of the Atlantic Ocean.

Dean leaned forwards, opened the window in front of him and threw the paper aeroplane outside. But the angles were all wrong and it fell limply to the ground. Dean slumped in his seat, disappointed. 'Next question,' he said.

'Do you know where Marcin and Anatol have gone?'

'No. But I doubt they've been murdered. Anatol probably went to get a pint of milk or something. And Marcin a packet of cigarettes. The simplest explanation is usually the correct one. Isn't that right? Occam's razor?'

'Occam's razor is just a motto,' said Janika. 'It doesn't

have any grounding in logic. Sometimes the truth is complicated. You should know that, Dean, you're an engineer. Occam never had to solve differential equations.'

'Right. Sorry.' Dean capitulated. 'Maybe they have been murdered then.'

Janika opened the top two drawers of the chest in front of her; she raised a leg and placed her foot halfway up the wooden shell, to prevent the whole thing from tipping forwards, then reached up and slotted her books inside, followed by her clothes. 'So does Anatol still want me to write a story? I assume that's why that typewriter's there.'

Dean nodded. 'Your names are in the display cabinet downstairs. But I think it's locked.'

'Who has the key?'

'Anatol,' said Dean. 'I'm not sure where he put it.'

'It doesn't matter,' said Janika. 'I wouldn't have time to write one anyway.'

Dean twisted around in his seat. He could barely move his upper body, but by turning his head he could just see Janika in his peripheral vision. 'I don't see why not,' he said. 'Even if it takes you five hours, you'd still finish before dinner. Just about. I'll make you a cup of coffee if you let me go.'

'I don't want to spend the whole day writing, Dean. Don't you like my company? Anyway. Everyone would know which story was mine, wouldn't they? If Anatol read the other ones yesterday, he would have to read out mine on its own.' Janika finished unpacking and closed her suitcase; she looked sadly at its fabric exterior. The mud along the bottom had dried to a yellow-brown dust. 'I can't believe I actually walked here.'

Dean turned back to the window. The sky was as bright as a cathode ray tube, so he couldn't see his reflection in the glass. But he knew that he must have looked guilty. 'Sorry,' he said. 'I wish I could have given you a lift, Janika. I'd have drunk a lot less last night if I'd known.' He tried a smile. 'Is that why you're keeping me prisoner here? As punishment?'

Janika closed the chest of drawers and moved her case away from the desk. 'You're free,' she said. 'You can stop complaining.'

Dean slid his chair back. He turned around and stretched out his legs. 'Anatol only read out three of the stories last night,' he said. 'The plan was to read three yesterday and three more today. If you did write one, he'd read yours out with the other two tonight.'

Janika was standing next to the bed, holding a clean pair of black jeans. She looked down despondently at the flourishes of mud on the ones she was wearing.

'I'm going to get changed,' she said. 'Don't look, Dean.'

'All right. Hang on a second.'

Dean moved his chair back to where it had been before, tight against the desk. Janika placed the suitcase behind him again. She took off her jeans and put on the new pair. As soon as she'd done so, her socks felt comparatively damp. She sat down on the bed, leaned over and found a clean pair of pink and purple argyle socks in the chest of drawers. They were rolled into a little ball, like a patterned hamster. Janika put them on.

'So where are the stories from last night?' she asked.

'I don't know.'

'Does Anatol have them?'

'Probably. Why do you want them?'

'To read them, obviously.'

'Why?'

'The ones I missed,' said Janika. 'Yesterday.'

'Yes. Why do you want to read them?'

Janika looked incredulously at the back of Dean's head. 'Why wouldn't I want to read them? I'm supposed to be writing one of them.'

'I thought you said you wouldn't have time.'

'I might.'

'But it's cheating if you read the other ones first,' said Dean. 'Nobody else did.'

'But I can work out what names I have if I read the other stories. What difference does it make, anyway?'

'All right. That's true.' Tentatively, Dean turned his head; he was relieved to find Janika fully dressed. 'But you'd need all five stories for that. And I've no idea where any of them went.'

Janika found Phoebe downstairs, sitting in the kitchen. She hadn't moved in the last half-hour. 'Do you know where the stories went?' asked Janika. 'The three that Anatol read out last night?'

Phoebe had finished the cup of tea that she'd made for herself and had started on the one she'd made for Janika. She hadn't wanted it to go to waste. 'No,' she said, between careful sips. 'They were in the drawing room. But they're not there now. I think Marcin took them with him when he went up to bed. Where have you been?'

'Upstairs,' said Janika, 'unpacking. Did Marcin go to bed before you?'

'Yes.'

'And you saw him take the stories?'

'I think so,' said Phoebe. 'But I'd been drinking. I can't remember exactly. Why do you want them?'

'Because I don't like feeling left out, Phoebe. And everyone has read them apart from me.'

'You're better off being left out. They weren't very pleasant.'

'Why not?'

'I don't know. They felt personal.'

'Is that why Marcin left this morning?'

'Maybe.' Phoebe shrugged. 'One of the stories was about Marcin. But it was tame compared to the one about me.'

Janika pressed on the glass-panelled doors of the display cabinet, but they barely moved. The silver tray was visible on the middle shelf, in front of a crowd of porcelain figurines, bordered by a dainty mosaic of Matchbox cars, but Janika couldn't think of a way to get to it. She could see the two slips of paper under their upturned cocktail glasses.

'I think I can make out the letter M,' she said, 'in green pen. That's probably Marcin.'

The doors' bronze lock was level with her belly. Janika tried pushing her finger inside it, but she soon gave up and leaned her head against the glass, feeling defeated. A cloud of condensation formed below her chin. She closed her eyes briefly and felt sleep flood her veins, turning her blood cloudy and thick. Her head started to slide down the frictionless surface. Then she was brought back to consciousness by the sound of Maya, behind her, scratching at a stuck cigarette lighter.

'You don't have any matches, do you?'

Janika steadied herself and turned around. Maya had moved one of the wingback armchairs towards the window and produced a packet of cigarettes from somewhere. The patio window stood wide open beside her.

'Sorry,' said Janika.

Maya tried the lighter again and eventually managed to light the cigarette, leaning sideways so that her head was outside the house; she took a long, decadent pull on it, then turned and exhaled into the garden.

'Do you know how to pick a lock?' asked Janika.

'It's a cigarette,' said Maya. 'I'm not a reprobate. Maybe we should search Anatol's room for the key.'

'I was just up there,' said Janika.

'Without me?'

'I didn't find anything.'

'But still . . .' Maya sank into her chair, her disappointment palpable. 'Snooping is an art form, Janika. You have to know how.'

'I wasn't snooping. I was looking for the stories.'

'Which stories?'

'The three that Anatol read out yesterday.'

'I wouldn't bother with those,' said Maya. 'They were all quite tame.'

Janika pressed on the doors again. 'I tried calling here last night, while you would have been listening to Anatol read them out. But the phone was unplugged. Was that so you could concentrate or because one of you didn't want me here?'

Maya shrugged. 'You should have tried Marcin's mobile.'

'I did. He didn't answer.'

'Maybe he didn't have any signal. What about Phoebe's?'

'I wasn't sure of her number,' said Janika.

'Why don't you smash the glass? There.' Maya was pointing at a heavy cloth-bound book on anatomy, on top of the display cabinet. 'Use that.'

'I'm not going to smash the glass,' said Janika.

Maya moved her hand back to the window, leaving a trail of smoke across the corner of the room. 'Then why don't you break the wood? You can glue it back together again afterwards. You'd just need to find something you can use as a crowbar.'

There was a brass companion set next to the fireplace. Maya pointed at it and her smoke made a zigzag. 'There. The poker. Hanging by the fire.'

'I'm not going to break anything, Maya, wood or glass.'

'You do like making things difficult, Janika.'

'I don't want to know my names that badly.'

'But now I want to know.' Maya threw the butt of her cigarette out of the window. 'Anyway. You can't have Marcin. Not in green pen. It's probably an A, rather than an M.'

'How do you know?'

'Because Marcin was my victim,' said Maya.

Janika was searching for the three stories in Marcin's bedroom. Tepid light came in through the windows. The walls were mint green and the carpet caramel. An imposing painting of St Sebastian, pierced by arrows, hung above the bed. It was the only wound in the room's otherwise cheerful countenance: his waxen body looked bleached by sunlight and slightly melted, like a used candle; the fuchsia bedsheets were almost black, as if flooded with his imaginary blood. Janika heard something and stepped over to the window.

Anatol was approaching the house, wearing a green wax

jacket and walking boots; the heavy sound of his footsteps on the gravel carried through the air like a shotgun blast. He disappeared behind the window frame and the footsteps stopped. Janika hurried downstairs. She opened the front door and found Anatol kneeling in front of her, picking at his soggy laces. A white scarf had been looped clumsily around his neck; it looked like a clot of dried toothpaste at the end of a tube. He glanced up at Janika and shook his head, feigning disappointment. 'I've been looking everywhere for you,' he said.

'Where?' asked Janika.

Anatol finished undoing his laces. He stepped out of the boots, bracing himself on the wooden door frame. 'Everywhere,' he said.

'I was at the train station,' said Janika, 'then I came here. Where did you look?'

Anatol leaned down and picked up his boots. They dangled from his hands, making his long arms look even longer.

'I went to the train station,' he said. 'I didn't see you there.'

'When?'

'About two hours ago. I asked the staff if they'd seen you. I even checked the café down the road. You weren't there.'

'So you arrived an hour late? I was there three hours ago. I stood in the car park for twenty-five minutes, waiting for you.'

'I stood there much longer than that, Janika. I waited for the train, then the one after. And that second one came in twenty minutes late.'

'But I was on the one before?'

Anatol nodded. 'I can see that now.'

'I told you three weeks ago what time train I'd be taking.'

'You can't blame me for forgetting, can you? Three weeks is a long time. I've had a lot on my mind since then. How did you get here from the station?'

'I walked,' said Janika.

'Through the fields?'

'Along the road. I had my suitcase with me.'

'That's bad luck. I went through the fields. We must have just missed each other.' Anatol turned over one of his boots and showed Janika the sole; it had a covering of mud thick enough to be hiding an ice skate. 'The ground was damp, but the dandelions are out. And there were the last few bluebells in the woods. If you'd gone that way, we would have run into each other.'

'I had a suitcase,' said Janika.

'I could have helped you carry it.' Anatol pointed at the open door with his boot. 'Can I come inside?'

Janika crossed her arms and refused to move. 'Don't you want me here?'

'Of course I want you here.'

'Then why did you walk? If you'd taken the car you'd have arrived on time.'

'I don't think it would have been safe to drive, Janika. I think I'm still drunk. I drank too much last night.' Anatol held out his hand with one of the boots hooked over his thumb. His long fingers were trembling slightly. 'Look. That's what grief does to you.'

'Then why didn't you ask Maya to pick me up? Why didn't you phone for a taxi? Why didn't you at least leave a message with Dean, so he could tell me what was going on when I called?'

'I didn't do any of those things, Janika, because I didn't know I'd got the train times wrong. Most of them wouldn't have helped, would they?'

'And why was the phone unplugged?'

'That plug needs replacing. It's always coming out.'

'I had a twenty-two-hour flight, Anatol. Plus a two-hour stopover in Singapore. I checked into a hotel near Heathrow yesterday evening. But I could barely sleep because my body is still on Australian time. I woke up this morning and took the train into Paddington, then the tube to Waterloo, then I caught a train out to Tisbury. That's another two hours. Exactly as planned. I did all of that so I could arrive here in time for your birthday. But instead you left me stranded at Tisbury Station with no way of contacting you. And you really don't have a better excuse?'

'You must be hungry. Can I make you some lunch?'

'Anatol.'

Janika took a step forwards. Anatol moved back, on to the wet gravel. He looked down at his feet unhappily. 'All right,' he said. 'I'll tell you what happened. Come with me.'

Anatol dropped his boots on to the doorstep and walked over to where his car was parked. Janika followed him cautiously, taking careful steps across the gravel in her socks.

'Where are we going?'

Anatol opened the door to his convertible. He got into the driver's seat, then reached across and opened the passenger door. 'It's not locked,' he said.

'I don't have any shoes on,' said Janika.

'No,' said Anatol. 'Neither do I.'

'Where are we going?'

'Nowhere. But it's private in here. If you want to hear what I have to say.'

Janika climbed into the passenger seat and pulled the door closed. 'All right. What?'

Anatol ran the back of his thumbnail down his philtrum, worrying at his stubble, while he worked out his confession. 'The truth is I've been distracted, Janika. I haven't been able to focus on anything.' He reached into the inside breast pocket of his jacket and pulled out a folded sheet of paper. 'Not since this came through the letterbox this morning.'

'What is it?'

Anatol unfolded the piece of paper and smoothed it over the steering wheel. He handed it to Janika. It was a white A5 sheet with three words printed neatly in the middle: 'I HAVE PHOTOS'. The letters were made up of short straight lines. They looked like they'd been drawn with a ruler.

'It's left me shaken,' he said. 'I know it might sound silly, but I don't really remember walking to the station earlier. I did it without thinking. I don't remember what time I set out. In fact, the whole day has felt like a dream. That's why I was late.'

Janika read the three words out loud. '"I have photos",' she said. 'What does that mean?'

'It means . . .' Anatol moaned, as if he was in pain. 'It means I'm being blackmailed, Janika.'

THREE WEEKS EARLIER
7 May 1999

Distant Relatives

Gus's funeral took place on a blustery Friday morning in early May, exactly two weeks after his death. It was three weeks before Anatol's birthday. The door of the stubby church in the village of North Hatch had been shackled to the floor, to keep it from closing in the wind. Phoebe was standing beside it, at the back of the church, counting the mourners as they came inside. She'd organized food for at least thirty-five, but Anatol had been vague about the number he was expecting and she was worried there wouldn't be enough for everyone. She'd reached seventeen when Dean walked in, holding the jacket of his suit closed across his stomach. His hair was in disarray, his black tie blown back over his shoulder. He sat down on the pew in front of Phoebe and tidied his hair using his wristwatch as a mirror, without realizing she was standing behind him. Then he got bored and started to fidget, balancing hassocks on hymnals and hymnals on hassocks.

Anatol was seated towards the front of the church.

The door was unhooked and allowed to close. It seemed like the service was about to begin. Phoebe stepped forwards and placed a hand on Dean's shoulder.

'Have a seat,' he said, looking around. 'This is the largest armchair I've ever sat in and probably the most uncomfortable. But it's nice to sit on something that's not pointed at the television. You know what Yulie's like.'

'Dean. There's something important I need to talk to you about.'

Phoebe squeezed in beside him and greeted him with a gentle prod to his firm, slender stomach. Somehow, Dean had managed to render his body lean and toned and muscular through nothing but dull, routine activities: Nordic walking on the weekends and a cycle ride to work each morning. But he was modest and unassuming and had no idea how attractive he was.

'I didn't think you were coming,' said Dean. 'I thought it was just going to be me.'

'Who do you think organized everything? If I'd left it to Anatol we'd be having champagne and oysters after the service.'

'Then the others won't be joining us?'

'It's just the two of us,' said Phoebe. 'You as his oldest friend and me as his most efficient.'

'Are you staying the night?'

Phoebe nodded. 'Someone has to eat all the leftover food. Are you staying as well?'

'Anatol asked me to. I didn't know you'd be here. What do you want to talk to me about?'

But their conversation was cut short when the service began. Later, when it was time for the mourners to gather up their things and file out of the church, Phoebe reached over and greeted Dean properly, with a lengthy hug. Since they'd already been sitting side by side for twenty minutes, it seemed gratuitous: indulgent, even. And Phoebe felt slightly ashamed for enjoying it.

'It's nice to see you,' she said in his ear.

The reverential silence soon filled with the rustling of clothes and the click of footsteps on flagstones. Anatol walked past, following the coffin. Phoebe smiled supportively, but he didn't notice. She took Dean's arm and joined the crowd behind him.

The burial took place in the newest section of the cemetery, a small square of land at the back of the churchyard, surrounded by cedar trees. When it was done, the mourners walked in a long thin line to Anatol's house. They'd looked relatively large in number when they'd been huddled together in the church, but stretched out along the roadside the group looked small. There were twenty-seven of them, to be exact. The road sloped upwards as it led them out of the small village, with a high, wild hedge on one side. Behind the hedge there were houses, hidden from the road. Anatol's house was the last on the right.

Phoebe and Dean stayed towards the back of the group.

'You wanted to talk about something?' said Dean.

He was staring down at the palm of his hand, peering at his fingers. They were walking so slowly that he wasn't bothered about watching where he was going, their pace set by the people in front of them.

'I do,' said Phoebe. 'Is your hand OK?'

'I was just thinking about food,' said Dean.

'There'll be lots of it. I planned for thirty-five.'

'But my hand is dirty, from picking up the soil.'

Dean had thrown a handful of earth on the casket five minutes earlier.

'There'll be cutlery,' said Phoebe.

'Is it the kind of food you can eat with cutlery?'

'I don't know. You can wash your hands, can't you?'

Dean looked up at the line in front of them. 'Yes. But there'll be a queue for the bathroom.'

'Dean.' Phoebe stopped and took hold of his hand. 'Let me have a look.' She found a tissue in her pocket and folded it over her finger, then spat on to its tip and wiped the damp white stub along the lines of Dean's palm, removing every trace of dirt. An old man passed them by with a knowing grin. 'There you go,' she said.

'Thank you,' said Dean.

When they started to walk again, now at the very back of the group, Phoebe kept hold of Dean's hand, grasping it with both of hers. 'I do want to talk to you about something. It's difficult though.'

'What is it?'

'Have you been avoiding me?'

'No,' said Dean automatically.

'I don't mean today. But over the last two weeks.'

Dean's hand curled into a fist inside Phoebe's. 'Look. It's nothing personal, Phoebe. It's just that Yulie and I are at war with each other. Temporarily, hopefully. And I don't want you to get caught in the middle.'

'I know,' said Phoebe. 'She told me about it.'

'What did she tell you?'

'That she'd cheated on you with someone from work. I was furious with her when I found out, if that's any consolation. I'm on your side.'

Dean laughed unconvincingly, breathing heavily as he did so. 'How could you be on Yulie's side? She doesn't even have a side. Her side was on her back.'

'I know. That's why I'm on yours. You can talk to me about it, if you ever need to. I mean it. I've been friends with you longer than I have with her.'

'Phoebe, come on. She's your sister.'

'It's true,' said Phoebe. 'We couldn't stand each other until we were in our twenties. And that's after I'd met you.'

She hugged Dean's arm, up to the elbow. He looked at her and laughed nervously and wiggled his hand free, then pressed it gratefully to the small of her back. 'I'd love to talk to you about it, Phoebe. It just wouldn't seem right.'

Phoebe was wearing a pleated black skirt, a white shirt and a black jumper. Dean's hand rested at the point where all three overlapped. It was the most sensual touch that she had felt in what seemed like a very long time.

The reception was held in the drawing room of Anatol's house, which, with the furniture pushed back against the walls, was just about large enough for the modest group. The table in the dining room across the corridor had been filled with trays of food, while paper plates and plastic cups were stacked on top of the sideboard. A small folding table had been set up in the corner for drinks. The most precarious antiques had been moved upstairs.

Phoebe had spent the morning getting everything ready, with little help from Anatol. Since they'd arrived back at the house she'd been hovering awkwardly in the corridor with a glass of white wine, watching the traffic between the two rooms, making sure that everyone had what they needed. When the stream of people passing back and forth had slowed, she went into the dining room and filled a plate with food. She took it across to the drawing room.

Dean was standing in a corner, surrounded by strangers. He saw Phoebe and excused himself. The two of them moved over to the window.

'I only have two topics of conversation,' said Dean. He

was holding his second bottle of beer. He hadn't eaten anything. 'How I met Anatol and what I do for a living. And neither of those have interesting answers. The only interesting thing is that it's the same answer for both. But no one believes that Anatol studied engineering. He's got the whole world thinking he's an arts graduate. I have nothing at all to say about Gus. I've got no anecdotes or memories to share. Only opinions, and those aren't particularly positive.'

Phoebe picked at her plate. 'At least you can leave, Dean. Go outside and go for a walk. I have to stay and make sure everything runs smoothly.'

'What if we just stand here and look deep in conversation? Maybe everyone will leave us alone.'

Phoebe nodded. She looked across the room at Anatol. He was with a group of elderly men half his size, sitting on a chair while the rest of them stood. He'd been busy talking to people the whole time they'd been at the house.

'Are you cold?' asked Phoebe.

She'd propped open the back door at the end of the corridor, so that people could go outside when they needed to, whether to smoke or to engage in more private conversations or just to sit by themselves and think. But the corridor had since become icy cold and, after a few trips back and forth for nibbles and drinks, some of the guests had put their coats back on, their black clothes covered with blues and greys and – in one notable case – a lime-green fox fur. Phoebe took it as a personal rebuke.

'Sorry,' said Dean. 'I don't have a coat. But if I did, I'd be wearing it.'

'Should I close the door then?'

'I can't imagine Anatol will do it.'

'It's his house,' said Phoebe, but Dean just shrugged.

The door could only be propped open or locked. Anything else would lead to it banging constantly back and forth in the wind.

Phoebe moved the brick that was holding it in place and pulled it shut. She went back to Dean with a fresh glass of wine. After five minutes they heard hammering on the window. Someone had gone outside to smoke and locked themselves out. Anatol was ignoring the sound.

'Hold this,' said Phoebe, giving Dean her wine.

She rescued the mourner, then came back with another new glass and a bottle of beer. She took her old glass back from Dean and gave him the bottle.

'Two drinks?' he said. 'You must be as miserable as me.'

The glass in Phoebe's right hand was lit by the crisp daylight coming through the windows, the one in her left by the garish yellow bulb in the middle of the room.

'It's been a long day,' she said. 'And it's only lunchtime.'

Dean downed the dregs of his old beer and opened the new one. 'So what exactly did Yulie tell you about the man she's been sleeping with? His name's Declan, I know that much. It's like my name, but with an extra two letters. A little cock and balls in the middle.'

By late evening the three of them were drunk, though they'd been picking at the food all afternoon. The last mourners had left between three and four.

Phoebe had filled the fridge with leftovers, then vacuumed the drawing room and dining room, while Anatol and Dean had sat drinking whisky. They'd decided to leave the task of putting the furniture back in place until the morning. No one had felt sober enough to handle anything delicate. Instead, they'd moved the large green sofa to the centre of the room and left it there by itself.

Phoebe, Dean and Anatol were sitting on it when the clock struck ten, their legs stretched out where the coffee table would normally be. Phoebe was in the middle, sinking towards Anatol. When he got up to freshen their glasses, her hand went to Dean's thigh to steady herself. There was nowhere else it could go.

'Whisky?' said Anatol on his return, giving them both a glass. 'Let's have a toast, then I'm going to bed. I haven't been sleeping much lately. I'm exhausted. But you two stay up, if you want to. Help yourselves to anything you need. You know where everything is.'

He raised his drink. 'To distant relatives.'

Anatol touched his glass against Phoebe's, then against Dean's, then downed his whisky and left the room. 'Good night,' he said as the door closed behind him.

Phoebe was taken aback by his sudden departure. She listened to the wind for several seconds, shaking the trees outside, then turned to Dean and bumped her glass against his. 'To staying up late,' she said. 'Don't you feel like you ought to be paid for your time here?'

'What do you mean?'

'I've spent the whole day running errands. I've hardly had any time with Anatol. He could have hired someone to do my job.'

'I'm just glad to get away from Yulie for an evening.'

'We're not going to talk about that all night, are we?'

'Sorry,' said Dean.

Phoebe got to her feet. 'I don't want whisky.'

She went to the kitchen and came back with a bottle

of chilled white wine, holding two glasses. She pointed one at Dean and he nodded feebly. When she'd filled them both, she placed the half-empty bottle on the floor by his feet.

'Dean,' she said. 'What are you wearing?'

His socks stood out clearly in the dim room: two blunt prongs of vivid magenta. 'Nothing,' he said. 'It was just an attempt to lighten the mood.'

Phoebe handed him his drink, leaving hers on the floor. Then she lifted one of his legs and sat down at the edge of the sofa with his foot on her lap.

'They're very loud,' she said.

'They weren't meant to be,' said Dean. 'They were meant to be quiet. A quiet rebellion against how earnest everything was today. All that stuff about God. And Gus. Christ. Don't think less of me, but I never even liked him.'

'No,' said Phoebe, pulling the sock from his foot and inspecting the pattern. 'None of us did. These are hideous, Dean.'

'I wear them at work sometimes when I'm in a bad mood. It's like giving someone the finger with your hand in your pocket. Do you ever do that? This is the same thing but with feet.'

'Sticking out your tongue,' said Phoebe as she draped the limp tube of pinkish purple fabric over her wrist. A line of frayed sausage dogs paraded across her palm. 'It's a bit passive-aggressive?'

'Yes. That's the point. I'm not very good at being aggressive. Maybe I should have worn them at my wedding.' Dean tapped Phoebe's knee. 'Sorry. I know you don't want to talk about that.'

'You can gossip,' said Phoebe as she struggled to get the

sock back on to his foot. 'Gossip is fine. Just don't go feeling sorry for yourself. I told you what my sister was like when you met her.'

'All right. I'll try to think of some gossip.'

'Have you ever cheated on her?' asked Phoebe. 'I won't tell her if you have.'

'No,' said Dean. 'Never. But that's the thing about cheating. It creates a disequilibrium. Because now I feel like I'd have to, if the opportunity ever arose. And then once we've both done it, what's the point in stopping? It's like an adultery arms race.'

Phoebe finished with his sock and tugged down on his trouser leg. 'Why don't you buy the right sized clothes?' she said.

'What about you? Have you ever cheated?'

Phoebe thought about the three long-term boyfriends that she'd had since university. Three attempts at adulthood that hadn't worked out. Yulie had always called Phoebe a serial monogamist. But she wasn't entirely monogamous. Two of the boyfriends had overlapped with one another.

'Yes. Once. But he never knew about it. And it's different, anyway, when a relationship is ending. Don't you think?'

Dean nodded thoughtfully. 'Let's see yours then, if we're judging each other's socks . . .'

Emboldened by the alcohol, he reached down over the front of the couch and grabbed Phoebe's calf, then felt along her leg to her foot. She held her breath as her dull shin came to life, his fingertips almost stroking her skin.

'I'm not wearing any,' she said. 'I was wearing tights earlier. But I took them off after the reception. I don't like tights. But you can't show your legs at a funeral.'

She could see the shape of Dean's stomach muscles, supporting him effortlessly as he leaned forwards.

'I don't know,' he said, his voice weakened by his folded belly. 'I don't think anyone would have objected. I wouldn't.'

Phoebe's hand moved to the small of his back. She still had his foot on her lap. 'What do we do now? We're tangled up together.'

'Yes,' said Dean. 'That seems to be the situation.'

His hand had settled around her ankle. He kept it there, the two of them in silent negotiation for several seconds, cradling each other's feet. Then he lifted himself back on to the couch, holding Phoebe's shoulder for support. Impulsively – and in no small part just to see what would happen, feeling reckless after drinking all day – Phoebe leaned across and kissed him. She placed her free hand on the back of his head. He tasted acidic, like sweet white wine.

They kissed for several minutes, Dean's hands first unbuttoning, then sliding inside Phoebe's shirt, and then moving down to her bare thighs in search of her underwear, while Phoebe encouraged him with subtle movements.

'It doesn't even feel wrong,' said Dean.

'No,' said Phoebe.

'In the circumstances, I mean. Since Yulie cheated on me. And it's nothing we haven't done before.' The two of them had slept together once at university. 'We were drunk then, too. And it didn't do us any harm.'

'Dean . . .' Phoebe laid a finger over his lips, and then kissed him again. 'You don't need to justify it, just let it happen.'

There was no question of stopping to consider the morality of the act. Since Phoebe had entered her late twenties, opportunities like this had become as rare as lunar eclipses: when one happened, you didn't sit and worry about it, you just got outside and gawped.

'Let's go upstairs,' she said.

'To the same room?' asked Dean sheepishly, pressing his lips to Phoebe's neck.

'Well, yes. Obviously.'

'I have a condom, for emergencies. It's in the car, in the glove compartment, tucked inside the driver's manual. You won't think I'm being presumptuous if I go outside and get it?'

'No,' said Phoebe. 'I'll be waiting right here.'

SATURDAY
29 May 1999

Poise and Pen

Phoebe picked up her bag and put it down on the bed. She took an envelope from one of the pockets, pulled a piece of paper from inside and handed it to Dean. He walked over to the desk, where the light was strongest, and laid it down on the wooden surface.

It was shortly before noon on Saturday morning. Phoebe had just arrived at Anatol's house. Dean had carried her bag upstairs.

'"I know",' Dean read from the note. 'What does that mean?'

Without the surrounding context – of the letter arriving anonymously along with the rest of the post – the note didn't seem particularly threatening. All Dean saw was a white sheet of paper with two short words written in the middle; he looked at them the way he'd look at someone's mad scribblings on the wall of a public toilet.

'I don't know,' said Phoebe. 'Someone sent it to me.'

'Who?' he asked.

'I don't know. It doesn't say.'

Phoebe passed Dean the envelope. He inspected both sides carefully. 'Someone in London,' he said, 'sometime on Thursday. Did it come crumpled up like this?'

Phoebe had been fretting at the envelope for the duration of her train journey. 'I think it must be from Yulie,' she said.

Dean shook his head. 'Yulie wouldn't do something like this.'

'But I think it's about us. And what happened at the funeral. Who else would send it if it wasn't Yulie? I think it's a warning. She doesn't want it to happen again.'

'Why do you think it's about that? It could be referring to anything.'

'Because I haven't done anything else, Dean. I'm a teacher and I live alone in a tiny flat in North London. There's nothing else worth knowing.'

Dean looked at the letter again. 'It doesn't even say it's something bad.'

'Why would anyone send an anonymous note accusing me of doing good deeds? Anyway, I haven't done any good deeds. Unless you count adopting a cat.'

Dean lifted his glasses and rubbed at his eyebrows. 'But if Yulie wanted it to be a warning, why would she send it anonymously? We'd have to know it was from her.'

'Plausible deniability,' said Phoebe. 'She knows I'd know who it was from anyway. Pettiness is like a signature. Especially between sisters.'

Dean scratched at the desk with his thumb. 'But I don't see how Yulie could possibly know. I didn't tell her. Did you?'

'It would have been something small,' said Phoebe. 'My perfume on your clothes . . .'

'I wasn't wearing any clothes.'

'And I probably wasn't wearing any perfume. That's not the point. It would have been something small, something we missed. It could have been anything.'

Dean held up the envelope. 'Can I hang on to this? I'd like to take a closer look. I've got a magnifying glass on my penknife.'

Phoebe nodded. 'But be careful with it. It's got my name on it.'

Dean handed the envelope back, but kept hold of its contents. 'I'll keep the bit that's not incriminating.' He read the letter again, studiously, as if it was more than just two words on a plain piece of paper. 'Yulie's not underhand like this, Phoebe. If anything she's overhand.'

'Normally. But this isn't a normal situation.'

'In-law-cest,' said Dean thoughtfully.

'Dean. I'm serious.'

'I know, Phoebe. I just don't think that this is from Yulie. She would have shouted at me if she knew about the funeral.'

'What happens next? If she does know?'

Dean shrugged. 'We'll be even, at least. She cheated on me.'

'And until then?'

'What do you mean?'

Phoebe flicked her eyes to the bed. 'With us,' she said, fretting at the envelope again.

'If I'm right,' said Dean, 'and the letter's not from her, it would be a shame to waste this opportunity. Not that I'd assumed anything was going to happen between us. But you did say you wanted to do it again.'

Phoebe nodded. 'We'll just have to be more careful this time.'

Though it wasn't in his nature, Dean knew instinctively when he was likely to be rewarded for being decisive. He knew it like a dog that had learned to perform a trick for a biscuit. Without waiting, he crossed the metre of carpet between the two of them and put his arms around Phoebe. She grunted, thinking it was hardly an appropriate time, but she leaned into him anyway. He moved his palms to the saddle-point of her waist.

'Your hands are cold,' said Phoebe quietly.

'Sorry,' said Dean.

Dean kept hold of Phoebe until he felt confident that their desires were aligned, then he leaned down and kissed her. The kiss was a pinprick of joy in the otherwise dismal room. His lips moved down her neck towards her chest.

'But what about the note, Dean?' Phoebe took hold of his head and tilted it upwards. 'If you're sure Yulie didn't send it then who do you think did?'

Dean composed himself and took a step back. 'I don't know.' He pushed his hands into his pockets. 'What about one of the children you teach? One of the teenagers? Could someone be playing a joke on you?'

An Author in Search of a Cigarette

'Once upon a time there was a man called Anatol...'

Marcin's lowest point came soon after lunch. He was sitting in the drawing room with Dean and Phoebe, his head resting on his palm and his elbow on the arm of his chair, holding his notebook up in front of his face, pretending to read. 'He made his friends do work on the weekend, so they killed him. The end.'

Phoebe put down her pen and looked across at him. 'Is that it?' she said. 'How did they kill him?'

'They drowned him. They held his head down in a bowl of washing-up water. He flailed around so much that when they pulled him out there were pieces of cutlery stuck in his face. He had a knife through his nose. And a fork through his cheek.' Marcin tossed his notebook on to the floor, in resignation rather than anger. 'No, that's not it. I'm stuck. I need to smoke. I don't know why I ever wanted to quit. Where did Maya go?'

'It's expensive. And it kills you.'

'But I have money, Phoebe, and I don't believe in hell.'

'It smells bad. It's unattractive.'

Marcin rested his pen lid between his lips and inhaled pretend smoke through the hole in the end. 'But it makes a good ice-breaker.'

'So did the *Titanic*,' said Dean.

'Marcin, do you want to go for a walk?' asked Phoebe. The sky was still overcast, but it had stopped raining during lunch. 'You might find the fresh air invigorating.'

Marcin breathed out sharply through the lid of his pen. 'Why on earth would I want to do that?'

The Piano Room

When Maya arrived back at Anatol's house, after visiting the cemetery, she kept her coat on and went straight to the kitchen. A locked door, halfway down the room, led through to what at one time had been a garage attached to the side of the house. Now it had linoleum flooring and a large set of double doors where the entrance from the driveway had been, with slim windows on either side. It was used mainly as storage space for things that were too large to fit anywhere else: an upright piano; a pool table with torn pockets; an old brass lectern; and a small collection of kitsch Americana, from a statue of Marilyn Monroe in fibreglass and resin to a set of restored nineteenth-century rawhide snowshoes.

Anatol had always called it the piano room. Maya associated it with the low points of long, structureless evenings in years past, when someone had wanted to play pool late at night and, rather than sit by herself, she'd felt obliged to go along and watch, which meant standing against one of the poorly insulated walls with her arms crossed against the cold, waiting to return to the comfort of the drawing room. And it was always cold, even in summer.

She slid back the bolts and tried the door. It was locked. She searched the nearby drawers for a key, but couldn't find anything except wooden spoons and spatulas.

'You won't find it there,' said Dean, standing in the archway.

Maya recoiled, taken by surprise. 'Dean,' she said. 'That's twice today you've done that.'

'Sorry. I just wanted to see if you'd work it out.'

Maya shrugged and slouched against the wall. Dean approached her with a look of concern. He reached up and took the key from the top of the architrave, then offered it to Maya.

'Sorry,' he said again. 'What are you doing, anyway? Do you want a game of pool?'

Maya took the key from him and put it in the lock. 'No. I'm looking for something.' She opened the door. A mass of cardboard boxes had taken over the room since Maya had last been there. There were hundreds of them, growing on everything, like a fungus. They were stacked on top of the pool table and the piano stool and slotted between the tacky antiques. They were even stacked on top of each other, forming rickety stalagmites around the edges of the room. Both windows were blocked out by boxes. There must have been over two hundred in total.

'You've heard of a box room,' said Dean.

'I knew they'd have to be somewhere,' said Maya.

A single step led down into the room. Some of the boxes were open, while others had been taped shut.

'So what are they?' asked Dean. He found one that was already open and pulled out a pair of tan loafers, then dropped them back in the box, as if they were toxic. 'Oh, I see,' he said. 'They're Gus's things?'

Maya nodded. 'I wonder what Anatol will do with them.'

'I think that's your answer.'

Dean was pointing at a piece of paper stuck to the wall opposite, with the word 'Destroy' written on it in lush red pen. Beside the door was a second sheet of paper.

'"Donate",' read Maya, taking a photograph. 'I'm not sure where the dividing line is . . .'

She lifted an old newspaper from the top of one of the boxes in the middle of the room and looked inside. It was full of clothes. She plunged her hand into a bundle of cold, crimson wool. The warm fabric felt alien and artificial at that temperature, but it was only a cardigan. Underneath was a pair of velvet trousers. 'This is probably donate,' she said.

She checked another box. Inside was a collection of worn old teddy bears. On top was a medium-sized bear in flushed pink, the colour of watermelon flesh. It was missing an eye.

'Destroy,' said Maya. She took out the bear and left it on top of the box.

'What are you looking for?' asked Dean.

'The radio,' said Maya.

'The one that killed him? I assume the police would have taken that.'

'Or anything else that's worth photographing.'

Dean reached over and closed the door. 'It'll be on the destroy side of the room. I don't think Oxfam takes murder weapons.'

'Murder?' said Maya.

'Sorry. That was a slip of the tongue.' Dean noticed a wooden chair against the wall, almost hidden by its cardboard accretions, and started working to uncover it. 'I should probably stay with you. At least that way we can pretend we came in here for a game of pool, if Anatol finds us.'

'I don't think he'd mind.' Maya wove her way towards the piano, on the destroy side of the room. She could feel spider webs brushing her arms as she walked. 'Will you do me a favour, Dean?'

'What?'

When she reached the piano, Maya pressed a few keys at random. She wasn't musical, but she liked prodding at things. The notes to her left groaned, while the ones on her right shrieked. The ones in the middle were boring and flat. 'Check the boxes around you. And tell me if you find anything interesting.'

Maya couldn't see Dean behind the wall of boxes, but she could hear the seashell sounds of his blue cotton jumper rubbing on cardboard. 'Christmas tree decorations,' he said. 'Does that count as interesting?'

'No.'

'Then what does?'

'Personal items. Anything from his childhood. Anything dirty or used . . .' Maya opened the box by her feet. It contained a collection of socks and ties. She tried the one next to it, which was filled with porcelain tableware: Victorian Spode in seaweed green. Every piece was chipped or cracked. A third had some old toiletries, including a toothbrush and a flannel.

'Maya,' said Dean, 'don't you feel like this is a little bit intrusive?'

'That's the point,' said Maya. 'It's art, Dean.'

Maya opened a fourth box and found a number of electronic devices inside, including a worn radio cassette player that looked at least a decade old. It was gunmetal grey, with a single speaker at one end, an empty tape bay at the other, and a radio tuning dial running above both. A thick aerial was clipped to the top and an equally thick wire emerged from the bottom.

'I've found it,' said Maya, holding the radio level with her chest.

Dean stood up, shaking his head. 'That can't be the same one,' he said.

Maya opened the cassette bay and turned the player upside down, hoping that a line of water would trickle out and drip to the floor, but nothing came. 'It's dry,' she said.

'I told you.' Dean sat down. 'The police would have taken the one that killed him.'

Maya put the cassette player back in the box. There were two other radio cassette players inside, identical to the one that she'd taken out. 'Why would he need three, though?'

'Three?' said Dean.

Maya nodded. 'Maybe he bought these ones to practise with . . .'

The Hamlet Plan

Phoebe emerged from the back door of the house, followed a moment later by Marcin. Both were looking up at the sky. They crossed the ring of gravel, on to the grass, and bumped into one another and stopped to confer.

'I don't trust that sky,' said Marcin.

The gentle breeze had thickened to a cold wind and the light was flickering at sluggish intervals as patches of cloud hid the sun, then revealed it seconds later.

'You don't trust anything,' said Phoebe, her tone half joking and half serious. 'We're not going far though, are we? We'll be fine.'

Phoebe made a point of walking onwards, but when Marcin didn't follow she turned and went back to him. They were face to face, a foot apart.

'You're the one with the umbrella,' said Marcin.

Phoebe smiled disarmingly. The umbrella's curved handle was hooked over the back of her left hand, its red and blue canopy folded and fastened shut.

'But I'm just being cautious. You're being pessimistic.' Phoebe walked away again. When Marcin still didn't follow, she turned and called out to him: 'Marcin, walking and talking aren't mutually exclusive. You of all people should know that. If you stand there all day, it's bound to start raining.'

'You're going in the wrong direction, Phoebe.'

'There is no wrong direction. It's a garden, Marcin.'

'Then why am I holding a handful of corn?'

Marcin showed her his open right hand. At the centre of his palm was a cobbled mound of apricot-coloured kernels. Phoebe dismissed his question by showing him her own right hand, which held a matching pile of grain. 'You can hold it for a few minutes more, can't you? I want to go the long way round.'

'It's making my hand sweat . . .'

But Marcin raised this objection purely to maintain the rhythm of their conversation. A few seconds later, he relented and hurried to Phoebe's side.

The garden widened behind the house, extending into what at one time had been a separate field, with a gentle downwards slope along its diagonal. Phoebe and Marcin turned to their left, which took them towards the top of the incline.

'I wonder if you could kill someone by locking them out in a storm.' Phoebe looked up at the stony clouds. 'If there was thunder and lightning . . .' She swung her umbrella as they followed the edge of the field, taking large strides through the uncut grass. The property was bordered on that side by a simple wooden fence, holding back an overgrown hedge of hazel and blackthorn. 'I don't think I've ever spent this much time thinking about death.'

Marcin placed his hands in his pockets, distracted by his own ideas. 'What do you think would happen if I wrote a story about Anatol murdering his father?'

'Marcin,' said Phoebe, leaving the two withering syllables to stand alone.

'I'm being serious. It works nicely as a motive. And he did say that anything goes.'

'But you didn't pick Gus's name out of the hat?'

'It was a cocktail glass, Phoebe. You could try wearing it as a hat, but you'd have to keep your head very still.'

'Marcin,' said Phoebe again.

'No. I didn't. But if someone found out about it then there'd be a motive for murder, wouldn't there? Another murder, I mean.'

'So who did you pick as your murderer? Not Anatol?'

'I can't tell you that, can I?'

'I don't want you to tell me,' said Phoebe. 'I'm checking that you haven't just told me by accident.'

'I haven't,' said Marcin. 'If Anatol murdered Gus it could have caused all sorts of other murders, couldn't it?'

Phoebe concurred with a subtle nod. 'I'm sure Anatol would see the funny side. He likes anything inappropriate. And I don't think he'd be offended, as long as it's not too graphic.'

'But I want him to be offended.'

'Marcin. Why?'

'It's just some gentle revenge for making us work on the weekend.' Marcin smiled. 'I've had a terrible week. Let me enjoy myself.'

'What's been terrible about your week?'

But Marcin walked on without answering. When they reached the garden's highest point, Phoebe climbed up on to the fence and sat on the top rail, her free hand holding the nearest post.

'It's beautiful, isn't it?'

Filling the distance in front of them were acres and acres of scarcely populated farmland, in vibrant greens and sandy browns, ridged with hedges and stone walls and roads, their corners darkened by cottages and farm buildings. It was a pattern that repeated all the way to the horizon, where a line of milky blue mist brought the land and sky together.

'It's chintzy,' said Marcin. 'I'd prefer something more minimalist.'

'I'm thinking about moving out of London. Do you think it would be nice to live somewhere like this?'

'No. Why? What's wrong with London?'

Phoebe sat and ruminated as the sky slowly shifted. 'London is like a bed of nails. It's impossible to settle anywhere. But I'm thirty now and I want a comfortable bed, literally and figuratively.'

'But you'd be all alone out here.'

'I know,' said Phoebe, feeling a slight, self-defeating annoyance at the fact that Marcin had cut straight to the heart of the matter. 'But I might not be single forever, Marcin. Has Anatol talked to you about his plans for this house?'

'No. Why would he talk to me about that?'

'I just thought he might have asked your advice. About money, inheritance tax. Things like that. He says he'll have to sell it.'

'None of you ever ask me for advice.'

'How much do you think I'd need to buy it?'

'I doubt you'd have enough.'

'I didn't mean by myself.' Phoebe lifted the umbrella and tapped him on the shoulder. 'You're too negative, Marcin. That's why we never ask you for advice.'

Marcin took hold of the end of the umbrella and glowered at her sarcastically. 'I'm not negative. I just enjoy pointing out the flaws in things. But enjoying it makes it a positive thing.'

'And what about plotting revenge on your friends?'

'I'm enjoying that too,' said Marcin, moving away but still clinging to the umbrella, pulling Phoebe down from the fence. 'Won't the chickens be getting hungry?'

'All right. Let's go.' They started to walk side by side across the field. 'Does Anatol ever talk to you about things like that?'

'Like what? Money?'

'Not just money,' said Phoebe. 'His long-term plans. Does he want to settle down, get married, have children? It's hard to imagine him doing any of those things, but he's getting older just like the rest of us.'

'He's never seemed particularly interested in being close to anyone,' said Marcin.

'He's close to us, isn't he?'

'I'm not sure. He seems to like having us around. But only up to a point. You remember his little one-bedroom flat at university?'

'So, what, he wants to grow old alone?'

'I don't know,' said Marcin. 'Maybe. We know he has a sex drive. He's had a few one-night stands. And Dean thinks he sleeps with prostitutes when he comes up to London.'

'Prostitutes? Is that normal?'

'I don't think so. Maybe for straight men? You'd be better off talking to Dean. Apparently, he disappears for hours at a time.'

'I can't believe that's true,' said Phoebe.

At the far corner of the garden, a chicken coop had been built on a patch of level ground. It had a wooden hutch and an open area, surrounded by wire netting. When Marcin and Phoebe reached it they found its tiny gate propped open and the occupants gone.

'Just put the food inside,' said Phoebe. 'They'll find it later.' She threw her handful of grain into an elevated metal bowl.

Marcin spotted the two chickens, pottering at the bottom of a nearby hedge, watching the coop intently. 'Didn't they belong to Gus?' he asked.

Phoebe nodded. 'Anatol got them for him as a present. That's why they're called Christmas and New Year.'

'I'm surprised they're still around,' said Marcin. 'Most of Gus's things have already gone. Don't you find that strange? He only died a month ago.'

'Strange?' said Phoebe. 'What do you mean?'

Marcin looked at her blankly. 'Nothing,' he said. 'I was just thinking about my story.'

'You don't still think that he murdered his father, do you? Not really? There was an inquest, Marcin. An investigation.'

Marcin shrugged. 'Watch his face when he reads out my story. Then we'll know the truth. It'll be like in *Hamlet*, when he puts on that play to accuse his uncle of murder.'

'*Hamlet*,' said Phoebe, 'only not as princely.'

The Piano Room (continued)

'Now help me take these out to the car.'

After fifteen minutes of searching through Gus's belongings, Maya had accumulated a number of interesting items. She'd left them sitting on top of their respective boxes. Now she began to gather them up, placing them in a pile by the door. Along with the pink teddy bear, there was a mediocre watercolour of the view from the garden, some notebooks filled with illegible handwriting, a pipe, a pair of gloves, a bundle of moth-eaten clothes and a cracked ceramic chamber pot, clouded with faded stains.

Dean watched her anxiously. 'Why? Are you planning to keep them?'

'Why not? I only took things from the destroy side of the room.'

'Yes, but ... Don't you think you should ask Anatol, at least?'

'Why?' said Maya. 'He might say no.'

'Exactly.'

'Yes, exactly,' said Maya. 'Are you going to help me or not?'

'What do you want them for?'

'I want to take some pictures, in better light. I told you. It's to help me process his death.'

'Will you give them back afterwards?'

'I don't see why,' said Maya. 'I'm perfectly capable of destroying them myself.' She put some of the smaller items in her coat pockets, while she arranged the larger items in a teetering stack. 'Will you hold the door open at least?'

She found her car keys and placed them between her teeth.

Dean stood and did as she'd asked.

Maya lifted the towering collection and carried it through to the kitchen, then into the hallway. When she reached the front door, she looked back at Dean and made a series of unintelligible noises. Saliva trickled down the length of her keys, the odd droplet falling to the floorboards. Dean opened the front door for her, and then followed her on to the gravel.

When they were by her car, Maya spat the keys on to the ground. Dean sighed and picked them up, frowning knowingly at finding them wet. 'Maya . . .'

'Can you open it for me?'

Dean unlocked the boot and pulled it open. Inside was a short promotional statue of the Michelin mascot, made of cast iron. Maya placed her new acquisitions beside it and emptied her pockets. She lifted the tartan blanket that had been waiting perpetually in the boot of her car for just such an occasion and laid it on top.

'There,' she said.

'Why do you need to process his death, anyway? I didn't think you were that close.'

'We weren't. That's what I want to process.'

'That doesn't make any sense,' said Dean.

'Gus was no saint,' said Maya dismissively.

'Why? What did he ever do to you?'

Maya closed the car boot with a thud. 'Dean. You told me it was the cleaning lady that found the body. But haven't you ever wondered why Gus was taking a bath when she was cleaning the house?'

'I don't know what you mean. What are you implying?'

'Why did he choose that time to take a bath?'

'I don't know,' said Dean.

'Well, think about it,' said Maya, patting him gently on the shoulder.

Ink Ribbon Red

At lunch, the large mahogany dining table had been covered with bread and meats and cheeses from the deli in Tisbury; antipasti and tapas; condiments, place mats and plates. But when Maya walked into the dining room late on Saturday afternoon, she found it cleared of everything except for two typewriters, placed across from one another.

Marcin was sitting at one of them, facing the window, with an open notebook on the chair by his side. He was typing fluently, his clawed hands keeping to a rhythm as they jabbed at the keys, never using more than his middle and index fingers.

The machine was an Olivetti Lettera 32, in muted turquoise.

'You're going to be the first to finish,' said Maya.

Marcin reached out and calmly pulled his work in progress from the platen. The paper stuttered, like a stuck zip. He slid it face down under his notebook. 'I haven't started yet.'

'Then what are you typing?' asked Maya. 'All work and no Players makes Marcin dot dot dot?'

'I'm brainstorming,' said Marcin. 'Free writing. I just wanted to type, to keep my hands busy. It's quite therapeutic. Bash bash bash. It's like taking a hammer to someone's skull. Exactly what I needed.'

'But you must be writing something?'

Marcin picked up the sheet he'd just discarded and read the last paragraph:

> 'Sunday afternoon. Heading towards evening. A soft landing. Pink skies. Cushioned clouds. The tang of lemonade in the air. Temperate. Middling. Turning. Thin jumpers. Brave shirts. A consensus on trousers. The end of spring. Half cold. Half golden. Winds that whisper. A husky breeze. The sugary mildew scent of lilacs in bloom. A meal outside. Sitting at the table in the garden. Peaceful. Idyllic. Blank kills blank by pushing over the chimney stack. Bricks sliding off the roof, pouring on to the table. The splash of a brick in a bowl of soup. Tomato sauce everywhere.

'You see? It's all nonsense.' Marcin put the piece of paper back on the chair. 'Have you ever noticed the chimneys here lean to one side?'

'No. But I like that idea,' said Maya.

'I'm not going to use it. It's too complicated. I want something simple. And I need to work Gus into it somehow. At some point I'm going to take this typewriter upstairs, shut myself inside Janika's room and not come out until I've finished.'

'Janika's room?'

'It's empty,' said Marcin. 'No distractions.'

Maya sat down in front of the second typewriter. She brushed a few crumbs to the floor with a sweep of her hand and laid her notebook down on the table beside her. Some of the crumbs stuck to her fingers. She put her feet up on one of the neighbouring chairs and placed an elbow on the tabletop. Then she swivelled the typewriter so it was facing her squarely.

'A Royal Quiet De Luxe,' she said, reading from an embossed metal plate at the back. 'It's been years since I used one of these. I hope I haven't forgotten how.'

She took a sheet of paper from a stack in the middle of the table and fed it into the top of the carriage. The typewriter's mechanism was hidden by its neat lead-coloured case, except for the crescent of typebars that showed in a line at the back, like the pipes of a church organ. At the head of each one the shape of a letter rose from a smudge of dried ink. The keys seemed to float in an empty rectangle at the front of the machine. They were connected to the typebars by long metal tendrils, but there was nothing behind them. Maya could see the table through the grey squares.

Some of the key caps were stained white, with what looked like dried salt or slug trails. Maya leaned down and inspected them.

'What's wrong with it? Is it mouldy?'

'It's just old,' said Marcin. 'Mine's like that too. The plasticizer leaks out over time, according to Anatol. Mine looks like it's been dredged from a lake.'

Maya scratched at the strange substance with a fingernail, leaving a line in the white mark. She licked the same finger and rubbed it over the plastic, but the stain didn't shift. Then she tentatively pressed one of the keys. The slug shot up and hammered the ink ribbon on to the page, while a series of internal levers moved the carriage along with a click. It felt like a bear trap springing shut.

Maya pressed another key, more confidently, and typed out a word. She looked at what she'd written. 'Why is it red?' she said. 'Is yours red too?'

Marcin nodded. 'They have two settings. Red and black.

They're both set to red. Don't change it or we'll know which story is yours. Anatol said the red ribbons were less worn. But I think red's more appropriate anyway. It's the colour of blood.'

'Blood is carmine,' said Maya, shaking her head. 'It's much darker than that.'

'All right. Then what shade is this?'

'I don't know. Ink ribbon red?'

'Ink ribbon red,' said Marcin. 'The colour of fictional blood.'

SUNDAY NIGHT
30 May 1999

The Sundial

Marcin and Maya could have been a pair of fireflies lingering near the house: all that could be seen of them were the pernicious orange dots of their twin cigarettes, dancing around their darkened bodies, and their cloudy breath, making the night look cold.

Marcin leaned his head back against the crumbling red brick and let out a plaintive sigh. 'I still think smoking cigarettes is one of the best things you can do with a human body. I know there are downsides to it, but . . .'

'We didn't come out here to make conversation,' said Maya.

'I thought we came out here to smoke?' Marcin held his cigarette up like a tiny lighthouse and looked at it with one eye closed. 'Cigarettes are the scaffolding of my calm disposition.'

'I'm tired, Marcin. What is it you want to tell me?'

'You're always tired.' Marcin turned sideways and scanned the house with narrowed eyes. With their flaking wooden frames, the windows looked like ears. But then everything looked like an ear to Marcin. 'Let's go for a walk,' he said. 'Away from the house.'

'I don't have any shoes on,' said Maya. 'What if there's broken glass?'

'We don't have to go far,' said Marcin.

He stepped off the paving stones into the knee-high grass and waited for Maya to join him. She walked over to the edge of the concrete and looked down doubtfully at the overgrown lawn. 'I can see things moving in there . . .'

Marcin ignored her and set off towards the middle of the garden. After a few seconds, Maya followed him, her shoulders hunched like a surly teenager's. When they were ten metres from the house, Marcin stopped.

'Someone knows what I've done,' he said. 'Somebody sent me a letter.'

Maya was staring down at her feet. She raised her head and squinted at Marcin. 'What have you done?' she asked. 'What are you talking about?'

'Insider trading, Maya. I told you about it before.'

'When?'

'At Christmas, remember? I told you about Regex Trade and my other investments. We were drunk on mulled wine.'

'Oh,' said Maya. 'That does ring a bell. But I didn't realize it was particularly serious. What did the letter say?'

'Of course it's serious. It made me a millionaire. And it's illegal. I could go to prison. I'd lose my job at least. And most of my money.'

Maya was unfazed. 'It's boring, though . . .' She dropped her finished cigarette into the darkness. 'Can't you commit a real crime next time? Something exciting?'

'What, like murder?'

Maya's eyes lit up. 'If you were a murderer, Marcin, I'd ask you to marry me.'

'If I was a murderer, I'd probably say yes. But I'm not, Maya. I'm a homosexual man. And we're getting off topic. I need to know if you told anyone else.'

'No. Of course not. It's not that interesting. Why did you tell me about it if you don't want people to know?'

Marcin threw the end of his cigarette into the spongy grass and immediately lit another. 'Everyone makes mistakes when they're drunk.' He started to walk further away from the house. 'But it was only once. I haven't told anybody else.'

'But somebody knows.' Maya was being dragged along behind him like a fishing net. 'Who do you think it is?'

They reached the Gothic Revival sundial that stood at the centre of the garden and stopped again and both rested their weight against its heavy stone plinth. 'That's the problem,' said Marcin. 'I have no idea. As far as I'm aware, it's only you that knows about it.'

Maya lit another cigarette for herself, using the bronze dial as an ashtray. 'Maybe that's who you should murder then, when you find out who they are.'

'I might,' said Marcin.

'How would you do it?'

Marcin shrugged. He tapped his cigarette on the top of the sundial. 'Do you think you could murder someone with this?'

'The cigarette?'

'No. The sundial.'

Maya looked at him sceptically. 'If you picked it up and threw it at them. But I'm not sure you'd be strong enough.'

'No,' said Marcin. 'If you used the gnomon like a spike. Then it would look like an accident, like someone had tripped and fallen on it . . .'

'The gnomon?'

'This bit that sticks up. That's what it's called.'

Maya rolled her eyes. She fingered the tip of the gnomon. 'I think it would hurt, but I'm not sure it's sharp enough to kill someone.'

'What if it hit them somewhere vulnerable? Like straight through the eye?'

'I'm not sure.' Maya gripped her cigarette between her lips and lowered her head to the mossy stone surface, so that her eye was level with the sundial's spike. 'Do the angles work?'

'I don't know. You tell me.'

Marcin reached across the sundial, wrapped his hands around the back of Maya's head and pulled as hard as he could. In an instant, the blunt bronze stub of the gnomon was thrust into her eye socket, catching on her cornea, causing the eyeball to compress and twist inside its orbit, until the optic nerve was pulled taut. Then it pushed onwards through the sphenoid bone, shattering it at its thinnest point, and plunged into the cranial cavity. There it scraped along the underbelly of the frontal lobe, tearing through the olfactory bulb, and ended up wedged in the middle of the brain stem, where it punched a tiny hole in the pons. Maya's major bodily functions failed within a few seconds. Her muscles twitched then went slack. She stopped breathing. Her cigarette fell from her mouth and landed on the sundial and, by sheer coincidence, accurately recorded the time of death.

Marcin let go of Maya's head and stepped back and shook out his aching arms. Her dead body stayed in place, hanging from its peg. He wiped the sweat from his forehead and appraised his work, finally taking the cigarette from his mouth. His hands were starting to cramp.

'I tried to make that quick, Maya. I hope it didn't hurt too much.'

SUNDAY
30 May 1999

Blackmail and Turmoil

Janika held the sheet of paper up to the windscreen, turning it translucent. 'Blackmail?' she whispered. The white sky was bright and uncomfortable; she squinted at the three words written in black. '"I have photos",' she read. 'But what photos?'

Anatol frowned. With one hand on the seat below him, he lifted his lap and took his car keys out of his trouser pocket. The convertible bounced when he sat back down. The rocking motion and the leathery smell of the car's interior made Janika feel sleepy. She closed her eyes for a moment and her head ratcheted forwards. Then she was startled awake by the sound of the engine starting.

'What are you doing?' she said. 'I don't want to drive anywhere, Anatol. I don't have any shoes on.'

'I know that,' said Anatol, pressing tentatively on the clutch. 'I don't have any either. I'm going to take us somewhere private, Janika. You keep waving that thing in front of the window. Someone's going to see it.'

'They'll see it if they hear a car starting and come to investigate.'

'Exactly,' said Anatol.

Janika glowered. 'Anyway. I thought you were too drunk to drive?'

'Three hours ago. But I've had a lot of fresh air since then.'

'I thought you weren't able to focus on anything?'

'And two cups of coffee, waiting for you.' Anatol hooked an arm around the back of Janika's seat and reversed jerkily into the middle of the driveway, looking over his shoulder. He changed gear and they began to crawl forwards. 'We're just going down the road.'

'You can die going down the road.' Janika looked behind them; the car's back window was beaded with raindrops from the night before. 'Nobody could read this from inside the house. No one's eyesight is that good.'

'Why not? They're big letters.'

'In thin pen.'

'Anyway,' said Anatol. 'Whoever wrote it wouldn't need to read it, would they? They'd recognize it, from the shape of the words. I don't want them to know I'm talking to you about it.'

'Why not?'

'Because it looks desperate.'

The ticking convertible rolled down the gentle slope towards the road and came to a sudden stop at the end of the drive. Anatol braced himself against the steering wheel, but Janika was sitting sideways without her seatbelt on. She was thrown from her seat on to the dashboard, landing heavily on her left arm.

A bright red car shot past the end of the hedge, heading out of the village.

'Sorry,' said Anatol. 'I told you I was struggling to focus.'

Janika picked herself up and felt along her bruised forearm: it wasn't broken, at least. She pointed limply back at the house. 'So you think one of them wrote it? Dean, Maya or Phoebe? Presumably you don't think it was me?'

Anatol pulled on the handbrake and switched off the

engine. The car settled where it had stopped, blocking the driveway. 'I don't think it was any of you.'

'Marcin, then? It might just be a joke. You know what he's like.'

'It's not a joke. It's serious, Janika.'

'How do you know?'

'Because you know when you're being blackmailed. And I know what photographs they're referring to.'

'All right. What photographs?'

A horse was watching them curiously from the field across the road, its right-angled head rising from a bramble bush.

'I'm not going to tell you that,' said Anatol. 'I've told you too much already. And only so you'd understand why we missed each other at the station earlier. I was still in shock.'

'You haven't told me anything,' said Janika. She'd dropped the letter when she'd been thrown from her seat. It lay on the floor, folded in half. 'They haven't asked you for any money?'

'No,' said Anatol.

'Then it's not actually blackmail, is it?'

Anatol reached between Janika's legs and retrieved the letter. 'It's not a birthday card, Janika. They're probably waiting to see how I react before they ask me for money. Then they'll know how much to ask for. That's why I don't want anyone to see us talking. I don't want them to think they've got to me.'

'So you do think it was one of the others? Here? At the house?'

Anatol shook his head. 'I'm just being cautious. Overly cautious, probably. Blackmail makes you paranoid. I think that's understandable.'

'But it can't have come through the post? On a Sunday?'

'It came through the letterbox. Not through the post. The envelope just had my name on it. No stamp. Someone must have delivered it by hand.'

'Then you know it can't have been me,' said Janika. 'I wasn't here last night. I can help you work out who sent it.'

Anatol looked angrily at the letter, then folded it away into his jacket pocket. 'I don't want your help, Janika. This isn't a crossword puzzle. It's my life.'

'If it wasn't one of us, it must have been someone local. How many people do you know around here?'

Anatol let his head loll back against the headrest. 'Someone came to the house,' he said. 'Late last night or early this morning. About five o'clock, I think. I heard them turn around on the drive. It woke me up.'

'A car?' asked Janika

'Yes, a car. But there were footsteps as well. You can ask Maya. Has Marcin come back yet?'

'No,' said Janika. 'Where did he go?'

'I'm not sure. But it would have woken him too. Anyone whose windows overlook the drive. They didn't leave quietly.' Anatol tapped his jacket. 'Then when I got up I found this on the doormat.'

'So you didn't see them?'

'I didn't look. I was half-asleep. I thought it was someone doing a U-turn.' He pointed at the road in front of them; the horse opposite ducked its head. 'We get that a lot. The road isn't wide enough here.'

'So you don't have any idea who it was?'

'I've told you everything I can tell you, Janika. I've told you too much.'

Anatol started the car again and, with his arm around

Janika's seat, reversed carefully up the slope. He parked haphazardly in front of the house.

'You haven't told me anything,' said Janika, for the second time.

'I have to say I expected more sympathy.'

'Why? You have to have done something bad to be blackmailed, Anatol. Bad or embarrassing or at least illegal. What did you do?'

Anatol waved the question away. 'It wasn't any of those things, Janika. It was something boring and technical. To do with tax.'

Janika shook her head. 'I don't believe you. How could anyone have photographs of that?'

Janika woke somewhere cramped and confined and thought at first that she was back on the plane or the train – since all travel is essentially by cage – before she realized that she was still sitting in the passenger seat of Anatol's convertible, blinking into its dim interior. She could taste the tang of dust in her mouth. She looked to her left and saw Maya's outline, moving away from her across the driveway. Her footsteps sounded like shaking dice. Janika blinked again and the form became flesh.

She rolled down the window and leaned her head out. 'Maya?'

Saliva came as she tried to speak, coating her palate with glue. Janika was furious with herself for wasting so much of the day.

Maya stopped and turned around. She was holding a varnished oak board level with her belly button. Mounted on top of it was a dead ferret, with an ashen face and bands of black and caramel fur. Its mouth was open, showing its teeth: two tiny rows of crescent moons. Maya held it up and crossed the driveway to Anatol's car, tilting the board back and forth in a pretend gallop. She reached Janika's window and put the ferret down on the bonnet in front of her. Its pointed face screamed through the windscreen.

'Look what I found,' she said. 'Isn't he horrible?'

Janika closed her eyes. 'Where did Anatol go?'

'He's upstairs, having a shower. He said you'd fallen asleep. But I didn't realize he meant out here.'

'I wish he'd woken me up. I feel like I've spent the night in a bathtub.' Janika's limbs were stiff; she tried to move and the car rocked like a boat. 'Now I'm welded to this death trap. How long have I been out here?'

'About an hour,' said Maya. 'Did you find out your names?'

Janika sighed. 'I hadn't finished talking to him.' She raised herself from the patched upholstery and stretched out her legs, then nodded at the ferret. 'Can you move that, Maya? It's going to give me nightmares.'

Maya turned the ferret ninety degrees. 'I found it in the cupboard under the stairs. Anatol doesn't want it.'

'I'm not surprised. What are you going to do with it?'

'It belonged to Gus.' Maya lifted the board, holding the ferret like a handle. 'I thought I might burn a few of his things, since I couldn't go to the funeral. I'll take some photographs. It'll be cathartic. You won't tell Anatol, will you?'

Janika shrugged. 'He left me stranded at the station. You can burn the house down, for all I care . . .' Her conversation with Anatol came back to her then. 'Maya. Did you hear a car turn around on the driveway, first thing this morning?'

'Marcin, you mean?'

'It would have been about five o'clock. It probably pulled off the road, turned around, someone may or may not have got out, and then it drove off.'

Maya nodded. 'That was Marcin, wasn't it?'

'Did Marcin leave at five this morning?'

'Closer to half past, maybe.'

'But Marcin never gets up that early. What time did he go to bed?'

'After everyone else. He stayed up late smoking my cigarettes. I went down for one in the middle of the night.'

'And it was definitely Marcin? At half past five?'

Maya nodded. 'It woke me up. I heard a car door slam. I looked at the clock, then I looked out the window. I could only see the end of the driveway, so I didn't see him get into the car. But I saw it pull out on to the road.' She tapped the ferret against her hip. 'I suppose someone else could have been driving.'

The back door slammed shut in the wind. Janika made fists against the cold and pushed them deep into the pockets of her cardigan, so that her elbows stuck out like a pair of parentheses. She looked around and spotted a head, floating above the lawn at the far side of the garden. Janika walked over to it and found Phoebe, lying on her back, holding a bouquet of wildflowers across her chest. She looked drunk or dead or like she'd been shipwrecked. An empty beer bottle stood upright in the thick, foamy grass beside her. Phoebe had picked the label from it.

'What are you doing?' asked Janika. 'Aren't you cold?'

'I'm picking flowers,' said Phoebe, showing her bouquet. She had gathered buttercups, catmint and cornflowers together with a trio of bright jug-eared poppies.

'I can see that,' said Janika. 'But why?' The stringy grass was wildly overgrown. Janika's shoes sank into the matted greenery. 'It's wet,' she muttered.

Phoebe felt the grass and shrugged. 'I was just killing time really. Until dinner.'

'Killing flowers,' Janika corrected her.

'Flowers go to heaven,' said Phoebe. 'These ones specifically are going to go in my bedroom. It's so empty in there, I can't stand it.' She picked up the beer bottle and slotted the stems of the flowers inside, then held it up and showed it to Janika. The green glass glowed like treasure. 'They'd only go to waste otherwise.'

Janika had kept her hands in her cardigan pockets. She pointed back at the house, making a webbed, woollen triangle with one of her arms. 'Anatol's back.'

'I know. I saw him.'

'Then what are you doing out here? Don't you think we should all have a drink together or something? To celebrate?' Janika checked her watch. 'It's been his birthday for seventeen hours now.'

'We had one,' said Phoebe. 'At midnight, last night.'

'But that was without me.'

'You weren't here.'

'It feels like everyone's avoiding me, Phoebe. Anatol gets back and you come out here. And Marcin's still missing. I've given up on him but you can come inside for a drink, can't you?'

'We're avoiding each other,' said Phoebe quietly. She planted the bottle in the grass and put her weight on it, pushing herself upright. She sat with her legs bent at the knees, resting a hand on one ankle. 'Did Anatol tell you that he's selling the house?'

'No.' Janika looked behind her at the crumbling building. 'Who's going to buy it?'

'No one, yet. But he has to sell it to pay the inheritance tax. I wanted these as a souvenir.' Phoebe held up the flowers. 'I'm going to press them and keep them forever.'

Janika pulled her cardigan wide, in a winged shrug. 'That makes my news easier, at least. I'm moving to Australia, Phoebe. At the end of the summer.'

Phoebe sagged; it was almost audible. 'Australia?' she echoed.

'Sydney,' said Janika.

'But you'll come back and visit us?'

Janika chose her words carefully. 'Not very often. Sometimes. Maybe.'

'And there I was worrying about what we'll do when Anatol sells the house.'

'It's the reason I came,' said Janika, 'this weekend. I'd like to have gone home and slept. But this was my last chance to come here.'

'Why didn't you say something earlier?'

'I was waiting until I'd got everyone together. I don't want to have to have the same conversation over and over, with different people.'

'Did you meet someone out there?'

Janika rolled her eyes. 'This is the exact conversation I didn't want to have, over and over, Phoebe. They offered me a job.'

'The university? Just like that?'

Janika shook her head. 'I was there for an interview. The conference wasn't real. I made that up. Conferences don't normally last three weeks.'

'But interviews do?'

'I was trying to get used to the city, deciding whether I'd like to live there or not.'

'And you would? Despite the beaches?'

'They're not compulsory.'

Phoebe looked sadly at the flowers she'd picked; they sprang untidily from the neck of the beer bottle. She took a hairband from her wrist and looped it around their stems, binding them tighter. 'All right. Then what's so good about the job? Is it more money?'

'It's less teaching. More research. I'm good at research. I'm not good at teaching. Teaching has too much small talk. Why should I be forced to do something I'm not good at, just because it's tangentially related to something I am? Where else would you get that? Two jobs glued together, with nothing in common?'

'You get that in every job,' said Phoebe. 'Why should I have to sit through meetings?'

'Anyway. I hate teaching. It's mindless.'

'I'm a teacher, Janika.'

'I know that. And I'm sure you're very good at it, Phoebe.'

Phoebe shook her head. She felt inside the pocket of her jeans. 'Do you think you can keep a secret, Janika? Just for the duration of the summer? When you get to Australia you can tell whoever you want, since it doesn't sound like we'll ever see you again.'

'I think I can manage that,' said Janika.

'Someone sent me a letter.' Phoebe pulled out an envelope and passed it to Janika. 'I'm trying to work out who sent it. You like mysteries, don't you?'

'I like puzzles.' Janika checked the envelope. It had been sent through the post, addressed to Phoebe's flat in Crouch

End. 'Puzzles have solutions. There's nothing in here, Phoebe.'

The envelope was empty.

'I took the letter out,' said Phoebe. 'But look at the handwriting. It was sent anonymously. I think someone is blackmailing me.'

ONE YEAR EARLIER
25 May 1998

Scarecrow

Turning on the shower was too much movement: it made Maya dizzy. She waited a moment for the cone of water to warm up, then crouched under it and vomited on to her knees. When she'd finished, she ran her hand through the mess of fibrous chunks, encouraging them towards the drain, and leaned her head back and let the shower water land on her tongue. She could feel the arch of her throat glowing.

It was just after five o'clock in the morning, on the late May Bank Holiday Monday, 1998: the year before Anatol's thirtieth birthday. Eleven months before Gus's death. Maya had spent the long weekend at Anatol's house, as usual. After roughly four and a half hours of sleep on Sunday night, she'd been woken by the sound of Gus flushing the toilet. His en-suite bathroom was directly above Maya's and the noise of the pipes had been enough to rouse her.

She was still drunk from the night before. She'd woken up with a throbbing headache and hadn't been able to get back to sleep.

It was just after sunrise. The sky was a jigsaw of thick and thinning clouds, patches of blue and red: it looked like the night was being taken away in an ambulance.

Maya stumbled back into the bedroom from the shower with a towel around her shoulders. She opened the curtains and stood hunched over in front of the window, her wet palms resting on the circular table, blinking into the early dawn.

She was trying to focus on the view outside – she'd be driving back to London in a few hours and needed to sober up – when she heard the soft creak of floorboards behind her. Anatol's house was always making noises, especially when it was empty, but it sounded like someone was outside her door.

Maya turned just in time to catch the light in the keyhole twitch; she crossed the room as quickly as she could, pausing halfway to right herself on one of the bedposts, and was about to open the door when she remembered the towel. She slid it from her shoulders and held it in a loose fist in front of her throat, covering her body down to her thighs. Then she opened the door, just wide enough for one eye, and looked outside.

But the landing was empty. The lights had been left on overnight. Maya shrank back from the bright taupe carpet and the perky yellow wallpaper, holding a hand up in front of her eyes. She waited there a minute or so, watching through the gaps in her fingers, but didn't see anybody.

She closed the door, wrapped the towel around her hair and returned to the window. She stared out at the fractured sky, trying to decide what to wear for the day. But it was hard to tell how warm it would be. The sun jabbed at a gap in the hedgerow.

Maya winced and lowered her eyes. The unloved borders at the base of the hedge were in full bloom, their shades made pastel by the paltry light. Looking at them directly, Maya noticed something she hadn't seen before. There was a scarecrow standing between the flowerbeds, with wiry white straw instead of hair. Its arms ran down the sides of its stomach, its hands tucked into the pockets of an old velvet dressing gown, worn shiny and thin. Its face seemed to be drawn on something flat, angled towards Maya like a mirror, though it bore no expression, only a slight gap between the lips. It had dark, indistinct eyes that she couldn't quite make out; they could have been looking in any direction. Maya saw all of this in less than a second. Then the scarecrow moved its arms behind its back, pulling its dressing gown open by the pockets.

Maya finally recognized Gus. His face was in shadow and he was standing with his hands held proudly behind him, exposing his broad dappled chest and the flaccid mass of his belly and genitals: bubbles of flesh in a froth of white hair, hanging between the wings of his gown, his legs and feet hidden by flowers. He pulled a hand from his pocket and touched himself.

Maya recoiled and yanked the curtains closed, snapping one of the plastic gliders. She crossed the room, took the key from her chest of drawers and locked the door. There was a brass doorstop in the shape of a duck. She picked it up and held it by its neck: a primitive weapon, blunt but heavy and oddly shaped. Then she sat down on the bed, wrapping the duvet around herself, and watched the door handle.

'Your father's dangerous,' said Maya.
'Gus?' said Anatol.
'Yes. Gus. Who else?'
'But Gus is harmless, Maya.'
Anatol was standing beside Maya's car, under the sprawling bank of hawthorn bushes. Maya was sitting in the

driver's seat, smoking a final cigarette before the drive home. The two of them couldn't see each other's faces, but were managing to hold a conversation through the open window. The cigarette rested on the lip of the glass.

'He's dangerous,' Maya repeated. 'I caught him watching me through the keyhole again.'

Anatol crossed his arms and gazed, dismissively, at the dormer window towards the top of the house. But Gus wasn't up there. 'If you give him something to watch, he'll watch it. Just treat him like a giant child. It's the way his mind is heading, anyway.'

'Haven't you told him to stop?'

'There's no point. I can't control him, Maya. It's his illness that makes him behave like that. It's nothing personal.'

'Then why is it always me he comes after?'

'He probably has positive memories of you, from before. You used to flirt with him.'

'I used to tolerate him,' said Maya. 'He liked my art. But he was always creepy. I never flirted with him.'

'Anyway,' said Anatol, 'you can cover the keyhole, can't you? Or leave the key in the lock?'

'That wouldn't be enough. Not any more. He was outside my window this morning, when I got out of the shower.'

'But you can close the curtains?'

'He had his cock out, Anatol.'

'But you didn't have to look at it, did you?'

Maya frowned. 'Of course I had to look at it. That's not the point. If he's standing in a flowerbed with his prick poking out of his gut, who knows what he might do next? What if he starts spying on me in the shower? His bathroom's above mine. What if he drills a hole through the floor? Should I start holding an umbrella while I'm using the toilet?'

'He won't do that,' said Anatol. 'He's not that rational, or that practical. He's more animal than man now, it's sad to say.'

'What if he goes in my room while I'm out? There must be a spare key. Do I have to check under the bed each time I'm in there? Search inside the wardrobe?'

A fringe of shifting shadows played on the silver roof of the car. Anatol spoke softly. 'I'm not sure what you want me to do, Maya. Lock him in his room when you come to stay?'

'Yes,' said Maya. 'That would be a start. Put something in front of the windows too. I don't like him looking at me.'

'Can you imagine what Phoebe would say? She doesn't even approve of the circus.'

'Phoebe wouldn't need to know. Gag him and chain him to the bed, then he can't make any noise.'

'What if there was a fire?'

The cigarette twitched. 'That's not a bad idea,' said Maya.

'So you want me to murder him?' said Anatol sadly.

Maya shrugged, though Anatol couldn't see her from where he was standing. 'Why isn't he in a home, at least?'

'Because he's not that bad, except when you're here to tempt him.'

'If you keep blaming me, Anatol, I'll castrate you with this cigarette.'

'Anyway. If I murdered him, I'd be the prime suspect. I'm the one that inherits everything.'

'Then maybe I should murder him.'

'All right,' said Anatol. 'How would you do it?'

The spent cigarette fell to the floor. Maya switched on the engine. A brace of starlings flew from the bushes above. The world had developed a dreamlike quality; neither Anatol nor Maya knew whether the conversation they were having was real or not.

'I don't know, Anatol. But I've got a three-hour drive to come up with something.'

SATURDAY
29 May 1999

Had We But World Enough

It was late afternoon. Phoebe was back at the beginning of her notebook, having torn out her previous efforts. The new first page had a margin of tatters and the book was beginning to look sullied and thin. Phoebe frowned at the mess she'd made, then forced herself to fill the page. When she'd finished, she put down her pen and massaged her hand. She was sitting at the desk in her bedroom. It was raining heavily. She closed her eyes and lost herself in the sound, seeking inspiration. Then she wrote down the sum of her thoughts: 'Could you drown in the rain if it was raining hard enough?'

The door opened and Dean came softly into the room. He didn't knock, but Phoebe heard the shifting floorboards and knew it was him. He walked to the end of the bed and leaned sideways against the mattress. 'How's it going?'

Phoebe didn't turn around but let her shoulders and back acknowledge his presence, tilting her head slightly towards him. 'Badly,' she said. 'I thought I'd be better at this.'

'You should take a break,' said Dean. 'It might help.'

Phoebe's handwriting was a tangle of blue barbed wire. Every time she looked at it, her eyes caught on something painful. She closed her notebook. 'Anatol has a gun in his car. If I can't think of a better idea, then my murderer is just going to shoot my victim. The whole story will be three words long.'

'I think you're overthinking this, Phoebe.' Dean's voice dwindled to a whisper as he approached her. 'It doesn't have to be a masterpiece.'

Phoebe snorted. 'My pride says otherwise.'

'Pride?' said Dean; it was clear from his voice that he was smiling. 'I had a different deadly sin in mind.'

Dean placed his right hand on Phoebe's shoulder and leaned down and kissed her neck. His bolder, less coordinated left hand traced the line of her throat, then slid into her jumper and found her breast. His fingernails caught on the cup of her bra. It was a clumsy manoeuvre, but it still felt good: the core of Phoebe's body was between Dean's two warm palms. She closed her eyes and wished that their other friends weren't there with them, that they'd died en route to the house in a series of cascading accidents – strangled by lampposts, blackjacked by caravans – or, better still, that they'd all just vanished.

'Do you like cats, Dean?'

'A reasonable amount. Why?'

Phoebe raised her hand and took hold of Dean's wrist, leaning her head back against his stomach. 'We can't do this now,' she said. 'There are too many people around.'

'Maya and Marcin are typing their stories.'

'I'm so behind,' said Phoebe.

'They won't hear a thing. Typewriters are loud. And Anatol's in the kitchen.'

'Directly underneath us?'

'I can be gentle.'

'That bed is noisy. Maybe later, Dean, when everyone's had more to drink.'

'When they're passed out in a pool of vomit?'

'I don't mind staying up late,' said Phoebe.

Dean removed his hand from her top and fell back on to the mattress. The steel frame whimpered. His chest was going up and down like an oil derrick.

'I should have given you a lift here,' he said. 'It would have been helpful to have someone navigating. I had to come through Salisbury. It's the only way I can do it without getting lost. But the traffic was terrible. If you'd been with me we could have stayed on the A303. It would have made sense, since we were both coming from London. And trains aren't cheap, are they?'

Phoebe was looking back at him. 'It would have made more sense if I'd come with Maya. Otherwise I'd have had to catch a train out to Kingston, but that means going through Waterloo anyway. Or Clapham Junction, at least. Then I'd have had to walk to your house. It would have been easier just to get on the train to Tisbury.'

'What if I'd come round to Crouch End to pick you up?'

'That's an hour in the wrong direction.'

'I know,' said Dean. 'But we could have stopped somewhere on the way. A few hours in a service station hotel and no one would have suspected a thing. Think how much we could have spent on sandwiches.' He sat up and put his hands in his pockets, trying to conjure some kind of casual charm. 'I could take you back on Monday?' He shrugged. 'I don't mind the extra driving.'

'We said we wouldn't do things like that. We said we'd be patient and wait for an opportunity. You've never given me a lift home before.'

Dean stood up and started to pace back and forth, taking long deep breaths. 'You know I'll always follow your lead, Phoebe.' He pulled his hands from his pockets and pointed at the nearby walls. 'But this is an opportunity, isn't it? We just have to be quiet. No one will come in without knocking. And I can hide underneath the bed if that happens.' He settled behind Phoebe and walked his fingertips down her spine. 'What else are you going to do with the next half-hour? Taking a break will probably help. You've got writer's block, Phoebe. Let me unblock you.'

With a heavy sigh, Phoebe opened her notebook and read through everything she'd written in the last fifteen minutes: three painful paragraphs. When she reached the end her confidence was crushed; each word had felt like another brick being loaded on her back. The French had a name for that kind of death.

Peine forte et dure.

Punishment hard and strong.

She pushed the notebook away, then reached back and felt for Dean's waist. 'All right,' she said. 'Take off your clothes.'

A Painful End

Maya had already finished her story. She was standing in front of the bathroom mirror, her bare shoulder angled towards the glass, peeling a dunce cap of dead skin from a spot that she'd squeezed the day before.

She reached for the light to get a better look. But when she pulled the switch – a yellowed length of string, hanging from the ceiling, threaded through a champagne cork – nothing much happened. There was a dull click, but no light came on. She tried again, then wandered through to her bedroom. The crown of dead skin fluttered to the carpet.

But the light in the bedroom wasn't working either. Maya opened the door to the landing and looked out. All of the lights were switched off; the taupe carpet was speckled with shadows. The steady sound of typing came from one of the doors at the far end of the corridor. It was the sound of mousetraps snapping shut. Maya left her bedroom and followed the noise to the door of Janika's room. She knocked on the wood. The typing stopped.

'What?' said Marcin.

Janika's bedroom was dim, though not as dark as Maya's bathroom had been. Marcin was sitting at the desk by the window, looking over his shoulder at Maya. His hands remained poised above the typewriter. He was wearing his reading glasses. 'What?' he said again.

'Can I try your light?'

Marcin was on the verge of finishing his story; he looked like someone about to sneeze. 'What?' he said, for a third time.

Maya tried the light switch, but nothing happened. 'I think there's a power cut.' She walked to the desk and scanned the horizon. 'I can't see lights in any of the other houses.' The nearest visible building was more than a mile away. Marcin refused to look at it. Maya went to the bed and sat down on the mattress. 'After all that fuss, you're going to finish before everyone else, Marcin. Everyone except me.'

'I'm not finished yet,' said Marcin. 'Where are the others?'

'Phoebe and Dean are writing in their rooms, I think.'

'Well. Can't you go and bother them?'

'And Anatol's downstairs, making dinner.'

'Anatol must have finished his story. He probably wrote his weeks ago.'

'I suppose so,' said Maya. 'You'll finish third, then.'

Marcin turned around in his chair. 'Did you know that he's going to sell the house? Phoebe told me he can't afford to pay the inheritance tax. Is he having money troubles?'

'He hasn't mentioned anything.' Maya glanced around the room. 'Who would buy it?'

'The same people that buy his antiques. Homophobes and fox hunters. Killers and vicars. Country people with delusions of grandeur.'

'So this is the last time we'll spend his birthday here?'

Marcin nodded. 'Unless the new owner turns it into a hotel.'

'Either way,' said Maya. 'Yulie's pregnant. Dean will have a baby by this time next year. If we do this again, I don't think he'll join us.'

Marcin raised an eyebrow. 'Well. Everything has to have an end, doesn't it? Apart from my story, apparently, now that you're here to distract me.' Marcin turned back to the typewriter and laid his hands on the keys. 'Look on the bright side, Maya. It means that we're safe to burn all our bridges.'

Fall Out

Dean's orgasm landed on his brain like an atom bomb. As he lay in a naked stupor on the floor of Phoebe's bedroom, he tried to take advantage of the sordid, quiet calm and use the time to think about murder. But all his imagination could conjure, lying on his back, was the image of someone drowning in a shallow layer of wet plaster the same shade as the ceiling above him.

Phoebe ran a finger from his throat to his belly button. 'We can't fall asleep,' she said.

Her prone body was lying parallel to his, but on top of the bed. One of her arms was hanging down, her hand gliding back and forth across his chest.

Dean grunted. He found the used condom on the carpet between his legs, held it up and examined its contents, the latex rim resting between his finger and thumb. It was open at the top like a test tube or champagne flute. A glass raised to his virility. He tied a knot near the opening, then gave the other end a few tentative squeezes. The texture was compelling, its wilted skin swelling whenever he pinched it. There was air trapped inside. Dean pressed it proudly: a sealed keepsake of his achievements.

'Dean,' said Phoebe, watching with quiet disapproval.

Embarrassed, Dean sat up and pressed the tangle of rubber into one of the pockets of his trousers, which he'd bundled under his head as a pillow. Phoebe swung her legs around and shuffled over to the edge of the mattress.

'One of us should go downstairs,' she said. 'Before it starts to look suspicious. I don't mind. I've been up here long enough.'

'I should go and finish my story,' said Dean. 'I've made some notes. I just need to type it out in full. Do you really not mind being murdered?'

Phoebe shook her head. 'I've got so much left to do,' she said glumly.

Dean pulled his boxer shorts over his ankles. 'But I need to talk to you about something first.'

'What?' said Phoebe.

'When we're dressed,' said Dean.

'Is it something bad?'

'It's not good or bad. Or maybe it's both. I don't know.'

Dean turned away from Phoebe and inched his toes into his grey chinos, laid out on the floor in front of him. He was dressing slowly on purpose. Phoebe found her underwear under the desk, the shapeless twists of fuchsia fabric like graffiti against the grey carpet. Her T-shirt was twisted into a loop. She found Dean's shirt and threw it towards him. Then she paused, with a sock in the middle of swallowing her foot.

'At least tell me the good bit,' she said.

Dean shook his head, disappointed with his choice of words. 'It's not like that,' he said. 'It's not something good and something bad. It's just one thing. But it's not a bad thing. There are positives and negatives.'

'You're talking in riddles, Dean. What's going on? Are you leaving Yulie?'

'Not at the moment.' Dean buttoned his shirt. 'Sorry.'

'Is she leaving you?'

'I don't think so. It's nothing like that.'

Phoebe frowned. 'What is it, then?'

When Dean was fully dressed and could delay no more, he walked over to the window and looked outside. The day hadn't changed in the last half-hour. It was still grey. He heard Phoebe sit down on the bed behind him. The steel frame wheezed. Something about the slow, heavy way she was moving told him that she was growing impatient. But he couldn't see her reflection in the glass, only his own.

'Yulie is . . .' Dean panicked. He stopped himself. 'Maya,' he said. 'It must have been Maya that sent that note. I'm sure of it. That's what I wanted to talk to you about.'

The next moments passed in silence. Dean pulled out the chair and sat down, facing Phoebe. He placed an arm on the desk beside him and rocked the chair on to its two back legs. He held that pose until Phoebe spoke.

'Maya?' She sounded indignant. 'Why would Maya send me a note saying "I know"?'

'Because that's what she's like,' said Dean defensively, holding his hands up. The tilting chair hit the floor with a slam. 'She takes things too far. She's like a child in a china shop. And she's friends with Yulie. It all fits together.'

'But Maya wouldn't send me an anonymous letter. Would she?'

'Maybe she thought you'd think it was a joke?'

'I doubt it.'

Phoebe lay back on the bed. Dean got up from his chair and joined her, sitting beside her with his back to her waist. 'It's not like the note asked for money or anything. There's no motive for sending it unless someone wants us to stop. And I can't think who would care, apart from Maya.' Dean ran a hand down Phoebe's flank. He squeezed her thigh. After twenty minutes of nudity, her rough blue jeans felt like set cement. 'This is unoriginal sin,' he continued. 'The only people that would care about it are Yulie and Yulie's friends. And it's more likely to be Maya than Yulie.'

'Then why didn't she send the note to you? You're the one that's married.'

'She didn't want Yulie to see it, probably. It makes sense. Maya knows about . . .' Dean slid his fingers across the bottom of Phoebe's stomach, where he thought her uterus must start. He caught himself before he finished the thought. 'Knows about us,' he whispered quickly.

'Does she?'

'Maybe,' said Dean. 'I don't know. I was just thinking out loud.'

'So what are the positives?'

'What do you mean?'

Phoebe frowned. 'This is what you wanted to tell me? You said there were positives and negatives. So what are the positives supposed to be? You're telling me that my best friend is sending me threatening letters, Dean. Aren't you?'

Before the Stories the Storm

Anatol ended up reading out the first three stories in darkness, late on Saturday evening; they'd eaten an early dinner while there was still some daylight, then Anatol had cleared away their plates. By the time he'd finished the sun had set. And the power was still out. Marcin, Maya, Phoebe and Dean had gathered in the drawing room and were sitting in the dark. Anatol stood in front of them, holding the stories: the first consisted of five sheets of paper, stapled together, covered in thousands of broken red letters.

'I picked this one at random,' said Anatol. 'It's as good a place to start as any.' He tried a light switch, but nothing happened. 'I suppose there's no rush, now that it's dark. Who needs a drink? Shall we open the champagne while it's still cold? There's plenty left. It belonged to my father. We might as well drink it. I'll start on the stories once we've all got a glass.'

'I'll get it,' said Phoebe, setting off down the corridor, feeling her way towards the kitchen.

Before they'd eaten, Anatol had found thirteen candles and an antique oil lamp and had lined them up along the coffee table.

Marcin watched in silence as Dean fussed over a candle with a cupped hand; Maya had moved to the window and was leaning over the telescope. Anatol went to join Maya, casting her face in shadow. The two of them stood either side of the tripod, forming an asymmetrical arch. Maya pressed her head to the eyepiece.

'What am I looking at?'

The window in front of them was half open, the wind outside wailing.

'Stars,' said Anatol.

There was a gap in the clouds above the horizon; the telescope was pointed towards it.

'They look like stars. That's why I asked. But shouldn't they be bigger?'

'They are bigger,' said Anatol. 'You can't see those ones without a telescope.'

Maya moved her head away from the eyepiece and looked along the line of the instrument. 'So magnifying them makes them look like the rest? What's the point in that? We should find something you can see normally and make it massive. Where's Venus?'

'I don't know, Maya. It's my first time using it. Dean, do you know where Venus is?'

'No,' said Dean. 'And close the window or these candles will blow out.'

The drawing room was on the side of the house sheltered from the wind, but they could still feel it tugging at their clothes occasionally.

'It's all right,' said Anatol. 'We have a lighter. We can light them again.'

'What about the moon?' said Maya.

'The moon's on the other side of the house. You wouldn't see it through the storm.' With one meaty hand, Anatol swung the telescope away from Maya, towards his waist. 'It's my birthday. I like the stars.'

Marcin was listening to this conversation with his eyes closed.

'Smart of us to get you the one gadget that doesn't need power,' said Phoebe as she reappeared in the doorway, holding a bottle of fizz and five champagne flutes. The glasses were all in her right hand: three of them dangled from between her fingers and two were clamped tightly between her thumb and her palm. 'It thrives on darkness, in fact.' She smiled and raised her tinkling paw.

'Like Maya,' said Dean, sitting back in the shadows.

At the sound of her name, Maya turned and walked over to the sofa. Dean stood and offered her his hand, guiding her through the unlit furniture.

'Before you sit down,' said Marcin, speaking at last, 'I think it's time for that cigarette we discussed earlier.'

'But, Marcin,' said Phoebe, 'you were doing so well.'

'I wasn't,' said Marcin. 'I was doing horribly.'

'You can last until bedtime, can't you? It's only a few more hours. Imagine the feeling of achievement you'll wake up with tomorrow.'

'You can't quit smoking while you're drinking alcohol,' said Maya. 'No one has that much self-control. You have to stay sober, otherwise it's hopeless.'

Marcin narrowed his eyes at both of them. 'You could at least confer before giving me advice. Can I have a cigarette, Maya?'

'You'll get drenched,' said Dean. 'I told you there was a storm coming.'

'I've got an umbrella,' said Maya.

'What about lightning?' said Phoebe.

'It's all right.' Maya shrugged. 'Marcin's taller than me.'

'Just don't be too long,' said Anatol loudly. His gaze was

still channelled through the eyepiece of the telescope, but his ear was pointed straight at the group. 'I want to read these stories before anyone gets too sleepy or drunk.'

'It's like we're in a story already.' Maya and Marcin passed through the ribs of moonlight that lined the hallway; a gust of wind brought a sheet of water crashing against the glass. 'You're not going to murder me, are you, Marcin?'

'Not if you give me a cigarette.' Marcin stopped to put his shoes on. But Maya had bare feet and didn't mind if they got wet. She didn't mind if they were struck by lightning, either. She thought it might be fun: peeling charred flesh from her extremities, once the pain had passed.

Marcin opened the front door and stepped outside. Maya followed him, keeping hold of the door handle, holding the door tight against her hip, so that it wouldn't blow open or slam shut in the wind. She had the pack of cigarettes in her free hand.

'Light one for me, would you?'

Marcin took the pack from Maya and placed two cigarettes side by side in his mouth, then gave it back to her. The lighter struggled in the strong wind, but Marcin sucked at them impatiently and managed to light both. He took a deep breath, then handed one to Maya.

'How does it feel?' she asked, struggling to be heard over the three-headed cacophony of wind, rain and leaves.

Marcin's lengthy exhalation was torn apart by the storm. 'It doesn't feel like anything,' he yelled, disappointed. 'I always think it's going to be like eating a meal when you're hungry. But it's not, is it? It's just going back to normal. Your lungs never feel full the way your stomach does sometimes. They're just two joyless organs. How many do you have left?'

Maya slid open the pack and counted. 'Fifteen,' she said. 'I want another one after this.'

'Are you sure?'

Marcin nodded. 'When the dam bursts, the village floods.'

The furious wind hacked at the trees surrounding the house. They were Scots pines: feathery towards the top, but bare up to the belly button.

'Marcin,' said Maya as she watched their milky silhouettes swing back and forth, 'did you get my note?'

'What note?'

'I left you a note.'

Marcin froze. 'Where?'

'You'll know it when you see it.'

'Did you send something to my flat?'

'No,' said Maya. 'I left it in your bedroom.'

'It wasn't a single sheet of paper folded in half, with capital letters written in the middle?'

'No,' said Maya. 'It was a yellow note screwed into a ball, with ash inside it. Anatol left it stuck to the door. So I used it as an ashtray.'

Marcin finally looked at Maya. 'I think we're talking about different notes.'

'Well, I only left one. It said something about going to the station to pick up Phoebe. And about the door being unlocked.'

'Where did you leave it?'

'In your bed. Under the duvet.'

'Why?' asked Marcin.

'I don't know. It amused me.' Maya held up her cigarette and stared intently at its glowing tip, as if she wasn't sure whether it was real or not. 'Now tell me about this other note, Marcin . . .'

SUNDAY NIGHT
30 May 1999

The Bolo Tie

It was the corner of the night and Maya was finding it hard to sleep. She was suffering from a mild toothache and had spent the last two hours pressing on the offending tooth compulsively, keeping herself awake.

She reached over and switched on the lamp beside the bed. She'd wanted to find her seashell compact, but the first thing she saw was a thin brown envelope lying on the carpet. It hadn't been there when she'd last had the lights on. Someone must have pushed it through the gap under her door, probably thirty minutes earlier when she'd been listening to music, trying to soothe herself to sleep with *The Best of Enya*. She'd had her headphones on and wouldn't have heard anything. But she couldn't imagine what it could be.

Maya rolled out of bed and picked up the envelope, then sat down on the floor and studied its exterior. There was no name or address on the front. There were no marks on the envelope at all, except for several smudges in one of the corners that vaguely resembled the outlines of fingers. Maya held it next to the lamp and the shapes lit up crimson. They looked like bloodstains. She flipped the envelope over, feeling its contents slide around inside, and saw a clear red thumbprint on the back. There was something in the envelope that was thicker than paper, something square and inflexible.

Maya opened it up and pulled out a pair of Polaroid

photographs, held together by a neon-green elastic band. The band was playing the role of a thong.

Underneath was a picture of Maya, naked.

All of the doors along the landing were closed. Maya walked over to one of them, treading carefully on the creaking floorboards, and rapped on the wood. The noise sank into the silence. The door stayed still. She waited half a minute, then knocked again. There was no response. It felt like she was throwing stones into a pond.

'Dean,' she muttered with her forehead against the frame.

The door opened a few inches and Dean looked out. He was fully dressed, in smart trousers and a Fair Isle jumper. The lights were on in the room behind him. 'You'll wake someone up,' he whispered. 'I was asleep.'

'You weren't,' said Maya. 'You're wearing clothes.'

'Did you expect me to answer the door to you naked?'

Dean's hand curled around the open door. He had a bandage of tissues wrapped around his thumb. Maya held up the envelope and waved it in front of him.

'What's this?' she asked.

'It's an envelope, Maya.'

'I know that, Dean. Where did it come from?'

'I don't know. The post office, probably.'

'Somebody slid it under my door.'

'Not me,' said Dean. 'I've been asleep since we went to bed. What's inside it, anyway?'

'It's covered in your blood,' said Maya. 'What happened to your hand?'

Dean tucked his thumb inside his palm, making a fist between the door and the frame. 'I caught the nail,' he said. 'That could be anybody's blood.'

'I recognize your thumbprint.' Maya showed Dean the back of the envelope. A few years earlier, she'd made a large sketch of the London skyline, seen from the park in Primrose Hill, with the different buildings on the horizon represented by fingerprints. She'd used Dean's thumb as the dome of St Paul's. 'It's hanging on my wall, remember.'

'No good deed goes unpunished,' said Dean, swearing under his breath. 'You didn't even pay me for doing that.'

'Where did it come from?' asked Maya, again.

Dean slumped heavily against the door, squashing his fist. He flinched from the sudden pain and stood up straight, shaking out his hand. 'I found it in my room,' he said. 'I had to open it, to know what it was. But I didn't look at the photographs any longer than was necessary. I thought you'd want them back. I was trying to be nice. No good deed . . .'

'Whereabouts in your room?'

'It's a long story.'

'Well?'

'It's late, Maya. Can't we talk about this in the morning?'

'I'm not tired,' said Maya. 'You can't post explicit photos of someone under their door, Dean, and not expect to be asked a few questions.'

'Explicit is an understatement.'

Maya pushed on the door until Dean relented. He didn't have the energy to fight her off. 'All right,' he muttered. 'Come in and I'll show you.'

Maya was curled into an ear on Dean's bed. Her whole face was throbbing with pain. The envelope was tucked between her thighs. 'Tell me where you found it,' she said.

Dean was sitting on the desk by the window. 'Don't speak so loudly. We don't want to wake anyone up.'

'Why not? I don't care.'

'There's a word called discretion, Maya. You should look it up.'

'I'll do that. In the discretionary?'

Dean patted the surface of the desk. 'This used to be up in Gus's room,' he said. 'Anatol must have brought it down here after he died. I used to have some kind of card table in here. Mid-Victorian, I think. Gothic Revival. Oak and baize. But I imagine that's been sold to someone. It was a very nice piece, but this is much more practical.'

'It's late,' said Maya, closing her eyes. 'Get to the point.'

The mahogany desk had two drawers. Dean stood up and pulled out the one at the bottom. 'So I had a look inside it, as you do. But of course Anatol's cleared everything out. Only I noticed that this bottom drawer doesn't pull out all the way. It's subtle, almost too subtle, but as an engineer you develop an eye for these things. The dimensions aren't quite right.' He pulled the top drawer out slightly, then tilted the bottom drawer down and lifted it out of the desk. 'There's a secret compartment here at the back.'

Maya opened her eyes and raised her head. Dean held up the drawer and showed it to her. There was an additional panel at the back, with a slot about an inch wide behind it.

'That's where I found your photographs,' said Dean. 'And this is what keeps it hidden . . .' He turned the drawer slowly and showed Maya the bottom: a rusty nail jutted out from the wood. 'It's designed to catch on the frame of the desk. But it's a daft way of doing it. It's lucky I just cut my thumb on that. The nail could have gone straight through my hand. It's sharp enough.'

Maya reached out for the drawer and Dean brought it over to her. She slid her hand inside the secret compartment.

'Where did you put the others?' she asked.

'What others?' said Dean, placing the drawer down on the carpet.

'The rest of the photographs?' said Maya.

'There were only two in the envelope. I gave them both back to you.'

'I doubt that,' said Maya. 'I took those pictures with Sepp. Do you remember Sepp? My ex-boyfriend, the architect? They were part of an art project. Exploring the extremes of the human body.'

'Exploring?' Dean went back to the desk and leaned against it. 'But did you have to make such a detailed map?'

'We didn't take the idea any further. It was just an experiment.'

'I'm not sure how much further you could have taken it. I'm no prude, but . . .'

'We took twelve photographs,' said Maya. 'So where are the rest?'

'Maybe Gus thought that two were enough,' said Dean. 'Or more than enough.'

'Why would anyone use an elastic band to hold two photographs together?'

'I don't know what to tell you. He only had two. How did Gus get hold of them in the first place anyway?'

Without moving, Maya reached out and opened the drawer of Dean's bedside table. She felt inside and pulled out a stack of ten square Polaroids. 'That was easy,' she said.

She slotted the photographs in with the others.

Dean watched with a pained expression. 'I was going to give them back to you,' he said. 'I just felt I should get some kind of reward for my trouble.' He held up his bloody hand. 'A finder's fee. Just a couple of thousand. Maybe five, maybe ten. I wasn't going to get greedy or anything. You'd sell a painting for more than that.'

'I'm not going to pay you for them, Dean.'

'I imagine someone could do some damage with those photographs. If they sent them to your friends and family and colleagues.'

'Yes. Well. They're mine now,' said Maya. 'I think I'll burn them. Or maybe I'll bury them.'

Dean picked at the tissue on his wound. 'The thing is,' he said, 'I do have copies. And you won't find them. They're not in here.'

'No you don't,' said Maya. 'You can't make a copy of a Polaroid.'

'You can with a scanner. If you have a computer.'

'Anatol doesn't have either.'

'But I do,' said Dean. 'I've got both at home. I scanned them back when I found them in your flat . . .'

Maya spotted a paperclip on the bedside table. She picked it up, placed it in her mouth and started to suck on it, ignoring the pain in her tooth. It was a bad habit she'd had since childhood. She shook her head.

Dean watched her, disgusted. He crossed his arms. 'Who do you think gave them to Gus?' he said. 'Gus didn't object to paying me for them. But that was years ago now. I'm going to need a bit more – for my trouble.'

'You're lying,' said Maya, pressing the paperclip into the roof of her mouth.

'I hope you're sure about that,' said Dean. 'Because if you don't pay me, let's call it five thousand, then the first thing I'll do when I get home is send a copy of those photos to everyone you know. And there's nothing you can do to stop me.'

'I could kill you,' said Maya.

'And spend the rest of your life in prison? You know they don't have sofas in prison?'

'Not if I made it look like an accident.'

'Right. But I don't think you're going to kill me,' said Dean.

Maya spat out the paperclip. It landed on the carpet with tooth marks in the steel. She got up and picked up the drawer from the floor, then walked towards the desk with it. 'How do I put this back?' she said.

Dean knelt on the floor by the desk and held up his hands to take the drawer from Maya. 'Give it here,' he said.

He tilted his head back, exposing his neck.

'You're making this too easy,' said Maya.

She pressed the drawer under Dean's chin, leaning into it with all her weight. The rogue nail pierced the base of his throat. Blood squirted out across the carpet. Dean tried to scream but couldn't open his mouth. The drawer was stopping him.

Maya moved back and the drawer stayed in place, hanging from Dean's neck like a giant bolo tie. He brought his hands up and flailed at the wood, but he was panicking too much to pull it out cleanly. He yanked it down and tore the wound open further. The blood-soaked drawer clattered to the floor.

'Maya,' said Dean, straining to speak, his voice just a croak. 'This doesn't look like an accident at all . . .'

He fell backwards on to the floor. Blood poured down the sides of his throat.

'No,' said Maya. 'But it's close enough.'

SUNDAY
30 May 1999

Marcin Was the First to Die

The window sash started to droop as soon as Janika had unlatched it; she felt the sliding glass smudge her knuckles and pulled her hand away quickly. The window fell and thudded into place, leaving the top half of the frame empty. A cold breeze flooded the room.

Janika sat down on the icy bedsheets. She stretched her legs out and looked at her jeans. A dark crown circled each cuff; they'd got wet while she'd been outside, walking across the overgrown lawn. Now they made a clammy set of shackles. Janika sighed and took them off. She moved to the chest of drawers and found her grey tracksuit bottoms in one of the drawers. She sat down again and pulled them over her feet; they were the third pair of trousers she'd worn that day, but she'd brought enough clothes to last her three weeks.

The door to her bedroom was open slightly. Someone knocked on it once, then it started to move. Janika put out her foot and stopped it.

There was a loud dull thump, of fabric against wood. Janika felt the impact along her calf. Then Dean stuck his head through the gap in the door. 'Janika?' he said.

'I'm getting changed,' she called out.

'Oh. Sorry.' Dean's head disappeared.

Janika pulled the tracksuit up past her hips. 'It's all right. You can come in now.'

Dean entered the room, walked over to the desk and

stood with his back to Janika, looking out through the window. One of his elbows was bent; in his right hand he was holding a vintage coffee cup, made of tarnished orange glass. It was filled with scalding black liquid, though the coffee stopped about two inches below the rim. The sleeve of his jumper was soaking wet and the bottom of the cup was dripping steadily.

'Sorry,' he said again. 'I didn't mean to intrude. I thought you might like a cup of coffee. I was just making one for myself. I know you were feeling tired, before.'

'You can turn around. I've finished getting changed.'

Dean transferred the cup to his left hand, holding it with one thumb on the lip and his index finger under the base. He held it out towards Janika. She nodded at the desk.

'Can you put it over there?'

'Don't you want it?'

Janika shrugged. 'Why did you bring it up here? I was about to come down.'

'You don't have to drink it. I'll just leave it here.' Dean placed the cup on the desk. Its steamy contents crawled up the window. 'Actually, there is one other thing I wanted to ask you.'

'What?'

Dean slid a sheet of paper from his trouser pocket. It had been folded and then folded again. He flattened it out and offered it to Janika. 'You're good at things like this, aren't you? Puzzles and things. I want to know if you recognize the handwriting.'

Janika took the note and examined it. '"I know",' she read. 'What does that mean?'

'Don't worry about the words. Do you recognize the writing?'

Janika had seen the same lettering twice before. Once on the note that Anatol had shown her and once on Phoebe's envelope. The characters had been drawn in black upper case. 'Not exactly,' she said, laying the note down on the duvet beside her. 'Where did you get it?'

Dean rubbed at his damp sleeve. 'I found it,' he said. 'I don't know whose it is. That's why I'm asking you. In case you can tell me. Do you think it could be Yulie's writing?'

'I don't know Yulie's writing all that well.'

'Can't you tell me anything, then?'

Janika held the note a few inches from her face. 'It's a gel pen,' she said. 'Whoever wrote it was obviously trying to remain anonymous. It was written with a ruler. It was done by someone in a rush, or someone impatient. They've lifted the pen from the page too quickly. Every line ends with a slight barb, like a fishing hook. Would you say that Yulie's usually impatient?'

'Sometimes,' said Dean. 'You don't recognize it, then?'

Janika glanced at the note again. 'Did it come in an envelope?'

'Not to me. I told you that.'

The note would fit the envelope that Phoebe had shown her. 'Then who was it sent to?'

Dean shook his head. 'I have no idea.' He searched the room for a change of subject. While she'd been outside, Janika had found the paper aeroplane that Dean had made earlier, when he'd been sitting at her desk. She'd brought it back inside and placed it in the bin. Dean picked it out and unfolded it. 'Is this the one I made?'

Janika nodded. 'It was caught in the roses.'

Dean smoothed the sheet on the desk and read out the words that he'd typed as a joke, earlier that afternoon.

'"Send help. I'm being held captive."' He shook his head, smiling. 'Yet I'm still here, talking to you, Janika. It must be Stockholm syndrome.'

'There's something on the back,' said Janika.

Dean turned the page over and checked the other side. 'You're right,' he said. 'I didn't notice earlier. It says: "Marcin was the first to die". Marcin must have typed that himself.'

'Marcin?' said Janika. 'How do you know?'

Dean passed her the piece of paper. 'It was him that put that typewriter there. He wanted to type with no distractions, so he came in here. That must be an abandoned version of his story. He wrote a single sentence, then gave up and threw it in the bin. That sounds like Marcin.'

'"Marcin was the first to die",' read Janika.

Six words in smudged red ink.

'But that doesn't make any sense,' she added.

A NOTE FOUND TORN INTO SEVERAL PIECES (CONTINUED)

I am not a murderer. And I'm not responsible for what happened this weekend.

The game was my idea, that's true. And it was me that wrote the story about Marcin killing Maya, by stabbing her in the face with a sundial. That is also true.

But I am not the one with blood on my hands.

You should blame the people demanding money from me.

PART FOUR
Lies

MONDAY, SUNDAY AND OTHER DAYS
May 1999

Storage Space

Janika was woken, late on Monday morning, by the sound of knocking. She blinked her eyes open and saw Anatol standing next to her bed, tapping his knuckles on the bedside table. She reached out and grabbed hold of his hand. 'Stop that,' she said. 'What are you doing?'

Anatol shuffled apologetically. 'Don't shoot the messenger. I need to make plans for the day. You can stay here and sleep if you like, but I didn't want to leave you stranded.'

Janika sat up against the headboard. She'd fallen asleep with a library book open on her chest and her nostrils were full of dust. There was another book by her side, sticking into her ribs. And there were pens everywhere. She'd only been there one night but she'd already turned the bed into a desk. Pale daylight came through the umber curtains. 'What time is it?'

'Just after eleven.'

'Eleven?' Janika slumped, bereaved by the loss of her morning, usually the most productive time of the day. 'Why didn't you wake me earlier?'

'I thought it would start an argument. You seemed tired last night.'

'Jet lag,' Janika said regretfully. 'But I hate oversleeping. I wanted to be home by now.'

'It's still early. When do you want me to take you to the station?'

'When are you taking Phoebe?'

'Phoebe's already gone,' said Anatol. 'Everyone else has already left.'

'Gone?' Janika slid to the end of the bed and stood and parted the curtains. There were no cars on the driveway, except for Anatol's convertible. That's when she noticed how quiet the house was. 'Without saying goodbye?'

'I think they thought it would start an argument. You did seem very tired.'

'I start arguments when people don't wake me up, not when they do.'

'We couldn't remember which way round it was.' Anatol checked his watch. 'The next train's in thirty minutes. Do you want to get that one or do you want some breakfast? I don't think there's time to do both.'

'I'm not hungry,' said Janika. 'I'll pack my things, then we can get going.'

'I'll be downstairs,' said Anatol. 'You can take some food for the train if you like. I bought too much. You may as well take it.'

'I can't believe they didn't say goodbye.'

Anatol tapped his chin with his finger. 'Leaving is a kind of goodbye.'

Janika undressed, changed her underwear and folded her pyjamas. She put on the same pair of blue jeans that she'd been wearing the day before, a new white T-shirt and the same black cardigan, then she gathered up the rest of her clothes, took her books from among the bedsheets, finding a third underneath the pillows, her slippers from the floor, and packed everything into her case.

She could hear the sound of a vacuum cleaner downstairs. Every few seconds it would rise in pitch, as the airflow became constrained. Somewhere there was a tap dripping. The emptier a house is, Janika thought, the more it seems haunted.

Then she opened her case again and took out her toothbrush.

After cleaning her teeth in the bathroom down the hall, Janika went into Phoebe's bedroom and sat down on the bed. The curtains were open, the bin had been emptied and the bed was made.

She looked out of the window at the garden. Both the trees and grass were the murky green of military equipment. The sky was a faint blue. A sparrowhawk circled the hedge at the end of the lawn, testing the camouflage.

'Janika? Janika?' Anatol threaded his neck through the gap in the door. He was holding a sandwich, wrapped in cellophane. He held it up like a white flag. 'What are you doing in here? We don't have long.'

'I thought Phoebe might have left me a note.'

'I don't think she did.'

'She shouldn't have gone without waking me up. We always take the same train. At least as far as Basingstoke.'

'Did she? Leave you a note?'

'No. I couldn't find one.'

'Where did you look?'

'In the drawers.'

Janika pointed at an off-white chest of drawers at the end of the bed. Anatol opened the top drawer. 'It's empty,' he said. 'Why would she leave a note in here?'

'What time did she go?'

'I can't remember. Nine, maybe.'

'There's a train at nine fifty.'

'That would have been it, then. Where else did you look?' Anatol handed Janika the sandwich. It was white bread with the crusts cut off, with thick slices of white cheddar cheese. The butter inside was also white. 'She could have written her note on that. Couldn't she?'

Janika peered down at the sandwich. 'What's that?'

'I was joking,' said Anatol. 'Because it looks like a piece of paper.'

'That,' said Janika.

There was a red smudge on one of the slices of bread.

'That's tomato,' said Anatol. 'But there isn't any tomato inside. It was on the chopping board. I made myself one too, with tomato. I didn't know if you liked tomato. You won't be able to taste it, if you don't.'

Janika placed the sandwich on the bed. It looked like a child's pillow lying next to its parent. 'Of course I like tomato,' she said.

Anatol tapped his thumb on his lower lip. 'You can take mine, if you like. The one with tomato in it. Are you coming downstairs?'

'In a minute,' said Janika. 'After I've packed my toothbrush.'

'There's no rush,' said Anatol. 'But we need to go soon.'

Before leaving the room, Anatol paused and looked down at the bed. He looked as if he was checking it for damage.

Janika waved her toothbrush. 'What are you looking at?'

'I was just wondering why Phoebe made the bed,' Anatol said quickly. 'I'm going to change the sheets of course.'

'Everything seems a bit strange this morning.'

Anatol smiled at her. 'Monday mornings are always strange.'

*

But Janika could tell when Anatol was lying. He must have noticed something unusual about the bed. She wondered what it was?

When he'd gone downstairs, she got down and stood where Anatol had been standing. She looked along the length of the bed and saw a tiny red stain at the bottom of the mattress. It could have been nail polish, or lipstick, but Phoebe would have stripped the bedsheets if she'd spilled something. Or it could have been blood. But Phoebe would have cleaned up if she'd cut herself. Janika lifted the duvet and checked the rest of the mattress. There were no other marks that she could see, but she found two strange lumps in the middle of the top sheet. Janika pressed down on them. They both felt firm. 'What's that then?'

The bed was built like a wooden box, with storage space inside. The top part of the frame, underneath the mattress, was attached to a hinge below the headboard and could be raised up to head height, supported by a pair of 800 Newton pneumatic struts. Janika wondered if there might be something large inside that was pushing up through the bedsheets. She held her toothbrush between her teeth, opened the catch and lifted the lid of the bed to her chin.

As the mattress rose, it pulled something out of the storage space. Janika turned her head, to keep her toothbrush from catching on the frame, and saw it in her peripheral vision. It was something that had the shape of a human body, attached to the mattress by its wrists, dangling like a cheap animatronic in a haunted house. Janika flinched away from it, but without recognition. She straightened her head and flinched again. Phoebe's immaculate dead body was hanging in front of her. Its throat had been cut. There were two pinkish lips where the wound had curled open. Both of its hands had been thrust upwards into the fabric of the mattress. Phoebe must have still been alive when she'd been locked inside the storage space, bleeding to death. Her last act had been to try and claw her way out through the bedding, forcing her fingers through the foam and springs.

Janika spat out her toothbrush in shock. Her white sandwich slid off the pillows and fell down into the pool of blood.

Anatol was standing behind her. 'Why didn't you just leave?' he said. 'I was going to let you go.' He caught hold of Janika's hair and moved her towards the storage space. He was holding a knife in his free hand. There was a slick of cheese still on the blade.

I don't need to tell you what happened next.

Janika Turns Detective

'This doesn't make any sense,' said Janika. 'How can the same person be murdered twice?'

She had accosted Anatol in the kitchen, late on Sunday afternoon. He was busy preparing dinner, adding papery slices of radish to a bowl of salad. The sweaty stench of meat drifted from the oven. 'Maya told me she had Marcin as her murder victim,' Janika continued. 'But Marcin must have picked himself as well. Look.'

She held out the piece of paper that Dean had made into a paper aeroplane and showed Anatol the six words Marcin had typed at the top, underlining them with her thumb.

'"Marcin was the first to die",' read Anatol, smiling. 'Poor Marcin, that's unlucky.' The smile segued into a frown when Janika didn't react to this half-hearted joke. 'You're not supposed to know what names Maya got,' Anatol added. 'Or Marcin.'

'But they're not supposed to have the same names.'

Anatol took the sheet of paper, read the few words on each side and handed it back. 'Have you written your story yet?'

'No,' said Janika.

'Then don't worry about it. I'm not going to read the rest of the stories anyway, unless Marcin comes back. It wouldn't be fair.'

'Why not? You read the first three without me.'

'Because you hadn't written one yet. And now you don't need to bother, Janika. It doesn't look like Marcin's going to come back tonight.'

'I don't have any intention of writing one,' said Janika. 'There isn't time anyway.'

'Good. Then we're agreed?'

Anatol turned back to the oven. A line of deadly implements hung from hooks on the wall: knives, sharpeners and cast-iron pans. He took down an innocent wooden salad server and held it by his side.

'No,' said Janika, tugging on his shirt, turning him around. 'This has nothing to do with the story I'm not going to write, Anatol. I'm asking how Marcin ended up with the same murder victim as Maya. That goes against the rules of the game. And it shouldn't have been possible, if there was only one of each name in each cocktail glass. Don't you want to know how that happened?'

Anatol placed his hands in his pockets and shrugged evasively. He was still holding the salad server. Its toothy end sprouted from his trousers. 'Well, I don't like to make accusations, Janika, especially when he's not here to defend himself, but I think it's clear that Marcin cheated. He didn't like whoever he'd picked as his victim. He was desperate to swap his names with yours, but I wouldn't let him.'

'So he took Maya's? Marcin? He took his own name, I mean, from Maya?'

'And now he's gone missing.' Anatol smiled again, more boldly than before. 'Let that be a lesson to anyone breaking the rules.'

'So which name didn't he want?'

The Apartment Complex

It was a warm evening, less than a week before Anatol's birthday. Marcin stepped off the Docklands Light Railway at Island Gardens Station and set out on the five-minute walk to his flat. The route took him through a cluster of frustrated apartment buildings that stood with their shoulders hunched and their hands in their pockets, queuing uselessly for a view of the river. They were blocked by the taller buildings that lined the peninsula. As he was passing through one of their pristine private courtyards, under pouting balconies, Marcin's mobile phone started to ring: a short ladder of melody, climbing endlessly in the otherwise quiet night. He pulled the phone from his pocket and saw Phoebe's mobile number stamped across the screen.

He answered the call.

'Where are you, Marcin?'

'I've just got home,' he said.

Phoebe sighed. 'Aren't you coming here?'

Marcin could hear the sounds of a bar behind her. 'Where?'

'Gordon's. We're going to buy Anatol's present tonight. I told you about it. I sent you a text, two days ago.'

'I didn't get it.'

'Yes, you did. You replied.'

'What did I say?'

'You said: "OK".' Phoebe spoke each syllable separately. 'Are you coming or not?'

'I'll be there in an hour.'

Marcin checked his post on the way into his building. There was a single handwritten letter in his locker. He turned it over and examined both sides. It was addressed to him, in upper-case characters; the letters looked like they'd been drawn with a ruler. But there was no return address. And nothing else on the front except a first-class stamp, franked indistinctly.

Intrigued, Marcin went into one of the waiting lifts. He'd torn open the envelope before the doors had closed.

An hour later, Phoebe phoned again. 'Where are you, Marcin? We're waiting for you.'

Marcin was still in his flat, sitting in a black Nordic egg chair, with a glass of whisky in one hand and a cigarette in the other, staring across the river at the spidery pylons of the *Cutty Sark*. It was the first time he'd smoked in more than three weeks. His phone was held between his cheek and his shoulder.

'I'm sorry, Phoebe. I can't make it after all.' He coughed unconvincingly. 'I think I'm coming down with something . . .'

Marcin looked at the letter that he'd opened in the lift. A single sheet of white paper lay on his lap, his cigarette poised above it like a pen. There were two words written in the middle, in scratchy black capital letters.

'INSIDER TRADING,' they said.

Janika Turns Detective (continued)

After leaving Anatol in the kitchen, Janika went upstairs; she was passing the open door to Maya's bedroom when a voice called out to her, lethargic and low in volume:

'Janika? Is that you?'

Janika stopped and took a step back. 'How did you know?'

Maya was lying on the bed with her sleeves rolled up, squeezing a mosquito bite on her elbow. The curtains were open. Watery daylight flopped in through the window, bathing her in a subtle brightness.

'Your walk,' said Maya. 'Those small, stressful footsteps. You're not the only one that notices things.' She rolled on to her side and looked Janika up and down. The pillows had better posture than Maya. 'Where are you going in such a hurry?'

'I want to change my trousers.' Janika's grey tracksuit bottoms felt too informal for the evening. 'Dinner is almost ready.'

Maya curled into a sitting position. She picked up a pair of tweezers and clapped their ends together compulsively. 'Do you have anything I can pluck? Or pick?'

Janika entered the bedroom and walked to the window. 'I'm not a stringed instrument, Maya. Were you with Anatol last night?'

'Anatol?'

'Were you in his room?'

'I go to lots of different places at night.'

'What does that mean?'

Maya tapped her forehead. 'Dreams, Janika.'

'I'm talking about reality, Maya. You told me you heard a car this morning. But you said you could only see the end of the driveway. I can see the whole thing from here.' Janika leaned against the glass. The gravel drive was laid out in front of her like a litter tray. 'The only room with an obstructed view of the driveway is Anatol's bathroom. What were you doing there? I don't want gossip – I just want to know the truth.'

Maya lay back on the bed. 'Yes. I was there. Do you want a diagram?'

Sweat on the Mezzanine

It was a sweltering Tuesday afternoon in May; Anatol lifted his naked lower body off Maya's crushed abdomen and collapsed on to the bed beside her. He was sweating so much he felt like he'd been flayed alive, while Maya had almost drowned underneath him. She found a packet of cigarettes under the pillows, lit one and watched it burn down as her breathing steadied, then put it to her lips and let the hot smoke flood her lungs.

'I'm sorry I couldn't come to the funeral,' she said.

It was three and a half weeks since Gus had died.

'Are you?' said Anatol.

'I didn't like him, but he was your father.'

Maya's bed was a double mattress on the floor of her mezzanine, overlooking the artful squalor of her studio flat. Anatol, who was too tall for most conventional beds, had always found it uniquely comfortable: one of his feet was resting on the top step of the wooden staircase, the other was pressed against the low curved ceiling. He held out his hand for the cigarette and took a tentative drag; it left him light-headed. He passed the cigarette back and turned on to his stomach.

'There's no doubt about that,' he muttered.

A narrow planter hung from the mezzanine's shortened bannister, holding a trio of philodendrons. It normally doubled as Maya's ash tray, but when she was sharing the bed she couldn't quite reach it, trapped in the triangle between Anatol's splayed limbs and the wall. She shrugged and stubbed the cigarette out on the ceiling instead, where a pattern of black marks served as an accidental tally of her sexual encounters, then threw the acrid butt across Anatol's reclining body, over the bannister and towards the front door, where she knew she'd be able to find it later.

'I really didn't like him, though,' said Maya brightly. 'Sorry, but I'm a lousy liar.'

'You don't have to lie. I didn't ask.'

Anatol accounted for roughly half of the burns on Maya's ceiling. The two of them had come to an understanding a few years earlier: when they were both single at the same time, they would sleep together every few months. It was an arrangement that they kept entirely separate from their existing friendship; none of their other friends knew about it and they never met outside of Maya's flat or Anatol's bedroom.

'You didn't have anything to do with his death, did you?'

Anatol grunted and turned away from Maya. 'We don't talk, Maya. We just fuck. I thought we'd always agreed on that?'

A line of spots crossed Anatol's shoulders, following the collar of his absent shirt. The hot weather had given them a shine. Maya couldn't help herself: she dug her thumbnails into the one on the end and squeezed out its sebaceous root. It came out like a sesame seed.

'Normally,' she said. 'But this is important. I'll understand if you did, but I hope you didn't do it for my sake.'

Anatol winced as her nails broke his skin. 'I thought you wanted me to kill him?'

'I wanted him to die,' said Maya. 'That's not the same thing. And it was a passing thought. A long time ago.'

Anatol looked back at her and, in a moment of atypical tenderness, ran a sweaty hand through her hair. 'You don't actually think that I killed him, do you?'

The flat was silent, except for the sounds of central London that were coming in through the open windows: children playing around the Barbican complex and cars queuing on the surrounding roads.

'Not really,' said Maya, 'I just wanted to hear you say it.'

'I didn't murder my father. There. I've said it.'

Maya nodded; she felt she owed Anatol a change of subject. 'I think Yulie might be pregnant,' she said.

Anatol was welded to Maya's mattress by the heat. Ten minutes had passed; the sheets were sticky with half-dried sweat and dragged at his skin whenever he moved. He was lying on his side, keeping still, watching through the railings as Maya gathered her clothes from the floor below. She'd been wearing almost nothing when Anatol had arrived: a white T-shirt, wet at the armpits, and a pair of pink knickers, twisted into a rope around her hips, while Anatol had been cooking in his heavy tweed jacket. She found both garments on the sofa, then vanished below the edge of the mezzanine. The doorways to the flat's dinky kitchen and diminutive wet room were directly underneath.

Anatol waited until he could hear the steady hiss of the shower, then rolled on to his back and looked between his feet at a squat bedside cabinet at the end of the bed; it was the only piece of furniture on the mezzanine, besides the mattress. A magnifying mirror stood on top of it, rising from a crowd of accoutrements and old coffee mugs, showing him his long naked body upside down. When the sound of the shower changed to a halting, erratic drumming, as Maya stepped under the stream of hot water, Anatol pushed himself on to his knees and shuffled down to the end of the bed. He placed one hand against the curve of the ceiling, leaned across the cabinet, opened the bottom drawer and felt inside. A glass of tepid water trembled on top as he moved things around. He found what he was looking for underneath an old diary: the clammy friction of an elastic band, holding together a stack of Polaroid photographs.

Anatol pulled them out and checked the picture on top of the pile. It showed Maya and one of her previous partners, tangled together, intimately. Anatol counted the photographs – there were twelve – and placed the stack down on the mattress. He found his clothes in an undignified pile pushed up against the wall. Lying down again, he pulled on his underwear and his corduroy trousers, then he slid the photographs into one of the pockets.

Their corners pulled the fabric taut.

Janika Turns Detective (continued)

The door to the utility room yawned open; Dean searched for it in the mirror above the sink, but from where he was standing he could only see his own head and shoulders. He sensed Janika's shadow in his peripheral vision.

'I'm not interrupting anything, am I?' she asked. 'The door was unlocked. You're not being sick?'

'I'm decent,' said Dean, shaking water from his hands. 'I was just washing before dinner. Why? Did it sound like I was being sick?'

The door to the utility room came off the hallway, at the halfway point between the kitchen and the stairs. It was a small, windowless space, crowded with furnishings. An antique toilet cistern was bolted high on one wall, trailing its two pipes like a pair of stilts. A row of white goods, badly discoloured, stood opposite: there was a chest freezer, a washing machine and a tumble drier. Beside the toilet was a boxy enamel sink, with unlacquered brass taps. And beyond the sink a shower curtain marked out one corner of the floor as a shower. An ominous drain had been set into the tiles: lacking a grille, it was just an empty eye socket leading down into the earth.

'No.' Janika perched on the edge of the freezer. 'But you're hungover, aren't you?'

'Not particularly,' said Dean. 'I'm just tired. These days I find drinking more exhausting than exercise.'

'So why couldn't you pick me up from the station earlier?'

Dean caught his involuntary grimace in the mirror in front of him; he corrected it quickly. 'I was hungover then. I'd woken up with a headache. But I feel a lot better now.'

'You didn't seem particularly hungover when I got here.'

'Not outwardly, maybe. But I was hungover on the inside.'

Janika shook her head. 'On the phone you told me it hurt to look at the light. But then you sat with me while I was unpacking, looking out of the window the whole time.'

'You didn't give me much choice, Janika. Your room isn't exactly roomy.'

'The sky was bright. But the light didn't seem to bother you then.'

'Where are you going with this?' Dean leaned over the sink and splashed water on his face, then took his time turning off the tap; the elongated squeak was slow and excruciating. 'The truth is I'd had lunch between the two, Janika, between you calling me and you coming here. Eating something made me feel a lot better.'

'Lunch?' said Janika.

'Hangovers can be fickle things.'

Janika rolled her eyes. 'You're hiding something, Dean. That letter you showed me earlier. Phoebe has the matching envelope. Is there something going on between you?'

The Applauding Tarpaulin

'Goodbye, Janika. I'll see you soon.'

Dean stood in the dark nook beside the staircase, early on Sunday afternoon, hoping his voice wouldn't carry to the drawing room. He was leaning against the grandfather clock: a mahogany box, two inches taller than him and a notch less narrow. He could have been leaning against his own coffin. The phone line went dead in his hand. 'Janika?' he said.

But Janika was gone.

Dean was attached to the wall by the red thread of the telephone cable. He picked his way through the indistinct furniture, towards the light, hung up the phone and then immediately took it off the hook again. He wiped the sweat from his palms and dialled his home number. He let it ring for a minute, but nobody answered. Out of habit, he glanced at the clock. Noon, it said. But it was just after one.

Dean replaced the phone and went to the window. The sky was a ridged, pitted white: it looked cold but at least there was no chance of rain. He continued to the drawing room and found Phoebe there, sitting in front of a full cafetière with both hands wrapped around it, watching the coffee grounds swirling inside, waiting for the optimal moment to depress the plunger. The liquid looked brown enough to Dean already.

'We've got an hour,' he said. 'Let's make the most of it.'

Phoebe glanced up at him. 'Who was that on the phone?'

'Janika,' said Dean. 'She's been waiting at the station. She's going to walk here. Wherever Anatol went, he's not with her.'

'Why is she walking? Didn't you offer her a lift?'

Dean shook his head, his lips pressed tightly together. 'She wanted to walk,' he said. 'Maya's in the bath. It's just the two of us, Phoebe. Do you want to go upstairs?'

Phoebe opened her mouth; she considered the question, spinning the cafetière slowly. 'I want to. But what if Marcin comes back?'

'We'll hear his car.'

'Somebody knows about us,' said Phoebe. 'What if we're being watched?'

Dean tried a smile. 'They can't find out twice.'

'But they could cause a scene.'

'I know somewhere we can go. Somewhere private, outside. We can have the coffee when we come back. It'll warm us up. When else will we get a whole hour to ourselves?'

Where his shirt had pulled away from his trousers, Phoebe could see the stark lines of Dean's abdominal muscles, rounding the tops of his hips like antlers. Her anxiety melted in the face of her desire. She reached out and pressed down on the handle of the cafetière: the steady motion was like a sigh of resignation.

'All right,' she said. 'Where are you taking me?'

'Empty your pockets,' said Dean. 'That way nothing will get ruined, in case it starts raining again.'

Phoebe patted the sides of her jeans impatiently. 'Nothing,' she echoed.

Dean was crouched by the back door; he'd paused over a pair of brogues that were unlikely to survive the conditions outside: it wasn't raining but the grass was still wet. But there was no time to tie plastic bags around his feet. Phoebe opened the door and stepped out on to the flagstones.

'One second,' said Dean. He tied his laces feverishly, getting minuscule friction burns on his fingers, then followed her out of the house; Phoebe had already reached the end of the patio.

'I don't want to risk being seen,' she said. 'Where are we going?' She was wearing a pair of Anatol's wellington boots. They were far too big for her. She had to swing her legs out to the side with each step, so they wouldn't come off.

'Not far,' said Dean.

He placed a hand on Phoebe's arm and led her to the edge of the property, where a wooden fence separated the garden from an adjoining patch of woodland. Dean climbed over and jumped down into the coarse vegetation on the other side, frowning as his shoes sank into mud. He helped Phoebe over the fence, took a moment to get his bearings, then guided her forwards.

Phoebe looked back and watched the house disappear. 'Is it much further?'

Dean moved behind her and put a hand over her mouth. 'Don't ask questions,' he said playfully. He put his other hand over her eyes. 'It's a surprise.'

Nudging her shoulders with his elbows, Dean managed to move her forwards while he steered her using her head. It was a clumsy endeavour: there is nothing more excruciatingly graceless than the sight of someone trying to make the world match a fantasy they've only imagined. But Phoebe liked the feeling of Dean's forearms on her shoulders and tolerated it until she couldn't any longer. She wriggled her face free, then felt she should say something to justify her escape. 'This is pretty. Did you do this?'

They'd reached a small hidden clearing, about twenty metres from the end of the garden. A vivid blue tarpaulin was tied to three of the surrounding trees, a metre and a half above the ground. Its fourth corner was loose and kept lifting into the air, folding over on itself. It was clapping in the wind. A second, matching tarpaulin had been placed on the ground underneath.

Dean picked up the lower sheet and shook it out, then took off his jacket and laid it down. '*Et voilà*,' he said. 'The coat d'Azur. I made this shelter with Anatol, years ago. We wanted somewhere scenic to smoke . . . you know . . . out of sight of his father. I came out here yesterday and fixed it up.'

'I didn't know you knew how.'

'I'm an engineer,' said Dean, recoiling slightly. 'That's my job.'

'I know that,' said Phoebe. 'But not with your hands.'

Dean looked down at his palms; he shrugged and started to unbutton his trousers. 'Well, I used to be a boy scout.'

'Do you know if somebody owns these woods?'

'Probably. We can go back if you want?'

Phoebe watched him undress. 'No, I don't want that.'

Dean kicked off his tattered brogues, then stepped out of his trousers on to the tarpaulin. He reached down and took something from one of the pockets. It was a damp pack of chewing gum, with a condom hidden inside.

Phoebe took off Anatol's monstrous boots and joined him on the mat. She knelt and helped ease his boxer shorts down past his thighs. The fourth corner of the hanging tarpaulin flapped frantically in the wind, applauding every movement. Dean was half erect. A hanging thread of sticky gossamer liquid joined the tip of his penis to the waistband of his underwear. Phoebe wiped it away.

'Like a spider,' said Dean, 'ready to spin a web inside you.'

Phoebe stood up. She sandwiched Dean's face between her two hands. 'Dean,' she said. 'I need you to understand this. Spiders aren't sexy . . .'

Twenty minutes later, they were lying naked on the tarpaulin with their elbows behind them and their torsos raised, watching tiny insects cross their bodies in short, exploratory arcs. Phoebe felt too exhausted to pick them off, but she kept an eye out for any that might bite. Dean found the used condom stuck to his knee. He tied a knot in it and threw it into the bushes, where it would linger for years, like a time capsule.

'I've got one left,' he said. 'It would be a shame to waste it. Do you think we'll get another chance?'

'Tonight,' said Phoebe. 'When everyone else is asleep. I'll make more coffee. Do you think you can stay awake?'

'Wild horses couldn't put me to bed.' Dean leaned across and kissed Phoebe's neck. 'But there's something I need to tell you first. Yulie's pregnant.'

A sudden surge of wind in the leaves above them sounded like radio static; all Phoebe had heard was a detuned voice. 'What did you say?'

Dean rolled on to his side, facing away from her. 'She's pregnant,' he said. 'You're going to be an aunt. I thought it was better that you hear it from me. But try and look surprised when she tells you.'

The next few seconds passed in silence. Dean traced lines in the soil. Then he felt Phoebe's arm around his waist, her palm pressed flat against his skin, her face against his narrow back. The gentle spike of her nose in his spine.

'I'm sorry,' said Phoebe. 'Who's the father?'

Dean understood her caresses then and took Phoebe's wrist in his hand, ready to flounce out of her embrace as though it was an ill-fitting robe. But he did nothing so confrontational. He was trapped between her and the ground, anyway.

'Me,' he said. 'I'm the father.'

'Oh.' Phoebe's grip slackened. 'Are you sure?'

She felt Dean's muscles shift as he shrugged. Then he moved her hand down and held it next to his stomach. 'Sure enough not to have given it any thought until now. Why would you think that I wasn't the father?'

Phoebe pulled herself free of his grasp. 'Did she say that you were?'

'No. But I didn't ask. She implied it.'

'How?'

'Wouldn't she have said if I wasn't?'

Phoebe sat up. She started to get dressed. Then she picked up a leaf and began pulling it apart. 'It's just that three weeks ago you said the marriage was in trouble. That you weren't even sleeping together. That she was sleeping with someone else. And now she's pregnant?'

Dean rolled over and watched her dress. The reasonableness of Phoebe's position frustrated him. 'That's all true,' he said. 'But it happened before that. Before I found out about the affair. It happened about ten weeks ago. And it takes a month to materialize, doesn't it? That's when Yulie found out. That's why she told me about Declan, so we could wipe the slate clean. It all fits together. You see?'

Phoebe's face was as blank as the sky behind her. 'She told you about Declan because I told her she had to. She didn't have a choice. Has she been to the doctor?'

'Yes,' said Dean.

'Did you go with her?'

'No. Why would I do that?'

Phoebe pulled on her jeans. The light had grown stronger in the last ten minutes, while the clouds were thinning. Shadows had formed in the hollows of her body. 'Where is she this weekend? She doesn't really have a cold?'

'She just didn't feel up to coming. And she can't drink alcohol anyway. It's hard work being pregnant.'

'That sounds like something Yulie would say.'

'It is what she said.'

'Aren't you worried she's with him?'

'Declan? You don't think he's the father?' Dean laughed out loud; it was high-pitched and forced. 'Who gets pregnant from an affair with a colleague?'

'I don't believe she's actually pregnant.'

'What do you mean?'

'She's lying, Dean. She told you she was pregnant so you wouldn't leave her. She cheats on you, the pregnancy brings the two of you back together, then something goes wrong. She's distraught. You can't leave her then.'

Dean didn't like the asymmetry in their states of undress. He felt vulnerable. He pulled on his pants and trousers. 'Maya knows too,' he said. 'She told me Yulie wasn't drinking, the last time they saw each other.'

'So she's a method liar. I know my own sister.'

'I'd like to think that I do too.' Dean belted his trousers and looked down at Phoebe: she was curled into a ball on the blue tarpaulin, clutching the tattered stem of a leaf. 'You're jealous,' he said.

'So what if I am?' said Phoebe.

'Is this just sex? Or is there something more going on? You know I've always had feelings for you.'

Phoebe shook her head. 'I don't know, Dean. But I think there might be.'

Janika Turns Detective (continued)

Phoebe looked cocooned inside her clothes: a colourful cable-knit jumper and a pair of faded blue jeans. She was lying face down on the bed, with her hands by her side. The sun was low in the sky and the bottle full of flowers that she'd brought in from the garden and placed on the windowsill cast a smeared green shadow across her back.

'What are you doing?' asked Janika, watching from the doorway.

'Nothing,' said Phoebe, as she turned on to her side. 'I was just resting my eyes. Is it time for that drink you wanted?'

'It's time for dinner.' Janika crossed the narrow room in a single step and sat down in the space between Phoebe's knees and her stomach. The bed tilted away from the wall; only three of its legs were touching the floor. 'Everybody's been lying to me, Phoebe. What's going on? Don't you want me here?'

Phoebe sat up at the implied accusation, placing a hand on the wall for support. 'I haven't,' she said.

'Haven't you?' asked Janika.

'What have I been lying about?'

'You told me that Marcin took the stories with him when he went up to bed. And that he went to bed before you. But Marcin was still awake when Maya went down for a cigarette in the middle of the night.'

'How do you know?'

'Because Maya told me.'

The white paint was webbed with fractures. Phoebe picked a flake from the wall and flicked it to the floor. It spun like an umbrella. 'Maybe Maya is lying. Maybe she took the stories.'

'Then you didn't see Marcin take them?'

'I did,' said Phoebe. 'Or I thought I did. But maybe he came downstairs again after I'd gone to bed. I don't know. I was just trying to be helpful, Janika.' She shook her head and ran a hand through her hair. 'I was drunk anyway. What difference does it make?'

A Desperate Act

It was late on Saturday night. Anatol had gone to bed, after reading out the first three stories. The power was still out and so were most of the candles. Maya, Marcin and Phoebe were sitting in the drawing room, banded with shadows. 'If I was actually going to kill someone,' Maya was saying, 'I'd take them somewhere remote, like the woods. One of those big woods like in Norway or North America, where you can get lost for weeks. I'd chain them to a tree, then I'd just walk away. No violence. No noise. No physical exertion . . .'

'That's cruel,' said Phoebe.

'It is,' said Maya. 'But why would I be kind to someone I'm killing?'

Maya stood up and stretched and yawned; it was the most energetic thing she'd done all day. 'I need to lie down,' she said. 'I'm going to bed.'

'Can you leave the cigarettes?' said Marcin. 'I'll replace them tomorrow.'

It was the first thing he'd said in more than ten minutes.

Maya picked up the cigarettes that were on the table and tossed them towards Marcin, too tired to take aim. They hit his chair, bounced off the arm and landed in the shadows under the sofa. 'Help yourself,' she said. 'They're on the floor somewhere.'

Then Maya left, leaving Marcin with Phoebe.

'Do you want another drink?' asked Phoebe as she shuffled along the couch towards him.

Marcin shook his head, tilting his bottle to show it was still half full. 'It's not like you to stay up this late. Has Dean gone to bed?'

Phoebe nodded; she looked at the stack of stories on the table. 'I won't be able to sleep,' she said. 'With all this talk of murder. I'll have bad dreams.'

'Just picture yourself somewhere peaceful, like the woods.'

Anatol had finished reading the stories a few hours earlier. He would read out the other three on Sunday night; they'd agreed to wait until then to discuss them. He'd left the three that he'd read on the coffee table. The white pages stood out clearly in the unlit room. Their broken red letters looked like tiny bite marks.

'You won't get any sympathy from me,' Marcin continued. 'It was you that wanted to play this game.'

'Anatol wanted to play,' said Phoebe. 'I just went along with it. Now I wish that I hadn't. I'll be up all night.'

'I wish that you hadn't too.' Marcin let the next minute pass in silence, then he reached out and moved the nearest candle further away from them. The light on both of their faces faded. It was a weak kind of privacy, but it made Marcin more comfortable. He sounded desperate. 'Are you blackmailing me, Phoebe?'

'Blackmailing you?' Phoebe had been holding an empty wine glass. She put it down on the sofa and let it fall on to its side. 'Why on earth would you ask me that?'

Marcin shrugged and swigged his beer. 'Someone is.'

'Who?'

'I don't know. Dean or Anatol. Maybe Maya. I didn't really think it was you. You're far too boring.'

'I'll take that as a compliment,' said Phoebe. 'What are you being blackmailed about?'

'I can't tell you. That's what makes it blackmail.'

'Someone's probably playing a joke on you, Marcin.' Phoebe brought her legs up on to the sofa. The glass rolled beneath her shins. 'Either way, I don't think we should be having this conversation drunk.'

Marcin made a point of raising his bottle. 'Ask me tomorrow, then.' He looked up at the ceiling and drank.

Phoebe leaned over the nearest candle. She breathed on it discreetly and the room went dark. 'Where's the lighter?' she asked. 'The candle's gone out.'

'With the cigarettes,' said Marcin. 'They went on the floor somewhere.'

'Can you find them?' said Phoebe.

'All right. Hang on.'

While Marcin sniffed out the cigarettes, Phoebe took the stories from the centre of the table. She felt for their staples, checking that she'd got all three of them, then folded them twice and pressed them into the pocket of her jeans. She pulled down her jumper to cover the lump. 'Don't worry about it, Marcin,' she said. 'It's time I went to bed anyway . . .'

When she got to her feet, the wine glass fell to the floor and smashed.

Toast

Only two things were discussed during dinner on Sunday night: Janika's new life in Australia and Anatol's hypothetical new house.

'Let's have a toast,' said Anatol, 'to Janika's promotion.'

The corralled friends crowded the dining table. Anatol stood towering above them, almost touching his glass to the ceiling. Dean and Phoebe were slumped in their seats, while Maya was sitting sideways with her legs resting on the chair next to hers. All three of them lifted their glasses.

Janika was sitting opposite Anatol; her feet were perched on the edge of her chair. She wrapped her arms around her knees. 'I wanted a drink, Anatol. Not a drink in my honour. And it's not a promotion. It's a new job.'

'If I'd known we'd have something to celebrate,' said Anatol, 'I'd have bought another bottle of champagne. But I wasn't expecting you to make it here. Not coming all the way from Australia.'

'I told you I was coming. I told you what time train I was getting. You were supposed to pick me up from the station, not cheer me on from the sidelines.'

'Yes. Well. I've apologized for that already, haven't I?'

'Then toast yourself,' Janika whispered. 'It's your thirtieth.'

'I think the toast might be done,' said Dean. His arm was still raised and was starting to ache. 'It might even be burning by now.'

'We're all here,' said Phoebe. 'Why don't we toast to that instead?'

'Except Marcin,' said Janika.

Phoebe rolled her eyes. 'Do you want a drink or a fist-fight?' Without waiting for an answer, she took a swig of champagne. 'Who else could turn a toast into an argument?'

The others followed Phoebe's lead. Maya tried to drink without bothering to lift her head from her arm, spilling champagne over her chin and sleeve; Dean drank a mouthful and gagged as his latent hangover came flooding back; Anatol sipped his champagne indifferently, as if it was water. It was only Janika that didn't drink. Her arms stayed locked around her knees.

'I'm only arguing,' she said, 'because I don't want to move to Australia. I have to, for work, but I don't want to. I don't know anyone there.' Janika swallowed her champagne in one. 'And you know I'm no good at making friends. The five of you are the only real friends I've ever had.'

Post Toast

A leaden sunset poisoned the sky, turning it first yellow then briefly blue then grey again and finally black; Janika excused herself to use the bathroom. While the others stayed in the drawing room, making paper cuts in their glasses of champagne, she stole upstairs to Phoebe's bedroom. Her emotions had been genuine, but there were still questions she wanted answered. Who was blackmailing who? And what had happened to Marcin? She searched the drawers of Phoebe's desk in the waning light, then looked underneath her pillows. Finally, with only a little reluctance, she knelt on the floor and pulled Phoebe's tan leather travelling bag from under the bed.

'I'm sorry, Phoebe,' she whispered to herself. 'But you lied about Marcin taking those stories, didn't you?'

She unbuckled the bag. Inside were a number of pieces of white A4 paper, covered in red ink. Janika pulled them out and flicked through the sheets. They separated into three stories of a few pages each, stapled together. Janika laid them on the bed, then closed the bag and nudged it back into the darkness.

She got up and moved to the window, taking the stories with her. The corridor outside stood silent and slack-jawed. Janika had left the door open, so that she would be forewarned if anyone came up the stairs. 'So what were you hiding?'

Without turning the lights on, relying only on the twilight

coming through the curtains, Janika held the first page a few inches from her face and started to read. But the paper looked like a pillow in the dim light; inevitably, her head started to droop.

Bad dreams hurtled towards her.

The Glass House

Art has a thousand different faces and death is one and disaster another. Early on Sunday morning, Phoebe was presented with a view of both. The Victorian glasshouse at the end of Anatol's garden was on fire. He had been using it, over the preceding few weeks, as a place to store some of his father's belongings. They'd been packed into cardboard boxes and stacked in towers near the door. The few plants that remained between the boxes had long dried out. It was his father's items and the plants that were burning fiercely; the building itself refused to light. The eight-sided oblong frame of the glasshouse was made of cast iron and stood on a knee-high base of bricks and mortar. Both the frame and the base were painted white. The panes of glass set into the antique frame were no more than one foot by two feet each. On a normal day the glasshouse would have been a froth of tiny white windows. But on the morning of Anatol's birthday, tall, papery flames filled the transparent structure, turning it into an ornate box of light, like a cut jewel or gemstone, tinted pink and orange, while soft white smoke daubed its empty corners with shifting, pearlescent textures. The sight evoked the human heart, imprisoned inside its ribcage, or maybe the trapped tigers at Marwell Zoo. Or was it a glowing yolk and albumen?

It was just unfortunate that the glasshouse hadn't been empty when the fire had started.

*

Marcin had been in the glasshouse, searching Gus's belongings for anything incriminating – diaries, accounts, letters or confessions – while Phoebe had been keeping watch outside. She'd heard a sound like a sudden gust of wind and turned just in time to see a burning tower of boxes collapse, taking two others with it.

'What happened?' asked Phoebe.

'I don't know,' said Marcin, still in shock. 'I tried to light a cigarette and it just exploded. It smells like someone spilled paraffin in here.'

There was a waist-high pile of rubble between them, blocking the doorway. It was burning brightly.

Marcin was trapped inside.

'Can't you get out?' asked Phoebe over the top of the blaze.

Marcin shook his head. He pulled off his jumper and wrapped it around his right hand. With this cashmere gauntlet, he started picking up boxes and throwing them towards the back of the glasshouse. 'No,' he said. 'Help me clear a path.'

But although those boxes that were only smoking could be moved easily, those that were fully on fire fell apart as Marcin handled them. Soon his jumper was in flames, abandoned on the floor, and his unprotected hands were throbbing, heavy with the weight of blood rushing into them. Marcin squeezed his tongue between his teeth. He was used to the pain of incidental burns, being a smoker, but he'd never seen his palms so shiny before. He could almost signal with them. He held them up high and waved them at Phoebe. 'Go and get a spade or something. Help me move this stuff out the way.'

'All right.' Phoebe looked around the garden. 'I'll be back soon. Just stay positive.'

'That implies I'm positive now.'

There was a long wooden trestle table running down one side of the glasshouse, with more boxes on top of it and several old plants. Marcin tipped it on to its side, sending dead leaves and plant pots flying, then took hold of its legs and turned it upside down. With one foot underneath the table, Marcin tried to use its far end as a large ineffectual shovel, pushing the burning boxes out through the door. But the table was unwieldy and most of the boxes had lost their definition. They fell apart when Marcin nudged them. Both of his hands started to bleed. He'd barely made a dent in the heap by the time the table itself had caught fire.

Marcin moved to the back wall of the glasshouse, away from the flames, and watched for Phoebe through the clouded windows. He couldn't see her anywhere. He looked around for anything else that he might be able to use as a spade, but it hurt to keep his eyes open. They felt as if they'd been dabbed with sandpaper. And his mouth tasted of charcoal. The whole glasshouse was growing thick with smoke. When Marcin breathed in deeply, it was like someone forcing a melted car tyre down his throat. 'Where are you, Phoebe?'

He kicked off his brogues and picked them up and slid his flattened hands inside them; then he punched out the windows along the back of the frame. He put his face to one of the now empty rectangles and inhaled rapidly. But the smoke continued to build behind him. Every breath still burned. Marcin climbed up the bars, closed his eyes and broke six of the panes of glass in the ceiling, flailing blindly with the heel of his shoe. Large shards of glass went crashing to the floor. But the panes above the fire were still intact, causing the smoke to spread sideways. He was still struggling to breathe. Desperate, he hurled both his brogues at a sheet of glass directly above the flames, but he missed twice and they bounced instead from one of the cast-iron bars and landed in the fire, blackened, and then shrank.

'Where the fuck are you, Phoebe?'

Marcin felt a few droplets of water tap him on the shoulder. He turned and saw Phoebe approaching, holding a garden hose. In her other hand she was clutching a rake.

'What took you so long?'

'The shed was locked,' said Phoebe. 'But I think I can move the boxes with this.'

'Don't worry about that,' said Marcin, each word coming out with a cough. He lifted his T-shirt over his mouth. 'Smash the glass, Phoebe. Let the smoke escape.'

Phoebe passed Marcin the hose and walked in a circle around the glasshouse, stabbing at it wherever she saw a pane of glass intact and retreating each time she needed to breathe. The hose was old and mouldy and the water coming from it tasted of rubber, but Marcin's throat was glowing. He raised it to his head and soaked himself, then tried spraying water over the fire. But it didn't seem to have much effect. The spray was too weak and the fire too big.

Marcin grabbed hold of Phoebe on her second lap, leaving a red handprint on her bright white jumper. 'Smash the ceiling,' he said. 'The smoke is going upwards.'

Phoebe looked above his head. 'Smash the glass ceiling,' she echoed, trying to lighten the mood. 'I didn't have you down as a feminist, Marcin.'

'This is serious, Phoebe. I'm going to die in here.'

Phoebe shrank back. 'I'm sorry, Marcin,' she said sadly. 'I've called the fire brigade. They'll be here soon. I'm sure you'll be fine.'

Without waiting to hear his response, Phoebe started to circle the building, thrusting the rake at the glass in the ceiling. But the angles were all wrong and she only managed to break a single pane. A thin thread of smoke corkscrewed into the sky.

Marcin stopped her again. 'Let me do it.' He yanked the rake away from Phoebe. The handle turned slippery with his blood. Marcin held its steel end over the flames, aiming it at the ceiling. But the long thin panes were harder to hit than he'd been expecting. They weren't much wider than the head of the rake. And everything in front of him was obscured by smoke. After trying for almost half a minute, he finally heard the sound of breaking glass. But by that point the wooden part of the rake was burned almost black.

He hit an iron bar and it broke apart.

Marcin turned to the frame behind him. The empty windows were roughly one foot by two feet. Marcin thought he might as well try and squeeze through one of them, though he knew it would be impossible. He'd tried everything else. Leaning down, he managed to get his head and an arm out, but his chest was too broad and his shoulders were too wide. He tried lifting the frame instead, but it wouldn't budge. Then he kicked at the bricks underneath, until his toes turned numb and cold and wet. He stepped back and stood on broken glass. Blood formed a puddle around his feet.

'Phoebe?' he shouted.

*

Marcin was standing in the corner of the glasshouse. He had been throwing things at the ceiling for more than a minute. Fragments of plant pots and old picture frames. But he hadn't been able to hit anything. He ran out of items and looked around for Phoebe. She'd gone somewhere to get more tools. But Marcin couldn't see her. The smoke was too dense. He crouched down and coughed and coughed. Every breath was now inadequate and painful. The heat inside had built up, too. It was like a weight pressing on his forehead and face, so hard that it tore and blistered the skin. His eyes were streaming, his eyelids acid. The situation seemed utterly hopeless.

It occurred to Marcin then that he should have run for the exit when the fire had started, scrambling over anything that stood in his way. Even if it had meant burning his legs or having his feet amputated or kissing his testicles goodbye. At least he would have survived. But that's the thing about fire. It turns every inconsequential decision you make into an instrument of torture and regret.

Phoebe's silhouette appeared like a vision, her small hands wrapped around the thin white bars. 'Marcin?' she said. 'Anatol's coming. He'll know what to do.'

'It's too late.' Marcin could hardly speak.

'Don't say that.' Phoebe sounded anxious. 'I didn't mean for any of this to happen, Marcin. I was just trying to teach you a lesson with the paraffin. You're not supposed to be smoking, are you? I was trying to help you quit. It was a bad idea. I see that now . . .'

Anger made Marcin stand up. He reached for Phoebe's hands but she backed away from the bars.

'You're not angry with me, are you?'

Marcin turned to face the door. He couldn't see it

through the cottony smoke, but he knew roughly where it was. He touched his back to the grid behind him and centred himself, facing straight ahead. The door must have been directly in front of him. What other possible hope did he have?

'I'm going to kill you, Phoebe,' he said loudly, but she couldn't hear him over the ravenous flames.

Then he held his breath and dashed forwards, as fast as he could, into the orb of orange and smoke. On his third step he fell.

It was like falling into boiling water.

*A NOTE FOUND TORN INTO SEVERAL
     PIECES (CONTINUED)*

*You should blame the taxman for what
happened to Marcin.*
 Or blame Marcin himself.
 *He is ultimately responsible for
his own decisions.*

PART FIVE
Truth

SUNDAY
30 May 1999

The Last Two Names

The telephone in Anatol's house started to ring late on Sunday evening. The shrill sound filled the dark hallway like a blinking neon sign. Janika had finished reading the three missing stories a few minutes earlier, sitting next to the lamp in Phoebe's bedroom, and her eyes were yet to adjust to the darkness. But she was wide awake with outrage. She walked past the ringing telephone and continued along the corridor, keeping a careful watch on the corner ahead of her, in case Anatol swung clumsily from the direction of the drawing room and collided with her in the low light. When she reached the safety of the drawing room doorway, she looked inside the brightly lit room. Anatol was kneeling by the window, fiddling with the telescope; he didn't seem to have noticed the phone.

Phoebe was watching him with her arms crossed. 'Aren't you going to answer that?'

'It won't be anything important,' said Anatol.

'It might be Marcin,' said Maya; she and Dean were sprawled on the two couches in the middle of the room, with magazines open on their laps. 'How about this one?'

Maya held her magazine upright, showing a page filled with glossy pictures of rural properties, and pointed at one of them.

'That willow tree is too close to the house,' said Dean, shaking his head. 'Its roots have probably wrecked the foundations. Weeping willow means weeping home-owner . . .'

Janika walked through their conversation and went to the display cabinet. She pulled firmly on the doors and felt a thin piece of wood break inside. The cabinet came open. Janika turned the two martini glasses over, took her names from the silver tray and unfolded them.

The phone stopped ringing. 'Anatol,' said Janika. 'I think we need to talk.'

Janika Turns Judge

The only light in the kitchen came from the moon.

'I don't think I'm meant to be a part of this story.' Janika was standing facing the window; Anatol was sitting at the table in front of her, drinking a glass of milk. 'This is a story about blackmail,' Janika continued. 'And you don't have anything to blackmail me with.'

She had folded the stories into the pocket of her cardigan, where they'd sprung open almost immediately. A triangular bulge jutted from her hip, hidden by the kitchen table.

Anatol chose his words carefully. 'I'm not sure what you mean.'

'There's no point denying it, Anatol.' Janika brought out the three stories and flattened them on her abdomen, then laid them on the table. 'I've read the stories you wrote. These are the three from last night. I understand now why Marcin had the same victim as Maya. He wasn't the only one, was he?' Janika showed him the names that she'd taken from the display cabinet: Phoebe in red and Marcin in green. 'I've worked it all out.'

Anatol flicked through the stories, then put them down. 'All right. I fold,' he said. 'I don't have any cards left to play, Janika. Except maybe the birthday card. You can't be angry with me on my birthday, can you? Not for something that was just a joke.'

'It wasn't a joke,' said Janika. 'It was a blackmail attempt.

I want you to tell me everything, Anatol. Then I'll decide how angry I am.'

Anatol shrugged; his wide shoulders moved in front of the moon. 'Where do you want me to start?'

'At the beginning. What happened at the station this morning?'

Anatol sighed. 'I was waiting there when you arrived, Janika. I was hiding in the bushes next to the car park. I watched your train pull in. But I didn't think you'd be on it. I'd left the phone here unplugged all night. I knew you would try to call and confirm, before you set off. I thought if nobody answered then you wouldn't bother coming.' Anatol cupped the flesh around his left nipple. 'My heart sank when I saw you step on to the platform. I watched you stand there for thirty minutes, like a little lost dog. I thought you were waiting for the next train back to London. Then you used the payphone. I thought you'd called a taxi. I didn't think you'd actually walk here.'

'A taxi would have taken thirty minutes to arrive. What did you do after I'd left?'

'Does it matter?' asked Anatol.

'I told you,' said Janika. 'I want to know everything.'

'I waited in Tisbury until the next train came, then the one after that. I went to a café and had a cappuccino and some cake. It's my golden birthday, Janika. I'm entitled to a piece of cake.' Anatol dug into the pocket of his blazer and pulled out a pointed nubbin of something dark brown, wrapped in a white paper napkin, dappled grey with grease. 'I've been saving that for later.'

'Cake?' Janika closed her eyes. 'Anatol, couldn't you have come up with a plan that didn't inconvenience me quite so much?'

'I told you. I didn't think you'd be on that train. I thought you'd take the chance to go home and sleep. You must be exhausted?'

Janika opened her eyes. 'Don't you want me here, then? You didn't reply to any of my emails. Were you trying to discourage me from coming?'

'Is that what's bothering you?' Anatol unwrapped the napkin; inside it was a thin slice of chocolate cake. 'I haven't been to the library lately. That's why I didn't reply to your emails. I've been too busy. It was nothing personal. Here, have this. We can bury the hatchet.' Anatol grinned shamelessly as he picked up the piece of cake and mimed chopping wood with it, before sliding it across the table to Janika. 'It might be a bit dry, but it should taste all right.'

Janika prodded the cake cautiously; then she picked it up and bit off the blade. 'That's what was bothering me this afternoon,' she said, her mouth full. 'Now I'm more bothered by you blackmailing our friends.'

'That wasn't anything personal either. I just needed the money.'

'They're your friends, Anatol. They're my friends too.'

'But they're not innocent, Janika. That's why I'm blackmailing them.'

'It has to stop.' Janika tapped the stories. 'You have to end this.'

'It's already ended. It never really began. It's not even blackmail, if you don't ask for money. That's what you said to me earlier, isn't it?'

Janika shook her head. 'It ends with you telling the others what you've done. You're going to gather them in the drawing room, sit them down in a circle and tell them everything. You owe them that.'

'That would mean revealing their secrets. How would that help anyone?'

'We're all friends here,' said Janika. 'If you don't do it, I'll do it myself.'

A glib smile lit Anatol's face. 'In that case, you can do it.' He pushed the stack of stories across the table; crumbs caught under their pages. 'You're a philosopher, Janika. You're far better at explaining things than I am.'

'Where are the other stories? The ones you didn't read out.'

Anatol reached into one of his oversized pockets and pulled out a stack of about twenty pages, folded up small. 'There.'

Janika picked up both sets of stories and set off towards the drawing room; she stopped in the archway and looked back. 'Aren't you coming with me?'

Anatol finished his glass of milk. 'I'm going to need a stronger drink.'

The First Three Stories

Janika wove her way through the furniture and sat down on the rug in front of the fireplace, making the coffee table her makeshift desk; she rested both arms on it and placed her chin in her hands. Her elbows drilled down into the wood.

'Marcin's being blackmailed,' she muttered.

She had no desire to stand and deliver a speech.

Dean lowered his magazine, leaving a finger on the page to mark his progress; Maya turned on to her side and tucked a hand under the sofa cushions; Phoebe left the telescope alone and leaned over the back of the green couch; all three of them were looking at Janika.

'By who?' asked Phoebe.

'Anatol,' said Janika. 'That's why Marcin went home this morning.'

'Anatol's actually blackmailing him? It's not just a joke? He wants Marcin to give him money?'

Janika nodded. 'Actual blackmail.'

'How do you know?' asked Dean.

'I worked it out.'

Maya was keen to ask the obvious question. 'So what's he being blackmailed over? It must be something serious.'

Janika pulled the stories from the pocket of her cardigan and placed them on the table in front of her. She picked one of them up and showed it to the group.

'It's all in this story,' she said. 'Marcin murders Maya by

pushing her head on to the prong of a sundial. He does it because she's been telling people that he's guilty of insider trading. There's a company mentioned, called Regex Trade. But Regex Trade is a real company.'

'How do you know?' asked Dean.

'Because I buy the *Financial Times*, for the crossword. Marcin really is guilty of insider trading. Maya hasn't been murdered, obviously. But the rest of the story is surprisingly accurate. It was Anatol that wrote it.'

Anatol's story was called 'The Sundial'. It had started, plausibly enough, with Marcin and Maya smoking outside. As they'd walked across the overgrown garden, to a stone sundial at the centre of the lawn, Marcin had accused Maya of spilling his secrets and telling people that he was guilty of insider trading. Patronizing Maya in her final moments, Marcin had explained the meaning of the word 'gnomon' ('this bit that sticks up') before pressing Maya's head down on to the sundial. The story had ended with a lengthy description of the passage of the gnomon through Maya's brain, written with the help of a dusty mid-century book on anatomy that Anatol had found in his father's room.

'That was the only story I liked,' said Dean. 'It's the only one I wasn't in.'

'This story,' Janika continued, 'was Anatol's way of letting Marcin know that he knew what he'd done. That he knew about Regex Trade.'

'How would Anatol know that?' asked Phoebe, sounding slightly insulted. 'I don't know about it and I'm usually the one that knows things. Don't tell me Anatol reads the *Financial Times*.'

'He knows because I told him,' said Maya. 'And Marcin told me. That part of the story was true, although I didn't realize I was doing anything wrong.'

Phoebe came around to the front of the couch. 'Where did you get these stories, Janika?'

'It's better that you don't ask, Phoebe.'

Dean shook his head. 'This still sounds more like a practical joke than actual blackmail, Janika. Anatol's always had a dark sense of humour. He was probably just playing with Marcin. Maybe Marcin overreacted?'

Maya pulled her hand out from inside the sofa, savouring the rasp of crumbs as it came. 'Someone sent him a note,' she said, pushing herself upright. 'Marcin told me that last night.'

'What kind of note?' asked Dean.

'He didn't say, except that it was sent anonymously, written in black capital letters.'

Dean turned to Phoebe. 'But that sounds like ...' Phoebe silenced him, placing her hand on his wrist. 'What?' he whispered. 'Anatol can't have written both stories.'

Janika sighed. 'I was trying to be discreet, Dean. Anatol wrote all three of these stories, including the two about you. That was obvious to me as soon as I'd read them. Didn't you notice the gratuitous descriptions of antiques he included? They weren't subtle. There's a "Gothic Revival pillar" in one, a "Gothic Revival sundial" in another and a "Gothic Revival card table" in the third.'

'He does like Gothic Revival,' said Maya. 'But why would Anatol write three different stories?'

'Because he's blackmailing all of you. Each of the three stories that he read out last night follows the same pattern.

Each one contains an accusation. And each of the accusations happens to be true.'

'But I'm not being blackmailed,' said Maya.

'One of those stories was about you, wasn't it?'

'Yes. But I didn't get a note. How am I being blackmailed?'

'You didn't get a note,' said Janika, 'because Anatol gave your note to me. When I challenged him on where he'd been earlier today, he told me that he'd lost track of the time after receiving a strange note through the letterbox. He was in shock. That was his excuse for missing my train. He showed me the note that he'd planned to give you, as proof. Luckily, I'm not that gullible. All it proved was his own involvement.'

'What did it say?'

'"I have photos".' Janika fished one of the stories from the pile and laid it down in front of Maya. 'This story,' she continued, 'is about Dean stealing a set of sexually explicit pictures of you and demanding money for their return. I assume that those photographs actually exist?'

'For the record,' said Dean. 'I would never do that.'

Anatol's second story, 'The Bolo Tie', had opened enigmatically with a brown envelope being slid underneath Maya's bedroom door late at night. Inside it were a pair of compromising photographs: part of an art project she'd undertaken with a former lover. Through some simple detective work, involving a cut hand and a bloody thumbprint, Maya had traced the envelope back to Dean. She'd immediately accosted him in his room and demanded an explanation. After a failed attempt at denial, Dean had told Maya the truth: he'd found the photographs hidden inside

Gus's desk and wanted money for their return. Instead of paying him, Maya had stabbed him through the throat with an oversized nail. Dean had died with a desk drawer stuck under his chin, like a giant bolo tie.

Hence the title.

'They weren't part of an art project,' said Maya. 'They were private. I thought I'd lost them.'

'Anatol has them,' said Janika. 'You're being blackmailed, Maya. Playing this game was just a ploy to get money out of you. Anatol even told me his plan, indirectly. At some point he would have sent each of you another note, specifying an amount. The worse your reaction to the stories, the more he would have asked for.'

Maya nodded silently. 'I'm going to kill him. Who else is he blackmailing?'

'Me,' said Dean, before Phoebe could answer. 'The third story was about me cheating on Yulie. That was the accusation. And it's true, I did cheat on her.'

'With me,' said Phoebe, taking Dean's hand. 'Anatol must have overheard us.'

'Everyone's sleeping with everyone,' said Janika. 'This is like a soap opera.'

Anatol's third and final story, 'Window Pain', had depicted a steamy tryst between Dean and Phoebe, in Dean's bedroom late at night. They had been planning to go for a walk in the garden. Dean had loosened one of the stones at the edge of the pond, earlier that day, in the hope that Phoebe would fall in and drown ('with a little assistance'). But Phoebe had refused to venture out into the rain ('I'm not Lady Chatterley') so instead Dean had pushed her out of the window ('It was four and a half metres from there to the ground'). Phoebe had returned to him a few minutes later, dazed and confused, and Dean had done it again. She'd landed in the same spot as before ('This time Dean didn't hesitate') and he had run outside to finish her off.

'And for the record,' said Dean. 'I wouldn't have paid him anything. Not for Yulie's benefit. It's not like she's innocent.' He raised Phoebe's hand to his lips and kissed it. 'Anyway, she'll have to find out eventually.'

'It doesn't matter. Marcin will pay me.' Anatol's resonant voice came from the doorway; he was filling the frame from top to bottom, holding an open bottle of champagne to his lips. 'Marcin rushed back to London first thing this morning. He wouldn't have done that if he didn't feel threatened. He's probably destroying evidence as we speak.'

'Anatol,' said Maya. 'What's wrong with you? You're as bad as your father.'

The Blackmail Plan

Anatol took a swig of champagne, then wiped his lips with the back of his hand. 'I wasn't blackmailing you, Maya. I wrote that story, but I never sent the letter, did I? I couldn't go through with it.'

Phoebe sighed. 'But you were blackmailing me?'

'It was nothing personal, Phoebe.'

'Of course it was personal. We're your friends, Anatol.'

'For the next few hours.' The champagne spilled as Anatol checked his watch. 'But we're not going to be friends much longer.'

'Why not? What do you mean?'

Anatol walked over to the window and parted the curtains; his arms were long enough that he could open them fully while standing still. The ripples on the back of his blazer formed a mangled face, winking and grinning as he moved his shoulders; he was killing time while he worked out his speech.

'I know what you all think of me,' he said at last as he stepped forwards into the middle of the room. 'I'm the convenient friend with the big house in the country. I'm the wealthy host. The grit in the oyster that caused the friendship group to form. But I'm not wealthy any more. And this was never really my house. So that means I'm back to just being grit.'

Anatol stood as tall as a flame curling from a campfire. 'Anatol.' Phoebe leaned forwards. Her wide eyes were like two white marshmallows. 'No one thinks you're grit, Anatol. No one has said that. I'm not going to let you invent things and blame them on us. We've spent the whole weekend doing what you wanted. We played that game, didn't we? We wrote those stories. And if anyone's the grit, it should be me. Most of you know each other through me.'

'So who's the pearl?' asked Maya absent-mindedly; she seemed upset, and even by her standards was unusually disengaged. 'Sorry, I wasn't listening.'

Dean groaned. 'Haven't we all just had a bit too much to drink?'

'I know what you all think of me,' Anatol continued. 'I doubt I'll see you again after you leave here tomorrow. Once I've sold the house, why would you bother? Friendship can weather anything except change.'

'What do you think we think of you?' asked Phoebe.

'You think that I murdered my father,' said Anatol. At that point the telephone started to ring. Anatol spoke over it. 'I've read the story Marcin wrote.' He stood and shrugged and walked to the door, glad of the excuse to end the conversation. 'I should answer that. It might be important.'

News of a Tragedy

It had been a weekend full of fictional death, but now reality was hammering at the door, screaming through the letterbox. The shrill sound shattered the silence. Anatol followed the trilling racket along the corridor to the bottom of the staircase, where his landline was located. He picked up the handset and the cacophony stopped.

'Hello?' he said, doubtfully, into the mouthpiece.

Reality spoke with a woman's voice. 'Anatol?' she said. 'I'm glad I got through, Anatol. Something awful has happened.'

Anatol recognized the voice, but he couldn't quite place it. 'Who is this?' he said. 'Who am I speaking to?'

'It's Marcin,' said the voice. 'Marcin is dead.'

Road Surface Red

'Why aren't the roads any other colour?'

Marcin asked himself this question as he was driving home from Anatol's house on Sunday morning. The road ahead of him was the exact same shade of grey as the sky. He was holding a lit cigarette against the steering wheel, trying hard to keep his thoughts light-hearted, imagining the tarmac in lavender or indigo, cream, crimson or canary yellow. A faint thread of smoke stretched from the window beside him. He pointed his cigarette towards the windscreen and continued his internal monologue.

'Why does everything have to be so fucking grey?'

Marcin was trying to keep himself awake. He'd dozed through Stonehenge and the new builds of Basingstoke. But it wasn't until he was approaching London, getting into lane for the M25, that sleep overcame him. He'd lit himself another cigarette – the last one in Maya's pack of twenty – and woke to feel it burning his thigh. He swore and knocked the cigarette to the floor, then brought his eyes back to the road. He swore again, significantly louder.

His car had drifted off the road on to the hard shoulder. A dumpy Highway Maintenance vehicle was blocking the tarmac ahead of him, moving slowly. Its broad back was chevroned in yellow and red. Marcin stamped on the brakes. An acrid gasp of black smoke curled from the tyres. His car slowed, but only slightly. Still moving at speed, it slammed into the back of the gaudy truck. The front half-metre of his car crumpled. Marcin was thrown forwards into the hugging metal. He felt the breath crushed from his lungs; then his vision went black. Both vehicles rolled to a stop. Marcin's heart stuttered and stalled. His right arm hung limp from the open window.

A trickle of blood turned the road surface red.

Janika Explains It All

Anatol hadn't returned to the drawing room after leaving to answer the telephone; instead, he'd gone to the dining room and had sat at one of the typewriters for several minutes, typing something; since then, he'd been sitting in his convertible, outside the house, with a bottle of champagne. The other friends were still in the drawing room.

'I don't think he's coming back,' said Phoebe. 'I wonder who that was on the phone.'

Dean had rolled his magazine into a baton and was holding tightly to both ends: in a cage of confusion, clinging to the bars. 'I still don't understand,' he said. 'What happened to the stories the rest of us wrote? And who did Anatol get when we picked out our names? He can't have taken three pieces of paper.'

'I've got your stories here,' said Janika. 'And the names meant nothing. That was just a magic trick. He showed you two glasses that he'd prepared in advance. The glass of victims had six slips of paper inside. Three of them had my name and three had Marcin's. The glass of murderers also had six. Three of them said Anatol and three said Phoebe, so no one could have got the same name twice. Anatol must have picked Phoebe and me. The stories that he'd written in advance had Maya, Marcin and Dean as their murderers, and Dean, Maya and Phoebe as their victims. So there was no overlap. He could read out those three stories last night without anyone realizing what he'd done.'

Dean shook his head, still puzzled. 'But how would he have read out the other three? The ones that we'd written ourselves. Some of those names must have overlapped.'

'Four,' said Janika. 'Five, if I'd bothered to write one.'

'Sorry,' said Dean. 'Four, then. Or five. One of us would have had to die more than once.'

'He never had any intention of reading those stories out,' said Janika sourly, 'because I was never meant to get here. I was never going to write my story. And that would have been his excuse for not reading the rest. That's why he left me stranded at the station. And that's why the phone was unplugged overnight. If I didn't come, the game could never be finished. My absence was a kind of collateral damage.'

Dean tapped the stack of stories with his impromptu wand. 'But what if we'd told each other which names we'd got? The whole plan would have collapsed.'

'That's against the rules of the game,' said Phoebe.

'Why don't we read the other stories?' said Maya. 'The ones that we wrote. It'll pass the time until Anatol comes back. Some senseless violence is exactly what we need right now.'

Dean sighed and shook his head. 'I'm going to go and talk to him.'

The Woods at Night

The car seat was uncomfortable; the air inside the car was icy cold. Anatol's coat was draped over his body like a blanket. The door to his left opened. Dean leaned into the vehicle with his knee on the passenger seat. Behind him, the brightly illuminated house loomed over the car like a birthday cake. 'How's the traffic?' he said. 'Do you want to be left alone?'

Anatol felt the car sink on its springs. He lifted the coat to his chin and shut his eyes. 'Are you getting in, Dean? It's cold.'

'Here. Take this.' Dean was pressing something smooth against Anatol's shoulder. It was a plastic flask. Anatol took it grudgingly, unscrewed the lid and sniffed its contents.

'Coffee?' he said.

'With whisky,' said Dean.

'Then why didn't you just bring the whisky?'

There was an empty champagne bottle under Anatol's feet.

'I thought you might want something to wake you up.' Dean clambered into the passenger seat. 'You can't sleep in here, can you?'

'I wasn't planning to sleep in here. I just wanted to spend the last hour of my birthday in peace. What do you want?'

Dean checked his watch; its silver dial caught the light from the moon. 'The last fifteen minutes of your birthday,' he said. 'There's something I need to ask you, Anatol.'

'Can't it wait?'

'Not really.'

'Can it wait fifteen minutes?'

Dean took the flask back from Anatol and poured himself a cup of coffee. His hands were shaking. 'This blackmail plan,' he said. 'It was mostly about money, wasn't it?'

'Blackmail is usually about money,' said Anatol.

'I know that. I just wanted to check.'

'But I wasn't blackmailing you, Dean.'

'You were blackmailing Phoebe – that's not so different. She means a lot to me.' Dean tried his coffee. 'And what about murdering your father?' he added. 'Was that mostly about money, as well?'

It had started to rain at some point; the downpour had the sound of television static, turned down low.

'My father was unwell,' said Anatol. 'Killing him was the kind thing to do. It wasn't murder, it was euthanasia.'

'That's what you told me at the time. But I don't believe you. Not after tonight. Not now I know that you've been blackmailing everyone. I think you did it for the money.'

'Why can't it be both?' said Anatol. 'Anyway, I hardly got any money from Gus. Don't you think that's punishment enough?'

'No,' said Dean. 'I lied to the police for you, Anatol. I don't want to spend the rest of my life with that on my conscience. I don't want to be your alibi any more. Not if it was just about money.'

Anatol sighed. 'Then what are you going to do, Dean?'

'I'm going to tell the truth. That's all. I was at work the

day your father died. You were staying at my house. But I came back home on my lunch break and you weren't there. I didn't see you. I don't know where you were. That's all I'm going to say.'

'There's something you should know, Dean. Marcin is dead.'

'What?'

'Marcin is dead,' Anatol repeated. 'He crashed his car on the motorway, driving back to London this morning. That was Octavia on the phone.'

'Octavia?'

'Marcin's mother.'

Dean swallowed the rest of his coffee; the sour taste lit the sides of his tongue. 'I don't believe you, Anatol. You're telling stories. You're trying to change the subject.'

'Marcin is dead. Gus is dead. I have no money and my friends all hate me. And now you're planning to send me to prison? Potentially for the rest of my life?'

Dean shook his head, struggling with the accusation. 'This isn't my fault, Anatol. You made me complicit in your father's murder. I didn't ask for that.'

'I told you, Dean. It wasn't murder. It was euthanasia.' Anatol started the car. 'We can't have this conversation here. Let's go somewhere private, where we can talk. Let's go to the woods.'

Heart Trouble

Anatol's father, Augustine, died of a broken heart. It was a warm, fresh morning towards the end of April. Anatol had been staying with Dean and Yulie in London. After they'd both left for work, he hurried to Waterloo Station and caught a train to Tisbury. He crossed the fields to his house, without being seen by anyone, and crouched in the border of trees and bushes that surrounded his driveway.

Mrs Novak, the woman who came to clean once a week, was leaning out from his bedroom window with a cigarette between her lips, reading a magazine. Anatol hid behind an abundant azalea in a bright, butcher's shop pink, and watched her turn the pages half-heartedly; when her cigarette had burned itself out, she threw the butt, like a dart, down three storeys to the gravel below, and disappeared inside the house.

Anatol studied the open window, trying to calculate her movements from the noises that she was making. When the strained suckling of a vacuum cleaner drifted down to him, he knew that it was safe to proceed. He untied his shoelaces and left his muddy Oxfords out of sight amongst the flowers, then gritted his teeth and walked across the gravel in nothing but his socks.

He opened the front door and padded up the staircase to one of the rooms on the floor above. It was the guest bedroom that Maya usually slept in. He opened a drawer at the bottom of the wardrobe and took out an extension cord, which he'd placed inside three days earlier: a compact plastic cylinder with two sockets set into the top and about eight metres of wire hanging loose. He carried it to the end of the corridor, then up a narrow staircase to the small attic nook where his father's bedroom and bathroom were located.

He dropped the bundle of wire on to his father's bed, then wasted no time in assembling his murder weapon. There was a small radio cassette player on the bedside cabinet, with a collection of cassette tapes in the cubby underneath. Anatol chose one of the tapes at random. He pressed it into the player, then plugged the machine into the extension cord and the cord into the wall socket next to the bed. He bundled both under one arm, walked across the room and flattened his head against the bathroom door.

He could hear his father inside, taking a bath.

Anatol felt his first pang of doubt, but knew that he couldn't afford to delay. He had to get back to London before anyone got suspicious. He opened the bathroom door and strode deliberately to the far end of the room, straight past his father's reclining body. The extension cord stuttered on the vinyl flooring. Gus cried out in shock and lurched forwards, shaken by the sudden intrusion. A surge of water spilled over the side of the bath. Anatol ignored it. He knelt and placed the socket in the corner by the toilet, where it might plausibly have sat if someone was using it. 'I'm doing this for your benefit, Gus.' Anatol spoke, facing away from his father. 'When you were well you would have wanted me to do this, if you'd known how bad things were going to get.'

Then he pressed play on the cassette player and turned around, keeping the device behind him. The second movement of Beethoven's ninth symphony started to spread from the small of his back, like a majestic set of wings. Anatol smiled when he recognized the melody.

'Beethoven,' he said, with a burst of enthusiasm.

But although Gus was looking vaguely at Anatol, his eyes were unfocused and he was breathing frantically. His hand had formed a fist and was thumping at his sternum.

'Gus,' said Anatol. 'What are you doing?'

But Gus only tilted his head back, opened his mouth wide, and allowed his breathing to become a strained, rattling hiss pointed towards the ceiling. It was the only sound he knew how to make. Anatol took a step forwards and looked down at his father's naked body, seeing it fully for the first time in years. His broad chest was trembling under the water; his legs were shaking; his genitals were flapping like a rooster's comb.

He was listing to one side, sinking slowly.

'Are you having a heart attack?'

Gus let one of his arms drop into the water, giving a horrid splash of affirmation.

'How bad is it?' asked Anatol. 'Are you in pain?'

Gus gave no answer. His eyelids were going like guttering candles.

Anatol had to get back to London before Dean and Yulie got home, otherwise his whole plan would fall apart. 'You see,' he said firmly. 'This is for your benefit.'

He dropped the cassette player into the bath. Gus started to convulse, like a freshly caught trout. His lips pulled back over his teeth; his eyelids went wide; Beethoven's ninth symphony wobbled to a stop. Anatol knew that he had to leave, before Mrs Novak came to investigate.

He took one last look at his dying father and walked out of the room, heading back to his Oxfords and the train back to London.

The Other Stories

Janika read out the remaining stories, sitting on the floor in Anatol's drawing room, with Maya to her right and Phoebe to her left, while they waited for Anatol and Dean to return.

Phoebe's story, 'The Scenic Route', had been set entirely in Anatol's car, as he'd driven Janika to the station on Monday morning. Anatol had spoken at length about grief and Janika had accused him of being a murderer. The confrontation had ended with Janika unbuckling Anatol's seatbelt and crashing his car into a chestnut tree. Anatol had survived the crash, bruised and bloodied; then he'd shot Janika in the back of the head.

'Anatol has a gun in his glove compartment,' Phoebe explained. 'I found it yesterday when he was driving me here, just after we passed a car that had crashed into a tree at the side of the road. That's what gave me the idea.'

Dean's story, 'Storage Space', had also been set on Monday morning. Janika had been woken by Anatol, only to find that their other friends had already gone home. Unable to believe that Phoebe would have left without her, Janika had searched Phoebe's room, finding her dead body stashed in the storage space under her bed. Anatol had caught Janika in the act and – it was implied – cut open her throat with a kitchen knife, though in an act of needless chivalry, Dean had declined to describe Janika's murder.

Maya and Phoebe agreed that the line 'a pair of 800 Newton pneumatic struts' gave away the story's author; only Dean would care about such an uninteresting detail.

Marcin's story, 'The Incest Paradox', had consisted of a long conversation between Marcin and Anatol, in Anatol's bedroom late at night. They had discussed the origins of chess and the mathematics of genealogy; Marcin had steered the conversation towards these topics, before accusing Anatol of murdering his father. Then Anatol had pushed him down the stairs. Marcin had landed at the bottom with a broken neck.

'It's a story full of maths,' Janika noted. 'I think we'd have known that it was Marcin's. I don't think anyone else would have been qualified to write it.'

'I would have known from the title,' said Maya.

Maya's story, 'The Glass House', had revolved around a fire in a (fictional) Victorian glasshouse at the end of Anatol's garden; Marcin had been trapped inside the structure, slowly asphyxiating. Phoebe had made several attempts at helping him escape, before confessing that she had caused the fire. She'd wanted to teach Marcin a lesson for smoking. Eventually, he had been defeated by the smoke and the flames.

'I wanted something visual,' said Maya.

It was the only story in which the death was long and drawn-out.

Janika placed the stories back on the coffee table. 'That's it,' she said. 'Those are all the stories. Everything else really happened.'

The Woods at Night (continued)

It was inevitable that Anatol would kill again. Guilt is gunpowder. And his mood, since his father's death, had been increasingly volatile.

He took off his watch and laid it along the length of the dashboard. 'Which hand hits the twelve first?' he asked. 'When it gets to midnight?'

He'd driven Dean to a small patch of private woodland, a mile from his house. Then he'd moved into the passenger seat.

'What do you mean?'

'Which hand on the watch gets there first?'

'It depends on the watch,' said Dean, sitting up straight. 'In theory, they should all hit twelve at the same time, shouldn't they? But you'd probably need a camera to know for certain, like Muybridge with his horses.'

'The same time?'

'Midnight, to be precise.'

'It's no longer my birthday,' said Anatol. 'Now we can talk.'

'Is it midnight?' asked Dean. 'So which hand hit first?'

Anatol took a small silver revolver out of the glove compartment. 'I don't know. I wasn't paying attention.'

At first, Dean thought the gun in Anatol's hand was too small to be real, but then the significance of their surroundings dawned on him. They were all alone in the middle of the woods. Every tree faced away from them.

He kept his voice calm and forced himself to smile. 'Do you get a lot of werewolves out here?'

Anatol showed him the gun. 'It's an antique,' he said.

Dean wondered whether he should try to run. He wished that he hadn't put on his seatbelt. 'Don't do anything you might regret.'

Anatol held the gun to Dean's head. 'I'm not going to let you send me to prison.'

It had been a weekend full of imagined murders. But now reality was swirling like a gathering storm, rattling the leaves outside. Anatol pulled the trigger and the right side of Dean's skull shattered immediately. A red asterisk appeared in the window behind him. The hot metal burned Anatol's hand; there was no doubting that he'd really done it.

Dean's body curled slowly into a question mark.

'Don't ask,' said Anatol. 'You know why.'

And Dean died with his hands in his pockets, curled up like commas.

As he was walking back to the house, Anatol remembered the note that he'd typed thirty minutes earlier, after taking the phone call from Marcin's mother. He pulled it from his pocket and read it through. The first sentence was no longer accurate. 'Dear friends, I am not a murderer . . .'

He tore the page into pieces, letting them fall to the ground.

A NOTE FOUND TORN INTO SEVERAL PIECES (CONTINUED)

Marcin's death is not my fault.
I know some of you will see things differently, but my conscience is clear.

Sincerely,
Anatol

A Final Confrontation

Janika took the stories upstairs after she'd finished reading them out, while Maya went up to Anatol's bedroom, in search of the photographs that he'd stolen from her. The two women met on the landing, a few minutes later. When they returned to the drawing room, they found the lights out and the room in darkness. Moonlight showed them the scene outside and the shape of the windows, but nothing else.

Maya felt her way to the velveteen couch and fell on top of it.

'Where's Phoebe?' she wondered.

'I'm here,' whispered Phoebe.

Janika switched on the lights. Phoebe was crouched on the granite-grey armchair, with a cut on her forehead in the shape of a pork chop. The coffee table had been moved towards her. The rug underneath it looked buckled and lumpy.

'Anatol's back,' said Phoebe, by way of explanation.

Then Anatol stepped out of the shadows behind her, holding a tiny revolver. He sat down, casually, on the red leather Chesterfield, resting his free arm on one of its lofty sides.

'Have a seat,' he said to Janika.

'Anatol, put that gun down before someone gets hurt.' Janika approached him; she was the same height as his seated form.

'I tried that,' said Phoebe. 'He did this to me.'

She pressed on her wound and blood seeped through her fingers.

'I didn't mean for you to hit the coffee table,' said Anatol. 'I was trying to keep you away from the gun. I don't want any of you to get hurt. I just want you to listen to me. I want to explain.' He poked the air with the end of the revolver and grinned at Janika, one last time, though his disarming smile was less charming, armed. 'Now sit down, Janika, or I'll shoot you in the leg.'

Janika fell on to the green sofa, crushing Maya's feet. 'Explain what?'

'I have some bad news,' said Anatol. 'Marcin is dead.'

'Marcin?' said Maya.

'He died, this morning, driving home. Still drunk from last night, presumably. He crashed into the back of a truck on the motorway.'

Phoebe was sceptical. 'And you're only telling us now?'

'That was his mother on the phone, Phoebe. She'd been trying to reach me all evening.'

'Octavia?' Phoebe slid her stocky mobile phone from her pocket. 'I haven't heard anything. She would have called me, wouldn't she?'

'Dean is dead too,' said Anatol.

'Dean?' said Maya.

'I shot him in the head. A few minutes ago.'

Phoebe leaned forwards. 'Don't be absurd, Anatol. Dean isn't dead. I don't believe Marcin is dead, either. Where are they?'

'Dean is in the woods, Phoebe. In my car. I wasn't thinking clearly. I shot him in the driver's seat. I didn't want to drive back sitting in a puddle of his blood, so I had to walk here.'

Anatol showed her his shoes. They were covered in mud.

'Anatol,' said Janika. 'Is this a joke? Another story?'

'No,' said Anatol.

'It sounds like a story.'

'I'm not going to try and convince you,' said Anatol. 'In fact, it's better if you don't believe me. That way you'll listen to what I have to say. And I'd like you to hear this. I don't want you to think I'm a bad person.'

Phoebe squinted at him. 'That's a line from my story.'

'And I wish you could have written the rest of what I want to say. This isn't easy.'

'Tell us, then.'

Anatol took a deep breath. 'Five weeks ago, I killed my father. But it wasn't murder, it was euthanasia. His illness was getting worse. There was no hope of recovery. He was a danger to himself, as well as to the rest of us. What choice did I have?'

Anatol thought back to that day in late April and saw the radio sinking to the bottom of the bathtub, while his father convulsed, under the water.

He shook his head and picked up his confession. 'I made it look like an accident. I wasn't going to try and explain to the police that I was doing what was best for Gus, so I told them I'd been at Dean's house all day. Only Dean had come home on his lunch break and knew I wasn't telling the truth. He lied to the police and said that he'd seen me there.'

Maya interrupted. 'Then why did you shoot him?'

'He didn't,' said Phoebe.

'I shot him,' said Anatol, 'because after tonight he was planning to tell the police everything. He wanted to send me to prison. I know that sounds like it might not matter, since it's all over for me anyway. But it felt like a betrayal. I wasn't even blackmailing Dean.'

'Anatol,' said Phoebe. 'Put the gun down, go and get Dean and stop telling us these silly stories. It doesn't matter about the blackmail. I just want Dean back.'

'You still don't believe me, Phoebe?'

'No.'

'What if I shot myself? Would you believe me then?'

Phoebe nodded heartlessly. 'Probably,' she said. 'Why? Are you going to?'

'Don't,' said Maya.

'But, Anatol,' said Janika, 'assuming, for the sake of argument, that you're telling the truth, you can only make a moral case for euthanasia when the person involved consents to die. You can't draw an equivalence between—'

Anatol raised the gun and shot himself in the head. Reality shattered. His body fell back against the sofa. Blood poured out of his broken skull.

And Maya was right: it was darker than ink.

Australia

Sydney, Australia, was a city of shark attacks and heartache; cultural landmarks and sun-bleached coffee shops; tree-lined streets and fingernail beaches. Janika and her friends were on the terrace of her house, looking out over the water. The setting sun looked like an egg yolk or an orange. Maya, having spent the day lying on the beach, was now lying in a hammock, brushing sand from her hair. Janika was reading to her from her latest publication. Phoebe had learned, over the last few days, how to use the milk steamer and was in the kitchen, making caffè lattes for everyone, with delicate hearts drawn on the froth. It was the late May Bank Holiday Monday.

Except in Australia, where there was no such thing.

'Is this story going anywhere, Janika?' Maya was lying on Janika's bed, while Janika sat on the floor by her suitcase. 'It's meant to have a murder in it. Otherwise what's the point? And it's supposed to be set here, not in Australia.'

Phoebe was sitting at the end of the bed with her knees tucked under her chin and her arms wrapped around her legs, a large plaster stuck to her forehead. The three of them had decided to pack their things while they were waiting for the police to arrive; they were taking it in turns, so they could stay together. None of them wanted to be left alone. Anatol's body was still on the sofa downstairs, with a mullet of blood running down his back.

'I was trying to lighten the mood,' said Janika. The top drawer of the chest of drawers was open in front of her. Janika reached up to it and yanked out her clothes. 'Being delicate isn't exactly my strength.'

'You can put in a murder,' said Phoebe quietly. 'We won't be offended. There's no point pretending that none of this has happened.'

Maya had cut off a sticky lock of Anatol's hair and was brushing it across her chin compulsively. 'I can't stop thinking about how small he looked.'

'Don't,' said Phoebe. 'I don't want to think about it.' She shook her head and pressed on her plaster. 'I just wanted a boring life. What am I going to say to Yulie?'

Janika felt something in the drawer that wasn't fabric. It was glossy and light and had the springiness of cardboard. She got to her feet and looked inside. The drawer had been emptied of everything except five small boxes of fudge.

Each one featured a garish illustration of a kangaroo.

'I've just remembered,' she said. 'I got you all a present from Australia. It's not much. Just something I found at the airport. You know I'm hopeless at buying gifts.' Janika passed one box to Phoebe and one to Maya; they both thanked her. 'It was just something to show that I hadn't forgotten you. And to say thank you, for being my friends . . .'

With guilt, with regret and – above all – with disbelief, Janika buried the other three boxes of fudge in her suitcase.

*

And then the sun turned a shocking red and Phoebe appeared on the terrace, brandishing a chainsaw in one hand and a flamethrower in the other. She cut the hammock in half with Maya still inside it and burned both ends to a crisp.

'There,' said Janika. 'Is that enough murder for you?'

Acknowledgements

When seeking an idea for the book to follow my first novel, *Eight Detectives* – a book that is itself heavily reliant on stories-within-stories – it occurred to me that it might be possible to write a mystery novel that builds its central mystery on the reader's inability to tell story from story-within-story. And so *Ink Ribbon Red* was conceived.

Realising this idea took me more than two years of long hours. I'd like to thank my partner, Georgina, for her patience. And thank you to my mother as well.

The major influences on the book are the remote-location mysteries of Agatha Christie and her imitators, the television programme *Friends*, and above all the novel *The Sundial* by Shirley Jackson, which I read multiple times while writing *Ink Ribbon Red*.

I would like to thank my editors, Joel Richardson and Serena Jones, my agent James Wills and rights director Rachel Richardson. Thanks also to Ellie Hughes, Hattie Evans, Beatrix McIntyre, Grace Long and the whole team at Michael Joseph, Zoe Affron and the whole team at Henry Holt, and my copy-editor Richenda Todd.

Loved *Ink Ribbon Red*?

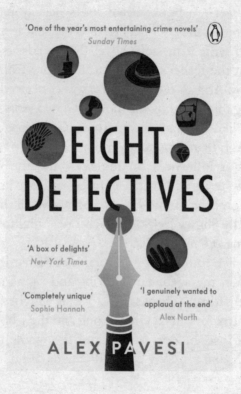

Discover another dazzlingly original mystery in *Eight Detectives*!

NURTURING WRITERS SINCE 1935